To Dawn—

Cover
Me
In
Darkness

Thank you for your gracious hospitality!

EILEEN RENDAHL

ISBN: 978-0-9906942-9-8

ALSO BY

Eileen Rendahl

Thriller
Cover Me in Darkness

Paranormal
Don't Kill The Messenger (A Messenger Novel Book 1)
Dead on Delivery (A Messenger Novel Book 2)
Dead Letter Day (A Messenger Novel Book 3)
Payback for a post-mortem (A short story from the Messenger World)
Dreidels and Demons (A Story from the Messenger Series)
Tinsel and Temptations (A Holiday Anthology)
Petals on the Pillow

Chick Lit
Do Me, Do My Roots
Dancing Naked Under The Moon
Un-Bridaled
Un-Veiled

Eileen Carr *Romantic Suspense*
Hold Back The Dark
Vanished in The Night
Veiled Intentions

Kristi Abbott *Cozy Mystery*
Kernel of Truth
Pop Goes the Murder
Assault and Buttery

Lilian Bell *Cozy Mystery*
A Grave Issue
If the Coffin Fits

ACKNOWLEDGMENTS

This book took its time coming to fruition. The idea for it started with something that happened in my hometown when I was a child and has been bubbling in the back of my brain since then. It's only been in the past few years that the bubbling moved from the back of my brain to the front and then out my fingers onto the page. Quite a few people helped it make that journey.

My sister Diane Ullman is an amazing scientist and was generous with both her wisdom and her life experiences. Her integrity shines in everything she says. Sulley Ben-Mahmoud has the patience of a thousand saints and the soul of a teacher. I am so grateful for his demonstrations in the lab and for him not laughing at me for not understanding basic biological concepts. Any mistakes in the science of this book are due to my faults as a student and not to his as a teacher. Thank you also to my cousin Jose Guarderas for giving me a tour of his lab and using all kinds of fancy science language that I could copy down and use.

Speaking of sisters, Marian Ullman is an amazing source of knowledge for how to kill people off in a book. Remind me never to truly piss you off, sweet sissy.

Thank you to my final workshop members and mentor at Antioch University in Los Angeles: Michelle Barney, Erin Raets, Claudia Ramirez, Lauren Strasnick. You helped me slow down and remember that emotion is as important as motion. While we're on the subject of Antioch, huge shout out to the Scirocco cohort! Whoo!!

Thank you to Aurora Publicity, especially the efficient and patient Stephanie, for helping me give this book new life.

Last but not ever least, thank you to Andy Wallace for putting up with all my crazy, for working out plot points, and for laughing at my jokes, but not at me.

.

CHAPTER

1

Friday, February 17

SOMEHOW IT SEEMED APPROPRIATE THAT I was drunk when I got the call. Well, not exactly drunk, but definitely a little bit…loose, like I'd been that night. The night everything had come crashing down. The night my world ended. This night, however, I wasn't a seventeen-year-old girl who had given a homeless guy twenty bucks to buy her a bottle of flavored vodka. This time, I was a twenty-seven-year-old woman who had gone out for drinks with people after work. Now I was a respectable drunk.

It was Friday and the atmosphere around the lab had been hyped up and giddy the whole day. Rumors were flying that big money was moving. Our little pipsqueak start-up might change from a choo-choo train to a gravy train. Bellefountaine Cosmetics might be bought out. Everyone's stock options might end up actually being worth something. Possibly a lot of something. Like, *life*-changing amounts of something.

At fourthirty, Jesse Garcia had stuck his head into the alcove off the lab that served as my office and said, "Hey, Amanda. Two -for-one margaritas at Pedro's. You in?"

I hesitated. Jesse asked me out for drinks approximately twice a month, and this was actually the third time in the month of February. I was starting to feel mean. It wasn't like it wasn't tempting. Jesse was funny and smart and good -looking enough for me to feel like he was out my league. While his attention was flattering, I had a pretty strict policy about dating people I worked with. That policy was not only no, but hell no. I looked down at the printout of results I'd been staring at for the past forty-five minutes. Something was wrong with them, but I couldn't figure out what it was. I brought it up in the Quality Control meeting the week before and no one else seemed to see what I saw. Actually, if it was something I saw, I could have explained it; this was more something I felt. About numbers. Even I knew it sounded crazy and I knew from crazy. Maybe if I read over them one more time…

"Melinda will be there and so will Sara." He smiled. It made the dimple on his left cheek appear.

I did really want a drink. February in Chicago was cold and dark and damp. I'd stared at the columns of numbers in front of me for so long that an ache had developed behind my right eye. A drink could be fun, festive, and practically medicinal, damn it. Pedro's was between the lab and my condo. I wouldn't even have to use a different train station. It was as if Jesse had picked the place for it to be convenient for me. If Melinda and Sara were there, then there was no way he could construe it as a date. Just work friends marking the end of the week, right? Where was the harm in that? Who could turn that down?

"Sure," I said and then felt bad about the way Jesse's face lit up. I shouldn't have that much effect on anyone. It wasn't safe for any of us.

"Great. See you there. I'll go early and get us a table." He gave a wave and left.

I really hoped this wasn't a mistake. I didn't generally socialize with my fellow lab rats at Bellefountaine Cosmetics. Not that there were any actual lab rats at Bellefountaine—we were 100 percent cruelty-free. Real or metaphorical rats aside, I liked to keep things separate. I liked to keep me separate. I was not going to go out with Jesse. Not ever, not nohow. It didn't matter that he had deep dark eyes, a dimple on his left cheek, and a set of shoulders that seemed to stretch the fabric of every one of his dress shirts. There were reasons I like to keep things separate and they were more compelling than the deepest dimple. I loved my work. I loved being in the lab. I loved the reassuring solidity of reproducible results and numbers. Cute, out-of-my-league guys wanting to buy me drinks weren't worth jeopardizing that, tempting as they might be.

It was already dark when I got off the L train at Van Buren. I stepped out onto the platform and the wind sliced through my coat, hat, and scarf like an icy razor blade. After the overheated, crowded train, the wind would have knocked me back a step, but there were so many people stepping off the train behind me that I was shoved forward against it. I adjusted the strap of my messenger bag over my shoulder, pulled the collar of my wool jacket up around my neck, and headed down the stairs, glad I had on gloves as I held onto the metal railing and even more glad that it was only half a block to Pedro's. I put my head down against the wind and walked.

I pulled open the door to Pedro's and the noise and the heat and the lights hit me in the face with the same intensity that the wind had a few minutes earlier. Again, there were too many people at my back to keep me from doing anything but moving forward. I was like a shark—move forward or die. I scanned the room and saw Melinda. She would have been hard to miss, as she'd stood up and done a full body wave to get my attention. I threaded my way through the other tables, trying not to whack anyone in the head with my bag. Sara and Jesse got to the table two steps before me, hands full with pitchers and glasses.

"Yay. You're here!" Sara reached an arm around me and gave me a quick squeeze. "I didn't believe Jesse when he said you were coming. You never meet us for drinks."

4

And probably wouldn't again if people were going to be giving spontaneous hugs before they were even drunk. What was up with that? Sara and I ate lunch together sometimes, but we were definitely not on hugging terms. I tried smiling anyway, hoping it didn't look I was baring my teeth. "Are there any chips? I'm starving."

"Coming right up," Jesse said and plunged back into the crowd.

Melinda leaned in. "Tell me you're going to put that poor boy out of his misery."

I shrugged out of my coat and draped it over the back of the high stool at the table. "What misery?"

Melinda and Sara both laughed.

"You have got to be kidding me. He follows you around like a puppy hoping for a pat on the head." Sara turned to watch Jesse lean over the bar to grab chips and salsa. "And I would totally rub that puppy's belly given half the chance."

I looked, too. It was a nice backside. Add it to the dimple, the shoulders, and the soulful eyes…was it enough to get me to knock down some compartment walls? I poured myself a margarita from the pitcher and took a sip.

Here was the thing about me and margaritas. They tasted like soda pop to me and I drank them like they were. Too fast. I was a third of the way into my second one and enjoying that funny woozy feeling I got from drinking when I felt my phone vibrate. I almost didn't look at it. Anna, Judy, and Bill had joined us. Judy

5

was doing a spot-on imitation of our CEO, Will Friedrichs, right down to the way his forehead never moved. "What we want is to help make women feel as beautiful on the outside as they are on the inside," she said. Priceless. I was having fun. Like a regular person. I looked at Jesse again. He smiled back at me. Something unfurled in the pit of my stomach, something sweet and warm, like spreading honey. Rules were meant to be broken, right? And there was that dimple to consider.

But then there was the phone. Who would be calling me on a Friday night? The answer was no one. The phone buzzed again. A shiver of uneasiness slithered through me. No one would be calling me with anything good, but that didn't mean that no one would call.

I pulled the phone out of my pocket. My stomach dropped when I saw the number on the caller ID. I'd been right. It wasn't going to be anything good.

"I have to take this," I said over my shoulder, already rushing out of the noisy bar onto the street to answer.

I knew it wasn't good to get a phone call after hours on a Friday from the facility where my mother was housed. I knew it was really not good when the person on the other end started the conversation with, "I'm sorry, Ms. Sinclair."

I listened as hard as I could to what the woman on the other end of the line was saying, hoping I'd absorb most of the information since I had no way to write it down. We said good-bye and I went back into the bar. All the talk and laughter and clinking of glasses seemed far away now, like I was listening to it through earmuffs and looking at the people through gauze. I stumbled through the bar like a ghost, passing unseen and unheard between the living as they went about their business. My heart was on fire inside my chest. I had to get out of there. I had to get home. I needed to go home.

"Amanda, are you okay?" Jesse's face swam into my field of vision.

Was I okay? I doubted it. Okay and I hadn't coexisted for a little over a decade, but we were farther apart than ever at the moment. I tried to answer but my teeth chattered. I wasn't really sure what I would say anyway. Telling them the news I'd just received would bring on a torrent of questions that would then bury me in an avalanche of shame. Better not to say anything.

"You're shaking!" Melinda picked up my coat and draped it over my shoulders. "What were you doing out there for so long? It's got to be way below freezing."

I gestured helplessly at my phone, hoping that would somehow be enough of an answer.

I pushed my arms into the sleeves of my coat. "I've got to go." I pulled a twenty out of my wallet and put it on the table, hoping it would be enough to cover my part of the bill. I snatched my bag and started toward the door.

Someone grabbed me by the shoulder as I reached the door. I whirled, jerking away from the touch. Jesse took a step back, hands up before him. "Let me walk you," he said.

I shook my head. The last thing I wanted right then was company. "It's only a few blocks."

"I could hail you a cab." He followed me out onto the street. "You don't look okay. Let me help."

That almost made me laugh. I couldn't quite imagine what could be of help at the moment. Not really. "I live like three blocks from here. The walk will clear my head. Thanks, though."

I pulled my collar up and started down the street. He fell into step beside me. "If it's only a few blocks, then let me walk you."

"I'm fine." I picked up my pace.

He kept stride with me. If nothing else, he was a determined bugger. "It'll make me feel better to be sure you're home safe. Humor me."

I didn't have the heart to argue more. My chest burned with the cold air I sucked into my lungs and with the news I'd gotten.

The streets were nearly deserted. An hour earlier, they'd been packed with people leaving the Loop. People heading to the L, to the train, to their cars, or to buses. They were gone now. Within a block, we were in the heart of the Financial District, the Chicago Board of Trade building looming up like a giant dam at the end of the concrete canyon we walked. The cold stung the inside of my nostrils and froze in the back of my throat. The strike of my boot heels echoed.

We stopped at the intersection of Wells and Harrison, waiting for the walk sign as a dark SUV crept down the icy street and a lone cab circled. Jesse grabbed my elbow to help me over the accumulated slush at the bottom of the wheelchair cut. I resisted the urge to yank my arm from his grasp. I didn't really want to be touched right then, not even through a bulky wool coat, but he was being sweet. Considerate. Solicitous. It wasn't his fault I was a freak and that the more he helped, the more I wanted to shove him down and run.

"It's a little creepy down here," he said as we crossed Polk. Wells dead-ends a block past my loft. There was no reason for anyone to turn down the street unless they lived there. Even with River City condos and shops across the street, it made for a quiet block. The dark SUV cruised to the end of the street, made a U-turn, and swung back past us again. Clearly, somebody's GPS was taking him or her on a scenic tour of Chicago's Printer's Row.

I was about to comment on having a higher threshold for creepy than most people when a man stepped out of a doorway into our path. "Change," he asked, holding out his hand. He had a rag wrapped around his head and rags wrapped around his hands. I had no idea how he would make it through the night without freezing to death.

Jesse put his arm around my shoulder and pulled me around the stranger. "Sorry." Jesse stepped up the pace.

"C'mon, man." The bum followed us. "It's cold out."

I slowed and started to fumble for my wallet. A dollar seemed like a small price to pay to get rid of the guy and not feel like a total asshat.

"Keep walking," Jesse hissed in my ear, pulling me along, and then calling over his shoulder, "Get lost."

"Fuck you, man," the man called after us.

I broke free from Jesse and stripped my gloves off my hands. "Here," I said. "Keep your hands warm at least."

He took the gloves from me, reaching slowly as if he thought I might snatch them away. I winced thinking about how he must have learned that response.

"Thank you, miss," he said.

Jesse took me by the arm and pulled me away. "Now what are you going to do for gloves?"

"I have another pair upstairs." I shrugged his hand off my arm and walked to the door of my building.

"Nice," Jesse said, looking up at the façade as I punched in the code to open the security door.

"Thanks," I mumbled. The door clicked and I pushed it open and stepped into the foyer. Jesse stepped in right behind me.

He pulled the beanie he wore off his head. Damn. He even looked cute with hat hair. It wasn't going to help him tonight, though. I needed to get away from everybody. Pronto. "Can I walk you to your door?"

I looked up at him. Could he truly be this clueless? "No. Thank you." I couldn't even stand the idea. What would be next? A request for a nightcap or a coffee? An examination of my loft? Fumbling attempts at seduction?

"You can't blame a guy for trying." He shrugged and leaned forward as if he was going to kiss my cheek.

I dodged and practically ran to the bank of elevators. He didn't follow, but he was still watching as I got on the elevator.

The doors shut and I slumped against the back wall. The heat of the car made the tops of my ears ache where the cold had bitten them through my hat. I covered them with my hands while I watched the numbers light up over the door. I didn't mind the pain. It kept me centered, kept me from whirling apart into a million pieces, kept me from sinking to the elevator floor to howl and kick like an animal. No one else got on and the car went straight to the eighth floor. I don't know what I would have done if someone had. I was no more capable of making small talk than I was of flying. I walked down the hall, pulling out my keys, and let myself into my dark apartment.

I shut the door behind me and listened in relief to the silence, to the sound of my own breath, to the beat of my own heart. The warmth seeped back into me. I dropped the messenger bag by the coat stand and dumped my keys into the bowl on the table. I didn't bother checking the lock. I'd known one girl who had to check and recheck the locks, sometimes more than five times a night. I understood the impulse. I also happened to know that the monsters could just as easily be locked up inside with you as on the other side of the door, so locks didn't make me feel safe. Tea, on the other hand, has been shown—scientifically—to reduce stress. I put the kettle on. Then I picked up the phone and dialed my brother's number.

Wherever he was, it was noisy. I wasn't surprised. He was in his junior year in college and it was Friday night and he wasn't quite the freak I was. He'd be somewhere with friends and noise and music.

"Amanda?" he yelled into the phone. "What's up, sis?"

"Dylan, get some place you can hear me." I wasn't going to repeat the message I had for him. I was going to say it once. I didn't have anyone else I had to say it to in the same manner, so the words would never have to come out of my mouth this way again. I wanted to keep it that way.

"Gimme a sec."

I waited, listening to the noise ebb and flow through the cell. Then finally a door shut and the noise was muffled. "Are you okay? What's going on?" he asked. He was a good kid. Still worried about his sister.

I took a deep breath and said, "Our mother is dead."

There was silence at the other end. I counted out the seconds, waiting for him to speak. One. Two. Three. Four. Then he said, "Good riddance."

CHAPTER

2

Saturday, February 18

I WOKE UP THE NEXT morning with my heart still burning. I'd slept. Perhaps that was one advantage of having survived my childhood—not much gave me insomnia. You don't have to stay up worrying about what might happen when the worst has already happened. And it had. Again. Too bad I hadn't also been able to stop dreaming. The night had been full of pleading eyes, hands reaching toward me, cries for help while I struggled against whatever forces keep you from moving in dreams like that.

I had one more phone call to make, and I wasn't looking forward to it. I should have made it the night before. I maybe should have made that phone call before I called Dylan. I'd put it off, though. It wasn't like it was an emergency. There was nothing he could do. It was cruel not to call him at all, though, and I tried not to be cruel. I wasn't always successful, but I did try.

I dialed and waited, trying to imagine what he was doing. It was Saturday morning. Early. Maybe he was playing golf. If he was, I'd get his voicemail. I pondered what kind of message to leave. Hi, Dad. Your ex-wife killed herself. Seemed a little harsh. Probably a simple call me would suffice.

But as luck would have it, Dad answered. He usually did. I suspected he also tried not to be cruel. "Good morning, Amanda. How are you?" his voice boomed. Healthy. Hearty. A good-natured dad to my two little halfsisters.

"I'm fine, Dad. There's something I need to tell you about, though." It was the best lead-in I could come up with.

"Shoot," he said.

I winced at the violence of the word. Not his fault. I knew that. Nothing was ever Dad's fault. "Mom is…Mom is dead."

Like Dylan, he didn't say anything at first. I could hear him breathing at the other end, so I knew he was still there.

"I'm sorry, Amanda," he finally said. "Is there anything I can do? Anything I should do to help?"

Not bad as responses go. Certainly more gentle than Dylan's. "Thanks. I, uh, don't know much about the arrangements yet. I just thought you should know."

"I appreciate that. Are you okay?"

Now I left a pause. "Yes, of course. I'm fine."

"Do you know how?" I could practically hear the wince in his voice. I got it. The wanting to know while simultaneously not wanting to know. I could so relate.

"Suicide." I let the word sit between us.

"Ah," was all he said.

"I'm leaving for Elgin in a minute or two. I wanted to call first. Sorry to start your weekend off this way."

"Amanda," he said, reproach in his voice, but he said good-bye and let me go.

I hung up the phone and sat with my head down on the table for a minute before shaking myself back into action.

The drive to Elgin from Printer's Row would take an hour if there wasn't any traffic. I doubted there would be any on a Saturday morning. At least I wouldn't have to sit on the Eisenhower for hours. It would totally be adding insult to injury if I had to deal with a traffic jam on the way to pick up my mother's personal effects. It was weird to be going out there without some little item for her. I always brought something. Some candy. A book. A new shirt. I'd be taking it all home with me now.

The homeless guy from the night before wasn't in the doorway down the block. I hoped he'd found some place warm to sleep. I walked the two blocks to where I kept my slightly disreputable Ford Escort garaged. I only drove my car once every couple of weeks, to the grocery store. Otherwise I didn't really need it in the city. I used to keep it in the open lot closer to my building, but after the third time someone broke into it and used it as a hotel room, not to mention absconding with the loose change in the console, I started paying the extra twenty-five dollars a month to keep it in the garage. It was cheaper than replacing windows.

I headed west on the Eisenhower past Rush Presbyterian and the University of Illinois. The sky was gray and the clouds hung low in the sky. According to the weather report, it wasn't going to rain or snow, but the clouds seemed ominous anyway. Or maybe that was my mood.

The city seemed to stretch on forever. Mile after mile of concrete and brick with frost-tipped grass in the medians and leafless trees dotted along the way. Bleak and cold. The burning cold sensation returned to my chest. I turned on the radio news but couldn't really focus on what the announcers were saying. The voices all blended into background noise.

My mother was dead. She'd committed suicide. It hadn't been her first attempt. I'd lost count of how many times she'd tried. Had this been her third? Her fourth? Something like that. Ironically, the attempts tended to come at times when she was improving, when she was more connected with reality than usual. When her delusions deserted her and she came face -to -face with what she'd done.

Unlike a lot of other mental patients, clarity was more of a nightmare for my mother than the twisting, turning logic of her illusions. Clarity was a slap in her face, at best. At its worst, it was a sucker punch to her gut.

Yet too much clarity hadn't appeared to be her problem when I'd visited two weeks ago. I made the trek out to Elgin every other week, if nothing else got in the way. I was her only visitor. Ever. That wasn't all that unusual; lots of people there never have anyone visit at all. At least I showed up, although it was hard to think of myself as much of a prize. My feelings toward my mother were a mixed bag, and sometimes the bag was filled with those cracked and dusty peppermint candies they give away for free with your bill at restaurants that aren't nice enough to spring for chocolate. I imagined her feelings toward me were no less conflicted.

Mom hadn't seemed all that clear on that last visit. I drummed the steering wheel and tried to remember exactly what she'd told me, exactly what she'd done. Exactly what I'd done, in case I was the one who set something off in her head that led her to finally managing to successfully kill herself. I may be a dusty peppermint candy, but I didn't want her to choke on me. I'd done enough damage to her as it was.

She'd told me a long, rambling story about a comb that had gone missing from her room and the woman she was sure was responsible, but who refused to admit her guilt or return the comb. I hadn't really listened. I'd gone out to CVS, bought a new comb, and made sure she got it.

She'd been flushed with self-righteous fury about the theft. For a minute, she'd looked almost like her old self. The high color in her cheeks and the brightness in her eyes eclipsed the graying hair and the crow's feet. I could almost see the old Mom. The Mom who would play tag and hide -and-seek with us for hours and build forts in the living room out of pillows and blankets. But also, unfortunately, the Mom who thought the neighbors were plotting against her based on how they piled the shoveled snow between their driveway and ours, who suspected the paper boy of being a spy, and who was convinced my father was sleeping with the new marketing assistant at his office. Although, of course, that last one turned out to be true. Even a blind pig finds the occasional truffle.

I pulled the car into the maze of buildings at the mental health hospital and maneuvered it to visitor parking. The lot was less than half full, adding to the feeling of desolation and isolation that hung around the place like a heavy shawl. At least it made it easy to find a space. I trudged over the ice-crusted lot to the snow-lined sidewalk, the cold damp numbing my toes inside my boots. I pushed into the lobby and stamped my feet on the linoleum to wake them up.

I walked up to the reception counter and waited at the window. The woman inside turned. For a second I froze. I didn't know what to say. Usually I said I was there to see Linda Framingham, but I wasn't, was I? She was no longer here to see.

Thank goodness I was a frequent flyer. I didn't have to say a word. Belinda, a middle-aged African-American woman with a round face and even rounder body, had seen me here too many times to count and recognized me. "I'm so sorry for your loss, Amanda. Let me call Dr. Ashmore."

I nodded and sat in the chair against the wall in the lobby area. I knew the routine—I always had to wait for someone to escort me. They can't let people waltz in and out of a locked ward, now, can they? It would kind of defeat the purpose.

Dr. Ashmore didn't keep me waiting long, which was good. I started to get bored and the urge to pull out my phone and play solitaire or sudoku was getting hard to ignore. Somehow that didn't seem appropriate for the daughter of a woman who had committed suicide. I was pretty sure I was supposed to be consumed with grief. Most daughters would be, no doubt. Most daughters would barely be able to function. Most daughters didn't have my mother. Most daughters weren't me.

Dr. Ashmore came out of the door to the left of the reception counter. I liked him better than my mother's last doctor, Dr. Hobart, who kept calling me "my dear" and acted like the idea of actually treating my mother was a novel one. He'd retired at the end of last year and Dr. Ashmore had taken over my mother's case.

He was young. Well, youngish. Older than me, but not by a lot. Maybe mid-thirties. Taller than me, too. Black hair that waved back from his forehead and blue eyes. The eyes stopped me in my tracks the first time we met. They were almost too light, a clear pale blue that pierced.

He stopped in front of me and crouched down so we were face -to -face. "Amanda, I'm so sorry."

I opened my mouth to speak, but no words came out. Suddenly my throat felt clogged. Was I finally going to cry? Here? In front of my mother's too-handsome-for-a-place-like-this doctor? I cleared my throat and managed to choke out, "Thank you."

He stood and extended his hand down to me. "Let's go to my office and talk."

I took his hand. It was warm. Or maybe mine was still cold. I stood and followed him through the security doors to his office.

I'd only been in it once before, when he first took over my mother's case. It had been a mess then, boxes everywhere, stacks of books next to the shelves. Journals slipping and sliding off stacks on the desk.

It was worse now.

Now there were three coffee cups and at least one half-eaten sandwich interspersed with the journals. The boxes were gone, but there were even more stacks of books. My fingers itched to straighten things up, stack the books more neatly so their corners matched up, align piles with the edge of the desk. The chair across from Ashmore's desk was clear, though. He gestured to it and I sat down.

"How did this happen, Dr. Ashmore?" I asked, not waiting for more small talk. "Shouldn't someone have been watching? She's always been a suicide risk. Always." I was a little surprised at the note of indignation in my voice. In some ways, my mother's death was a

20

release. A release for her from this institution. A release for me from feeling responsible for her. But it was not a release from guilt. I didn't think there would ever be a release from the guilt. Where did that anger come from?

He rubbed his hands across his face. "I know, Amanda. It never should have happened. Another patient became extremely violent that night and the staff were all focused on subduing him. It's no excuse. They should have been able to handle a crisis without endangering other patients. We're reviewing our protocols now."

Fat lot of good that was going to do my mother. Then something in what he'd said struck me. "Wait. When did it happen?"

"We're not one hundred percent sure. She was fine at the ten o'clock bed check, then as I said, the staff got distracted. No one did the two a.m. bed check. She was found in her room the next morning at six." He said all this with his gaze fastened securely on me. No wavering. At least he wasn't trying to sidestep the screw-up.

"She was found at six in the morning and no one contacted me until six that evening?" I asked.

"I apologize for that, too. A lot was happening here. First, there were life-saving efforts, although to be honest, there was no chance they were going to work. Then, as I'm sure you can imagine, the rest of the ward became very…volatile. Staff was needed to keep that situation under control so no one else would get hurt." He rubbed his face. "It was a long, hard day for

21

everyone, but you're right. You should have been contacted sooner."

I sat with that information for a moment. What would I have done? What help could I have been? Part of me was glad they'd waited to call until I was off work. I can't imagine having received that phone call in the lab in the middle of the afternoon. It would have been agony. "Do you have any idea what set her off? Did she leave a note?"

He shook his head. "No, she didn't, and I don't know what happened that led her to make this decision. It took me completely by surprise. I'd reviewed her file and I knew what kinds of things usually precipitated an attempt. I wasn't seeing signs of any of them."

I leaned forward. "What kinds of things were you watching for?"

He grimaced. "Anything that brought your mother face -to -face with the incident that brought her here, really. As long as she could cushion herself with her delusions, she was okay. It was when she was improving her grasp of reality that she seemed most likely to self-harm."

I nodded. It was what I thought, too. At least he understood.

"What about the date? Is there anything significant about mid- February? An anniversary? A birthday?" Dr. Ashmore leaned forward, resting his elbows on the desk. The sleeves of his white dress shirt were rolled up and I found myself staring at his wrists while I thought.

"No. Not that I can think of." I'd wondered about that, too, but nothing came to mind. Jackson's birthday was in May. Dylan's is in August, and mine wasn't until October. Mom and Dad's anniversary had been in June. When exactly had Dad left us? Had it been in February? I shook my head. I didn't think so and whatever that date had been had never seemed to be terribly important to Mom.

And the incident, as Dr. Ashmore so delicately put it? That had been in the spring, too, about a month before Jackson's fourth birthday.

"What about Collier?" I asked. Patrick Collier had been my mom's "spiritual advisor" at the time of her complete unraveling. Collier was the leader of Children of the Greater God—COGG, as those in the know called it. Part preacher, part life coach, he'd swept my mother into his church and taken over our lives. More than anyone else, he'd set in motion the events that had finally broken us completely. His name was sour in my mouth. Regardless, none of what happened could ever be laid at his feet legally. They did manage, however, to lock him up one some kind of financial charge, misuse of funds, money missing from he church coffers. "He's up for parole soon."

Dr. Ashmore frowned and shook his head. "We would not allow him any contact with your mother whatsoever. He certainly hasn't been in contact with her by phone or mail. We keep a close eye on all that."

"Could she have seen something about him on the news?" I asked. He'd been popping up here and there lately.

He shrugged. "It's possible, but there hasn't been much coverage of it. I didn't even know he was up for parole until about a week ago."

What did it say about me that I had a Google alert on the name of the man at whose feet I laid most of the blame for what happened to my family? If Collier hadn't come into our lives, my mom would still have been crazy but maybe not lock-her-up-and-throw-away-the-key crazy. Dylan disagreed with me entirely. He said that if it hadn't been Collier, it would have been something else. He said our mother was a ticking time bomb with a hair trigger and he did not care about mixing metaphors. He said I was almost as crazy as Mom for placing blame anywhere but squarely on her shoulders, although he did reserve a little soupcon of responsibility for our father.

He didn't blame me at all. Then again, Dylan didn't really know everything that had happened back then. He'd only been eleven. He wouldn't have understood then, and later, well... What difference would it have made?

The office was warm. The chill had finally left my bones. I slipped out of my coat. "Then I've got nothing. Last time I was here she was all twicked out about one of the other patients who she thought was out to get her. Something about a stolen comb, I think."

Dr. Ashmore suddenly got very still. "Did you say comb?"

"Yeah, why?" Why was he acting so weird about a comb?

He drummed his fingers against his desk. "She used a comb that she'd sharpened to slit her wrists."

CHAPTER

3

ALL WARMTH FLED FROM MY body. "What did you say?"

"I'm so sorry." Hadn't he said that to me before? He hadn't had that look on his face before, though. Before when he'd said how sorry he was, it was perfunctory, what he was supposed to say, what he was required to say. Now he looked like he meant it. He didn't pull any punches, though. "It's how she killed herself. She'd somehow sharpened a comb and used it to...well, I think you understand."

I did understand. All too well. I'd given my mother the instrument she had used to kill herself. I couldn't speak. My lips were numb. A buzzing noise filled my ears.

Dr. Ashmore came out from behind his desk and knelt in front of me again. "You know if it hadn't been the comb, it would have been something else. It's incredible what the patients here have fashioned into weapons. Toothbrushes, pencils, spoons, you name it."

I looked down into the cool, pale lakes of his blue eyes. "But it wasn't a toothbrush or a pencil. It was a comb. A comb I gave her."

He took my hands between his and rubbed them. I supposed they must be cold. They certainly felt that way, but I wasn't sure of anything at the moment. "It's possible she manipulated you into giving her the comb, Amanda. She was quite capable of that."

As if I didn't know that. Mom almost never asked for anything directly. She could never simply say what she wanted. I think it was one of the problems between her and Dad. Well, that and the fact that she was literally certifiably nuts.

Mom was always trying to work an angle to get people to do what she wanted. Could she ever ask for someone to take out the trash? No. She had to make some little drama about how the trash was overflowing and she was so darn busy making dinner she didn't have time to take it out. Instead of asking me to babysit my little brother, she'd walk around sighing and talking about how she could use a little time to herself. It was maddening. Enraging. And, sadly, very effective. We were all likely to succumb to her manipulations.

Except toward the end. We all got a little tired. I knew I, for one, was freaking exhausted.

She wasn't as good at it as she used to be, either. Her long -range planning had suffered greatly

27

with the medications that kept her wilder fantasies at bay. Most of her recent manipulations centered on getting me to bring her food she generally couldn't get inside the locked ward: Frango Mints from Marshall Fields, Italian beef from Johnnie's, caramel cashew popcorn from Garrett's. That kind of thing. Setting up a scenario to get a comb to sharpen to use two weeks later to kill herself? Impressive. Even for my mom. Also outrageously cruel.

"This wasn't a contraband snack. It was the thing she used to kill herself." My face suddenly went from cold to hot. "She made me bring her the weapon she used to kill herself."

I started to rock in my chair. I couldn't stop myself. I was aware of Dr. Ashmore watching me, holding my hands, murmuring to me, but somehow it seemed to be happening to someone else far away. Somehow I seemed to be viewing the whole thing from a deep well, looking up into the room as it whirled around me. Anger. Guilt. Shame. Frustration. Grief. They all swept in at once, threatening to drown me.

Then, just as suddenly, I snapped back into myself. I took a deep breath, shuddering as it entered my lungs, and extricated my hands from Dr. Ashmore's.

I missed their warmth immediately.

"Sorry," I said. "I don't usually fall apart like that."

He cocked his head to one side, looking up at me from his crouched position. "Under the circumstances, I think it's pretty normal."

I shook my head, rubbing my hands up and down my arms, hoping to warm myself again. "Not for me. Not when it comes to my mom. It's been a long time since she's been able to surprise me."

Dr. Ashmore rose to his feet. "I suppose that's true."

"What about the…the body?" I didn't know what to call her now. She wasn't my mother anymore. She was the shell that encased the wild craziness that had been the woman who'd raised me for seventeen years before doing the unthinkable and unforgivable.

He sat on the edge of the desk. "There'll be an autopsy. It's the law. Then the medical examiner will release the body to you. Do you know what her wishes were?"

I shook my head.

"Do you need to consult with other family members?"

I couldn't help it. I laughed. "No. I doubt any of them will want to get involved." Most of them couldn't understand why I was still involved. I wasn't going to enlighten them; no one else needed to know what part I played, what my contributions had been to the destruction of my family, what burdens lay on my shoulders. Besides, there wasn't anybody else, was there? I was her oldest child, her only daughter. She'd always turned to me. Always. That was part of my horror. Even at her worst, at her lowest moment, she knew there was something inside me that she could count on.

Dr. Ashmore pulled a couple of pamphlets from one of the stacks on his desk. "These might help you start with your decision-making process. The ME doesn't generally take too long, so you might want to make the decision sooner rather than later."

I nodded and took the pamphlets, sliding them into my purse without looking at them. I'd look at home. I didn't trust myself not to fall apart again when faced with making the decision about what to do with my mother's body, and I didn't want to do that in front of Dr. Ashmore again. I didn't want to do it in front of anybody.

Ashmore picked up the phone and hit a button. "Could you have Lois bring in Ms. Framingham's belongings?"

He turned back to me after he hung up the phone. "I had one of the nursing assistants pack up your mother's belongings. I hope that's okay."

I nodded. I was grateful, but I also suspected that they needed my mother's belongings out of the way so they could use the bed. Dealing with the medical establishment had made me a little cynical. More cynical would be more accurate, I guess. By the time my mother was actually locked up here, I'd had most of my illusions destroyed. I walked into the situation pretty jaded. Still, it was nice not to have to think about going through my mother's drawers. "Thank you."

We waited a few minutes in silence and then there was a soft knock on the door. "Come in," Dr. Ashmore called.

A pretty young nursing assistant came in struggling a little with a large cardboard box. Ashmore came out from around his desk and took the box from her. "Thank you, Lois."

She smiled up at him. She was pretty. Seriously pretty. Blonde hair parted in the middle framed a heart-shaped face sporting a spray of light freckles across the bridge of her nose and on her cheeks. She looked young and fresh and wholesome and open. I probably was only a few years older than her, but I felt dried up and desiccated in comparison. Crabbed and dark, twisted in on myself.

She turned, her big hazel eyes focusing on me. I'd seen her before when I was visiting my mother, but not a lot. "You're Amanda?" she asked.

I nodded.

"I'm so sorry. I hadn't worked with your mother for very long, but I was getting to know her. She was so creative, so talented. I made sure to put some of her drawings in here." She motioned to the box.

"Thank you." I didn't know what else to say. She was right; my mother was talented and creative. She'd painted murals on all of our bedroom walls when we were kids. It never seemed to matter what we asked for, she could paint it. Dinosaurs playing soccer. Underwater castles. White puffy clouds on blue skies. Mom would get out her brushes and whatever scene we wanted would appear on our walls.

"It's such a shame." She bit her lip like she was thinking about saying more and then changed her mind. "Again, my condolences."

She left the room, patting my shoulder as she passed by me to exit.

Dr. Ashmore hoisted the box up. "I'll carry this out for you."

I nodded and retrieved my coat and gloves. "It's freezing out. Don't you want to put on a coat?"

He shook his head. "It'll do me good."

We retraced our steps back to the lobby and then out the door. He stopped for a second as we walked outside and the cold air slammed into us. "That is…brisk."

I put my gloved hands on my cheeks, which were already burning with the cold. "I warned you. I can probably take it from here." I reached for the box.

"I'm fine. Just making an observation." He walked down the steps and turned toward the visitor lot. I hurried to keep pace with his long stride, the ground crunching beneath our feet.

"I'm right here," I said, gesturing toward my Escort. I unlocked the doors and opened the trunk. Ashmore placed the box inside. I shut the trunk and turned toward him, almost bumping into him. I didn't realize he was standing so close.

He took my hands in his. I could feel their warmth through the wool of my gloves. "I'm so sorry, Amanda. I really am. I know your relationship with your mother was…fraught, but that doesn't mean you won't be grieving. I hope you'll call me if you need to talk." He dropped my hands and took a card out of his pocket. "Here are all my numbers. All of them. Call any time."

Then he turned and headed back to the hospital. I got in my car and left, the crouching hulk of Elgin Medical Center forever in my rearview.

I drove the hour back to downtown Chicago with the sky still pressing down on me. After punching the buttons on the radio too many times, I finally turned it off. Everything set my nerves jangling. Even easy listening was like fingernails on a chalkboard. The silence soothed me, but it also left me alone with my thoughts.

After nearly ten years in a locked forensic unit, my mother killed herself using a comb that she may or may not have deliberately manipulated me into giving her. Was there a message there somewhere? According to Dr. Ashmore, she hadn't left any other message. No note. No manifesto. Just a sharpened comb down the long line of her slender wrists. Mom had been delicate, a fact that probably saved Dylan's life that night ten years ago. If she'd been stronger, she wouldn't have needed my help. She wouldn't have woken me, and I wouldn't have called 911.

I remembered that night with such clarity, the edges sharp and hard, everything else in relief. I'd woken to someone shaking my shoulder. I'd slapped the hand away, but she hadn't given up, even after I'd told her to leave me alone. I felt sick, like I might spew. The vodka had tasted good going down, but I knew it wouldn't be so fun coming back up.

33

"Amanda, baby, wake up. Wake up, honey sweetie pie." Mom. Mom was cooing in my ear. Mom was shaking my shoulder. Mom, still reeking of bleach from her manic cleaning episode earlier in the day.

I pulled the blanket up around my ears, but she pulled the blanket back down. "No, Amanda. I need your help now." Her voice had turned stern.

I asked if it could wait until morning, trying to keep my eyes shut against the spinning of the room. Mom laughed. That had been the first alarm bell that had gone off in my head. That laugh. High and trilling. Bright and brittle. It was never a good sign. Worse even than the bleach.

Mom smoothed my hair, tucking it behind my ear. Her touch soft, the caress of a mother's love. "I need your help with Dylan."

I was confused. Dylan was eleven. Jackson was the one Mom usually needed help with. "Do you mean Jackson?" I asked.

"No, honey, no. I took care of Jackson. Jackson's all settled." Mom frowned. "It was hard, though. Much harder than I thought. Look. I think he bruised me." She showed me a blooming purple spot on her arm.

"He hit you?" The fog in my brain started to clear. Jackson didn't hit.

"Not on purpose. He didn't understand, so he struggled." Mom shrugged. "I think probably Dylan won't understand either and he's much bigger, much stronger than Jackson. That's why I need your help."

"Wait. Understand what?" The inside of my mouth tasted like I'd been licking garbage cans. I tried to work some spit into it to wash it out.

"Why they need to go to God now. Why it's time. You can't explain something like that to a three-year-old. Even an eleven-year-old won't be able to grasp it. But you, you're a big girl. A woman already, really. Seventeen." Mom laughed again. This time the sound made the hair on my arms stand on end. "You know I'm only doing this to protect them."

My heart raced. "Protect them from what, Mom?"

"From all the evil in the world." Mom cocked her head to one side and smiled almost coquettishly. "It's too late for you and me. I'm so sorry about that. I should have been more watchful. I should have kept you innocent and pure. But it's not too late for your brothers. They're still innocents. We can save them. We can send them to God. I sent Jackson, but I don't think I can send Dylan without your help."

"So Jackson's already gone? Gone to God?" I'd forced the words out of my throat although I'd felt like it had swollen shut. She couldn't have been saying what I thought she was saying. My mind raced to find other explanations, other interpretations. There weren't any. I knew what going to God meant. I'd fought the urge to scream.

"Oh, yes. You can come see him. He looks so peaceful now, like a little sleeping angel." Mom held her hands to her chest and beamed.

"You're sure he's not just asleep?" Please, I'd begged in my head. Please let him only be asleep. Please let her not have done what I *think she's* done.

She laughed again. "Oh, I'm sure. He's gone. And now we need to send Dylan."

Dylan. Happy, funny Dylan. If I couldn't do anything for Jackson, I could at least do something for Dylan. I looked at my mom. We were the same size. Could I overpower her? Hold her down? Then what? I needed help and I needed it fast.

"Okay. Just let me pee first." I slithered out from under the blankets and stood, sliding my cell phone off my bedside table as I did. I went into the bathroom and locked the door. Inside, I turned the water on in the sink, but didn't splash it on my face or brush my teeth. Instead, I dialed 911 on my cell. It had taken four rings before someone answered. I thought I'd die in that time, but I didn't. I didn't die. My heart kept right on beating. Air kept moving in and out of my lungs.

Finally, a woman's voice said, "911, what's your emergency?"

"I need the police. I think my mother hurt my baby brother." Then I gave my address.

They came fast. I could hear the sirens by the time I came out of the bathroom. Mom had stared at me and in a whisper asked, "What have you done, Amanda? What have you done?"

I dodged her grasping hands and ran downstairs to the front door with her hard on my heels. That was fine with me. If she was chasing me, she wasn't hurting my brother. She caught me before I made it to the door, grabbed my hair and pulled me back, wrenching my neck. It hadn't mattered. The police were on the other side of the door. They heard me screaming. They broke down the door.

They found Dylan hiding in his closet. They found Jackson, lifeless and blue, in his bed.

They wouldn't let me hold Jackson's body. They'd said he was evidence, that they needed to examine him and investigate. What could there have been to investigate? Which pillow Mom had used to suffocate him? I'd longed to hold him in my arms, to feel his weight against my shoulder, to fold him against me one last time. I begged. They still said no.

So instead I sat outside his bedroom door and rocked and cried.

CHAPTER

4

I SHOOK MY HEAD AS if I could shake the thoughts out of it. If only it was that easy.

I parked the car back at the garage and carried my mother's box back to my apartment. It was heavy and ungainly enough to make me consider putting it on the ground to kick it along the slushy streets to my place. I didn't. It was not the kind of thing dutiful daughters did with their mother's effects, and I at least wanted to look like a dutiful daughter. Instead I carried it and ended up uncomfortable and sweaty under my coat. I was almost to the loft when the same homeless guy who'd asked Jesse and me for a handout the night before slipped out of the doorway that he'd clearly taken over as his.

"Please, miss. Some help?" He stretched out his hand, covered by my gloves. I set the box down, dug in my coat pocket, and came up with two quarters that I handed over. "Stay warm."

He looked over my shoulder and glared. I turned, catching a flicker of movement going around the corner. Whatever or whoever had been there was gone. I turned back to the man in front of me. His face had become impassive again. "Bless you. I'll do my best." He slinked back into the doorway.

I thought about Jesse's reaction to the guy the night before. A decisive strike against poor Jesse. Being mean to homeless people was a deal-breaker for me. So was being mean to waitstaff. Or animals. In fact, meanness in general knocked a person out of contention for my affections. It was one of the reasons I worked for Bellefountaine. No animal testing of products, completely cruelty-free. We used artificial human skin to test our products. It was expensive, but Friedrichs was willing to spend the money. Decisions like that made me respect the man, not something a person could always say about a boss.

Once I was finally inside my apartment, arms aching and sweat starting to drip, I plopped the box down on the dining room table, flung my coat over the couch and rummaged around in the fridge and the cupboard. It was close to two o'clock and I was starving. I focused on making my lunch, but the box was like a living, breathing thing behind me, a pulsing hulk squatting in my living space.

I snapped on the TV while I ate and watched a rerun of a stupid sit-com that didn't require much concentration on my part. It also did nothing to lessen my awareness of the box. I should have put it in the Dumpster by the garage. I couldn't imagine any memento of my mother I would actually want to hold onto. I knew for a fact there wouldn't be anything in there Dylan wanted. And Dad? Well, any reminders he'd had a wife before Jessica were not welcome. And yes, sometimes that included Dylan and me.

Yet I'd lugged the stupid box the two blocks from the garage with the wind blowing down the back of my neck, carried it into the elevator, and lumped it down the hall to my apartment. I'd probably passed three Dumpsters. Any one of them would have done. I supposed part of me would always hope to find some shred of that other mother. The fun Mom. The sweet Mom. The Mom who laughed and rolled in the grass with me and fretted with me about what to wear to school dances and was baffled by my math homework by the time I was in eighth grade, but still tried to help.

The Before Mom. Before Jackson was born. Before she would spend entire days in bed. Before she would go days without showering or brushing her teeth or eating. Before Dad left. Before Patrick Collier welcomed her into the waiting arms of the Children of the Greater God.

I knew I could put myself out of my agony by opening the box to see what was inside, but part of me was afraid of what I'd find. Dr. Ashmore said there wasn't a note or any indication of what prompted my mother to finally successfully take her own life, but maybe he didn't recognize whatever it was. He'd only been her doctor for a few months; I had been her daughter for twenty-seven years. If I recognized a sign or a message or a warning, how would I feel? How bad would the guilt get if I knew I had missed her cry for help on top of providing her with the tool she used to end it all?

My guess? Pretty freaking bad.

I did the dishes, vacuumed the loft, cleaned the bathroom, sorted the laundry, and still I could feel the presence of the box. It was nearly six by then. Well after five, I reasoned. I opened a bottle of wine. Who was there to judge me anyway?

Armed with my liquid courage, I got a pair of scissors from my desk and cut through the tape sealing the box. I pulled it open and jumped back a little, as if I expected Gwyneth Paltrow's head to be in it or for snakes to jump out. I shook my head. My mother's story might have the makings of a good horror movie, but she was long past being able to create those horrors. Her ability to do that had gone ten years ago, when the police arrived at our house and took her away in handcuffs as she shrieked at me for betraying her and God and told me I would always be unclean in the eyes of the Lord.

I peeked into the box. No severed heads. The bathrobe I'd given her for Christmas was on top. I pulled it out and set it aside. Some lucky Goodwill shopper would be happy for a nearly new L.L.Bean flannel bathrobe, because I sure as hell wasn't going to wear it. Then there was a lot of junk. Toiletries in a plastic bag. Those I tossed on top of the bathrobe. Some colored pencils. A journal I set aside to look at later. A sweater. I poured another glass of wine. A folder that held some of her artwork.

As I tossed the folder onto the journal, something slipped out. A photograph. I flipped it over and this time I stepped back for a reason. It was a picture of Jackson taken maybe a month or two before he died. He was wearing the Spiderman pajamas he'd gotten for Christmas and that he practically lived in. He was sitting on Mom's lap, smiling up at the camera, an impish grin on his face, grasping a little Spiderman toy that had come from a McDonald's meal. That toy that had briefly been the bane of our existence. He wouldn't go to bed without Spidey, and it was so small it was constantly getting lost: in the car, between the couch cushions, under Dad's desk. I couldn't count the hours we'd all spent searching for Spidey so Jackson would go to bed. We couldn't get another one, either. McDonald's had stopped giving them out.

I tried to imagine what that photo was doing in Mom's stuff or what seeing it would have done to her. One of her most self-protecting delusions was that Jackson simply didn't exist and never had. A photo like this could have easily cracked the protective shell she had woven around her.

A flash of anger surged up in me. No way had she gotten hold of this photo on her own. No way. I certainly hadn't sent it to her. Neither would have Dylan. He may have hated her and wanted nothing to do with her, but he wasn't cruel. Dad? No, Dad was way more into denial than that. In a way, he handled the situation the same way Mom did. For Mom, Jackson didn't exist. For Dad, Mom didn't.

I racked my brains for who else would or could have sent it. No one—and I mean no one—kept in contact with Mom. Whatever friends and family she hadn't alienated with her mood swings and crazy accusations before everything came crashing down had pretty much fled by the time of her trial. By the time she came to Elgin, there really wasn't anyone who wanted anything to do with her. Who could blame them? Not me. I'd have run if I could have. I'd been seventeen and in high school without a clue as to how to get away from my mother or how bad things were going to get.

None of the people who had fled from us had the kind of sadistic streak it would take to send her that photo of Jackson, though. No one actually wished her ill, they just didn't want to have any of her crazy cooties get on them.

I opened the folder. The top two pieces of paper were thick smooth Bristol, covered with colored pencil. My mother's usual still lifes. A coffee mug with a drooping daisy next to an apple. A bruised-looking pear with some fall leaves. I sifted down through more of the same. Some of them in watercolor, but most in pencil. Then I hit newsprint. A page of the Chicago Tribune, still fresh and unyellowed. I unfolded it and my hands started to shake.

I recognized the photo before I read the headline. Patrick Collier Up for Parole. I'd read the article when it had been printed in the Trib a week ago. It had infuriated me. Patrick Collier was going to be a free man. He was going to step out of prison and right back into his role leading the Children of the Greater God. They still existed. Oh, their numbers had dwindled, but they were around. Every once in a while I saw members collecting money at intersections or L stops. Always adults now. Not teenagers like there had been when I had been a member of COGG. Still, they were there. I had no idea what the prospect of Patrick out in the world leading others, influencing others, guiding others to God, would do to mom. How would she have felt seeing the man she had trusted, had followed, had loved, getting out of prison with virtually no hope of the same for her?

People think that when someone is found not guilty by reason of insanity (NGRI, for those of us in the know), that they're somehow getting away with something. The truth is, most people found NGRI spend more time incarcerated than if they'd been found guilty and gone to prison. You can't get out unless you're cured, and proving you're sane when you're in a locked ward isn't easy. Plus, with my mom, getting close to sanity always meant having to face what she'd done,

44

and that didn't exactly work for her. Hence the repeated suicide attempts. She wasn't ever getting out of Elgin unless she went feet first.

Which she had.

By using the comb that I'd brought her.

Beneath the article from the Tribune was a photocopy of an even older article. The headline on this one read Highland Park Mom Kills Toddler. I didn't read the rest of it. I knew what it said. I remembered all too well the weeks and weeks of articles about my family that ran in the news. Not just the local news, either. We were a hot topic everywhere. CNN. NBC. ABC. CBS. NPR. BBC. They all did features on our family. They all begged for interviews. They all massed on the street outside our house for weeks. They all ran after our car shouting, shoving microphones at us, pointing cameras at us.

I remembered looking at the photos of me that had run in the newspapers and magazines and wondering who that girl was.

I looked down at the photo of Jackson, the article about Collier, and the article about Jackson's death. I was reeling. Nauseated, shaking, pulse pounding. If seeing these things did that to me, what would they have done to my mother? Maybe, just maybe, I wasn't totally at fault here. Somebody brought those things to her. Someone who must have known what they would do to her. Someone who knew how to get things through the guards. Someone inside Elgin. Someone who damn well should be punished.

I pulled Dr. Ashmore's card out of my pocket and dialed his cell. He answered on the fourth ring. I could hear a lot of noise in the background. "This is Dr. Ashmore," he said.

"This is Amanda Sinclair. Linda Framingham's daughter. I'm going through the box you gave me and all I can say is, what the hell, doc?" It felt good to have a target for the anger. My lungs felt shuddery. I rolled my shoulders like a prizefighter.

"You're going to need to be more specific, Amanda. What the hell about what?" The noise lessened on his end. Was it just a TV?

"There's a photo of my baby brother in this box and a news article about when it happened and another news article about Collier coming up for parole. You want to know what might set my mother off? What might make her sharpen a comb and slice through her veins with it? I'm pretty sure I have an answer for you." I was breathing hard.

Now there was silence at his end. "I assure you, Amanda, no such things were found in your mother's room. We wouldn't have allowed them."

"Yeah, well, allowed or not, they're in the box of her belongings. Care to explain that?" I actually hopped on my toes.

"I can't, Amanda. I can't explain it at all." He paused. "Would it be possible for me to see these things?"

That brought me up short for a second. "I don't see why not, but I'm not driving back to Elgin tomorrow." As far as I was concerned, I'd made my last drive to Elgin.

"I'll come to you. Where should we meet?" he asked.

I sat back down at my dining room table, all the fight abandoning me, and looked at the photo of my little brother. The idea of showing that photo to Dr. Ashmore in a Starbucks under the eyes of curious strangers while jazz-classic Valentine's music played more than didn't appeal. "Come to my apartment."

Now it was the doctor's turn to hesitate. I could see why he might want to think twice about coming alone to the apartment of his former homicidal and suicidal patient's angry daughter, so I gave him a moment. "Sure," he said. "I'll be there at about two."

I packed everything except the flannel bathrobe back into the box. I threw that into a bag in the closet that was headed for donation land. My closet is not particularly tidy. There have been some studies linking childhood trauma and OCD. I wish I thought that lining up my shoes just right or washing my hands over and over would protect me and the people I cared about. My mother proved to me that I could wash the whole house down with bleach and bad stuff would still happen. At least I didn't have to waste time keeping things crazy tidy. As I shoved the bathrobe into the bag, something slipped out of one of its pockets, something shiny. I knelt to pick it up and almost couldn't stand back up. It was a necklace. Silver. A thick chain with a shiny silver cog hanging on it like a pendant. The symbol of the Children of the Greater God. All of Patrick Collier's followers had worn one of these. Men. Women. Children. My mother had worn one. For a brief time, I had worn one.

Shaking, I picked it up and put it in the box. I couldn't bear to leave the other stuff lying on the table exposed. Every time I walked past the photo of Jackson, it stopped me short like a leash had suddenly pulled tight around my neck.

I didn't keep photos of Jackson around. They were too painful. I'd been in junior high when he was born and as far as I'd been concerned, he was my baby as much as anyone else's. I'd been a little slow to mature and I'd only just finished playing with dolls when Mom and Dad presented me with a real live baby doll to hold and feed and rock and love.

Dad took me to the hospital to see him before Jackson and Mom came home. Dylan must have been there, too, but I don't seem to remember him. I don't really remember Dad or Mom being there, either. Just Jackson. He'd been crying. Screaming, really. His little face was screwed up and red with anger. I'd reached for him, and his tiny little hand had grabbed my finger. I know now that he couldn't have known it was there, couldn't have known how to grab hold, but that's what happened. Then he pulled my finger into his mouth and started to suck on it.

It made me believe in Cupid's arrows. At that moment, I was shot through the heart with love.

So no, I didn't have photos reminding me of his absence. Then again, I didn't have photos of any of my family displayed in my apartment or at my office. Not perhaps for the same reason, but does that really matter?

Isolate. Compartmentalize. Control. That's my motto.

CHAPTER

5

Sunday, February 19

SUNDAY MORNING I DID WHAT most of America does—I got a little cardio in. I opted for the gym in the basement of River City rather than a run along the lake since it was still only about fifteen degrees outside. I showered. I read the paper. I drank coffee. I checked my email and my Facebook page. I made a shopping list. I folded my laundry.

I did not reopen the box.

Dr. Ashmore showed up at five minutes after two. I buzzed him into my building and met him in the hallway after he got off the elevator. He had on jeans and boots and a peacoat over some kind of thick off-white sweater. He looked like a model for a catalog. He smelled good, too. Kind of soapy.

I felt a little self-conscious in my yoga pants and long-sleeved T-shirt. Whatever. It wasn't like this was a date, after all.

"How are you feeling?" he asked as he walked down the hall. He didn't ask it in that breezy *How ya doing?* tone. He asked it as if he really wanted to know, like a doctor.

I opened the door to my apartment. "I'm not really sure."

"It takes a while for things like this to sink in," he observed, stepping inside and shrugging out of his coat.

I took his jacket and led him into the main room of the apartment. He looked around. "Nice place."

"It suits me," I said.

He nodded. What the hell did that mean? Suddenly I felt a little too exposed and I wasn't talking about the way my yoga pants fit. Do shrinks ever not shrink? Was he looking at my apartment and analyzing why I would pick such a place? What did my big, open, empty loft with giant windows on one end say about me? How about the lack of anything on my walls? I pulled the box out from under my desk where I'd stowed it.

Dr. Ashmore took it from me and put it on the table. "Okay if I open it?" he asked.

I nodded. I really didn't want to go through my severed -head routine again, especially not with an audience. He undid the flaps. I'd left the photo of Jackson on top.

"Your brother?" he asked, holding it up.

"Yeah. That's Jackson. The one...well, you know." Ten years later and I still had trouble saying it out loud.

Dr. Ashmore sat down, gazing at the photo. "I've never seen a picture of him before. There weren't any in your mother's file." He looked up at me, those blue eyes of his way too piercing. "He looks like her. He looks like you."

I sat down across from him. It wasn't like I didn't know that. Both Jackson and I took after Mom. Dark straight hair. Brown eyes. Chins that were a bit too pointed, mouths a bit too wide. Otherwise, unremarkable.

"How old was he again?" He set the photo down.

I picked it up. "Almost four."

He reached back into the box and pulled out the newspaper clipping. "This is the other thing you mentioned?"

"I thought you said there was no indication of what might have set her off. I thought you said she didn't have access to this kind of stuff. I thought you said that you monitored her." My grasp tightened on the photo of Jackson. I felt the spark of anger ignite again. My mother was crazy. She was a murderer. There was blood on her hands, but she didn't deserve to be tortured.

"We do." He shook his head. "At least, I thought we did. I have no idea how these got into her room,

52

Amanda. I really don't. No one mentioned that they were there."

"So you didn't clean out her room yourself? You didn't go through her things?" Now there was a catch in my throat. What the hell? What was it about this guy that made me choke up?

He shot me a look. "No. I don't clean out the rooms of patients, Amanda. I'm pretty sure you know what my client load is like."

I bit my tongue. I supposed it would be like expecting me to mop the lab after hours. I let that one slide. "Do you know who did?"

He leaned back in the chair and rubbed at his chin. He was clean-shaven and not all stubbly. No one wanted a doctor to be trendy. At least, I didn't. "I'll find out," he said.

"Well, I think we have our answer regarding what might have set her off, but I still would like to know who gave her these things." Dr. Ashmore knew I was Mom's only visitor. That meant whoever decided to torment my mother with Jackson's photo and the news article about Collier's parole had to be on the inside at Elgin. It had to be one of his people.

"So would I." He rubbed at his forehead with his thumb and index finger. "Would you let me hold on to the photo of your brother?"

Reflex had me pulling the photo toward my chest, as if he might snatch it away from me. "Why?"

"I'd like to show it around. See if anybody else at the center saw it or saw your Mom with it." He drummed his fingers on the table. "I'm not sure what else to do."

I slowly slid the photo across the table to him. It was the one to appear in a lot of the newspaper articles around the time of Mom's trial. I didn't know why I'd grabbed it back. I was about a decade too late to protect Jackson, and Mom was clearly outside of my circle of care as well. In fact, being in my care seemed like it might be a death sentence. Good thing I didn't have any houseplants.

"Thanks," Ashmore said, taking the photo and looking at it again. Then he looked up at me. "Are you all right?"

"I'll be okay." I always was, wasn't I?

He cocked his head slightly to one side. A shock of dark hair fell across his forehead and he brushed it away. "That wasn't what I asked. Are you all right now? Is there something I can do to help you?"

I couldn't imagine what that might be. I'd been beyond help for a lot of years. "Find out who was tormenting my mother, okay? She was no angel, but she didn't deserve that." I stood up to seal up the box. The Ziploc bag with her toiletries in it had popped open and spilled its contents inside the box. I started picking up the items and putting them back into the bag before I shut the box again. A toothbrush. A lipstick. Deodorant. A comb.

My fingers stopped. A comb?

I drew it out of the box. "I thought you said she used the comb to, uh, to hurt herself."

Dr. Ashmore reached out his hand for the comb. "She did."

"Do you know that for sure? Or are you going on hearsay for that, too?" I asked then regretted how bitchy I sounded.

He grimaced. "I saw it myself." It clearly was an image he didn't want to revisit.

I handed the comb to him. It was the one I'd bought my mother two weeks before. I'd written her name along its spine before I left and it still had her name written in my crabbed script. "Do you remember what color the other one was?"

"Pink."

I tried to remember if my mother's last comb was pink. I always bought her things light in color so it would be easy to write her name on them. This one was beige. Boring, I knew, but my choices had been limited. "Well, this is the one I bought her two weeks ago. I'm sure of it."

He turned the comb in his hands, making it look tiny next to his big fingers. "Amanda, this is very strange."

Strange, but a bit wonderful, too. Maybe I hadn't bought the instrument my mother used to kill herself. The burning in my chest went down a notch.

"We keep pretty close tabs on resident belongings. We do it to avoid, well, what happened with your mother. If this is the comb you bought her two weeks ago, where did the one she sharpened come from?"

I didn't have any more of an answer to that than he did. "Are you guys absolutely sure she did this herself? Could someone have..."

The look of pity on Ashmore's face was almost more than I could stand. He reached across the table for my hand. "Amanda, why would anyone want to hurt your mother? She wasn't a threat to anyone."

I pulled my hand out from under his. I knew he was right. She wasn't a threat. Not anymore. Not even to Collier. Even if my mother could have said something to hurt someone, who would have believed her?

Ashmore handed me back the comb and stood. "Thank you for calling me, Amanda. Thank you for showing me these things. I'll let you know what I find out.

I picked up his coat and walked him to the door. He shrugged into his jacket and stopped. "Look—I know this can't be easy for you. I can only imagine what you're thinking and feeling. I don't know if you're treating with anyone, but I hope you'll call me if you need to talk."

I bit back about a dozen snarky comments that tumbled into my mouth. He didn't have to come here. He didn't have to look into anything. A woman committed by the state who had made several previous suicide attempts had finally succeeded. It wasn't exactly the kind of event that launches a major investigation.

"Thanks," I said. "And thanks for coming, Dr. Ashmore."

"Sam." He smiled. "Please, call me Sam."

"Okay," I said, grabbing my coat and grocery bags. "I'll walk you downstairs, Sam. I'm leaving now, too."

We rode down in the elevator in silence. He looked like he had more to say, but I didn't encourage him. I'd had about as much sharing as I could stand for the day. Possibly the week. Maybe even the month. We shook hands at the front of my building and I headed over to the garage to get my car.

As I walked to the pedestrian entrance, a black SUV came barreling out of the garage exit, not pausing as it rolled over the sidewalk and into the street. I jumped backward to avoid being sideswiped, but my heel caught in the sidewalk crack and I ended up tumbling down. I sat on my ass and watched the SUV turn up the narrow street, tires screeching as it made its turn at way too high a speed.

"You okay, miss?" A man was taking my arm.

Instinctively I grabbed it back.

"Easy there," he said. Red-faced from the cold with a watch cap pulled down on his forehead, he could have been half the artist's sketches of people wanted by the police. Instead of grabbing my purse and running, he helped me up and brushed at the dirt on my coat.

"Yeah. A little surprised, I guess." And embarrassed.

"Too bad there weren't no cops around. Jerk coulda killed you. He never even slowed down." The man shook his head at the perfidy of SUV drivers or perhaps people, in general.

I smiled. "Well, all that's bruised is my dignity."

"You're lucky," he said, shrugging inside his plaid jacket and then walked on.

Yeah. Lucky. That's me.

Driving to the nearest Jewel supermarket, something kept rattling in the back of the Escort. As soon as I parked—no small feat on a Sunday afternoon in Lincoln Park—I walked around the back to see what was loose. It only took a second to spot it: someone had broken into the trunk of my car. I couldn't believe I hadn't noticed it earlier, although nothing in the front seat had been touched. Then again, I'd also been a little preoccupied. "Damn it," I said, trying to get the lock to work. Whoever had done it hadn't been subtle. They'd used a crowbar or something to pry the trunk lid open and then shut it again. The edge of the trunk was mangled and wouldn't close all the way, but it wouldn't lift easily either. I worked at it for a few minutes and finally got it open.

Sitting in the middle of the trunk of my car was a note typed on a piece of paper, small letters on an otherwise blank sheet: Keep your mouth shut. Jaw dropping open, I picked it up. Underneath was a little Spiderman figure with its head broken off.

CHAPTER

6

MY FIRST INSTINCT WAS TO slam the trunk shut and back away, which almost got me creamed by a white Chrysler 300 that came out of nowhere in the Jewel parking lot. So much for first instincts. That was two brushes with vehicular death in one day. My second instinct was to call Dr. Ashmore and make him come look at it. Luckily I had time to stop myself from doing that. What on earth could he do about this? No way had this happened out at Elgin. I would have heard that rattle on the way home no matter how deep in funk and misery I was, and I would have seen it when we were putting the box in the trunk. Whoever had messed with my trunk and left me such a pointed message had to have done it when my car was parked in the garage.

With a little wrangling, I got the trunk to open again and took a picture of the headless Spiderman with my cell phone. At second glance, it was actually kind of funny. Who did something like that? If I had a bunny, would they have boiled it?

I glanced around to see if anyone was watching me. Would whoever had done this follow me to watch me find it? Why else leave me such a cryptic message except to get their jollies watching me find it? The parking lot was a madhouse. It was Sunday afternoon and everyone wanted to get their shopping done for the week. Everyone wanted to get home and enjoy what was left of the weekend. Could someone have followed me here? I'd have noticed someone in the parking garage, but once I was out on the streets? I'd been focused on the traffic ahead of me, not what might be behind me.

Then I thought about that black SUV. Hadn't there been one circling my block when Jesse walked me home on Friday? Of course, there were a few thousand black SUVs in Chicago. I was getting paranoid. Some jerk plays a nasty little joke and suddenly I'm convinced someone is out to get me? No.

I wouldn't mind knowing who was messing with me, though. No candidates sprang to mind. I hadn't thought anyone knew who I was or why that little Spiderman toy would be significant, let alone hate me enough to poke me like that. Well, fine. They'd gotten what they wanted, they made me jump. I wasn't going to let this turn me into a sniveling mess, though.

I shut the trunk again, went into the store, and did my grocery shopping. I bought some brown paper lunch bags as well as the other items on my list. When I got back to my car (no, I didn't need assistance, thank you very much), I slid the headless Spiderman into one of the paper bags and folded the top shut. I watched cop shows on occasion. I knew that fingerprints could be preserved that way. I wasn't sure who might want to dust a tiny Spiderman figurine for fingerprints, but if anyone ever did, I'd be ready. I was so prepared I was practically a Boy Scout.

I picked my way home through the traffic, parked my car on the fourth floor of the ramp, and heaved my groceries out of the mangled trunk. There was no one in the garage office on a Sunday evening to whom I could report the break-in. I'd have to stop back during the week. I trudged home, two grocery bags hanging off each hand and my purse periodically slipping off my shoulder. I really needed to get one of those rolly carts all the old ladies in the neighborhood used.

The sun started to lower in the sky. The wind picked up and it was as if I could feel the water it picked up from the lake pouring down the neck of my coat. My shadow lengthened in front of me, turning blue as it crept along the snow piled on either side of the sidewalk.

Suddenly it struck me as ridiculous that I was tramping along the icy sidewalk hauling Honeycrisp apples and Lean Cuisine dinners. My mother was dead. Someone tormented her with pictures of her dead son and stories of her soon-to-be-released-from-prison religious leader until she committed suicide. Then someone left a weird threatening message and a headless action figure in my car. What was I doing? Why was I bothering to go through the motions of my solitary pathetic life? I stopped walking, barely feeling the whoosh as another black SUV swept past me, splattering slush as it turned the corner ahead. See? There were dozens of them cruising the streets of Chicago. None of them had anything to do with me.

The handles of the plastic bags cut into my cold, bent fingers, making them ache. No matter how ridiculous it was, I was here. That has always been my burden. I was here. Jackson wasn't. Now Mom wasn't either. Back in the day, Dad hadn't been. But I was. I was alive. I was breathing. I was working. And I had to eat, didn't I? I resumed my march, managing somehow to punch in the code on the front door without taking off my gloves. I was trying to shoulder the door open when someone pulled it open from behind me. I turned to say thank you and came face -to -face with the homeless guy.

I wish I could say I said thank you with dignity and went on in, but no, I reacted as if he'd pulled a knife. I skittered backward like a mouse into a corner.

He held his free hand up. "No, ma'am, no. Just trying to help."

My heart slowed back down to maybe a Gloria Estefan rhythm. "Oh. Sorry. Thanks. I, uh, didn't mean to…" To what? I asked myself. Imply that because he was homeless, he was also violent and criminal?

He snorted. "Don't worry. I know. Just wanted to do a good turn for you since you did one for me."

And then he was gone.

And I was alone again.

And that was when I started to cry.

One little act of kindness and I was completely undone.

So, crying was exhausting. No wonder I didn't do it more often. After the homeless guy held the door open for me—an act of kindness out of nowhere—and I started blubbering, I made it into the elevator, stumbled down the hallway, and fell into the safe silence of my loft. I couldn't stop the tears from pouring down my face. What's worse was that it felt like the sobs were coming from somewhere deep down in me, down in my solar plexus, making me nearly double over as each one wracked me.

I dropped the groceries in the entryway, ripped off my hat and scarf and gloves and coat as I crashed to my bed, and gave myself over to the tears.

I woke up forty-five minutes later. Apparently I'd cried myself to sleep. I got up, splashed some water on my face, tried not to look at my puffy creased eyes, and rescued my groceries from the front hall. Luckily I kept the loft at sixty-eight degrees in the winter and the ice cream had only started to get a little soft.

I felt a little like the ice cream. Halffrozen but also deeply empty. I'd heard people talk about feeling cleansed after a big boo-hoo session. I felt drained and desolate. If this was catharsis, they could keep it. Still, I had at least three calls to make. The first was to the cops to report that my car had been broken into. Shockingly, the Chicago police were not terribly exercised over this occurrence. They were, in fact, blasé.

"Anything missing from the car?" the bored officer on the other end of the line asked.

I hesitated. Nothing was missing, was it? If I told the cops about the Spiderman figurine, there would be a lot of questions, most of which I wouldn't be able to answer. Most of which would make me sound crazy. Most of which the cops would do nothing about. "No. Nothing missing."

"So you're reporting this for the insurance claim, right?" she asked.

"Yeah. For the insurance claim," I confirmed.

"Got it, then. Here's your report number." She rattled off a series of digits and letters I scrambled to write down. "Call us if we can be of any further assistance."

She hung up before I could say thank you.

My next call was to Dr. Ashmore.

"Amanda? Are you okay?" he asked instead of saying hello.

If I hadn't felt like a basket case before, I did now. "Yeah. I'm okay, but can I text you a photo?"

"Of...?" Now he sounded amused.

"Of something I found in the trunk of my car this afternoon." I was only a little sorry to burst his bubble. I wasn't going to be sexting my mom's shrink anytime soon. Probably.

"Sure."

I hung up and texted him the photo of the Spiderman toy. He called me back in less than thirty seconds.

"Did you call the police?" There was no more amusement in his voice.

"Yes," I said, realizing I was only technically answering his question.

"What did they say?"

"Not much. I didn't actually tell them about the note or anything. I reported the break -in so my insurance would cover the broken trunk." I picked up a pen on my desk and tapped it against the note pad I kept there.

"You're joking, right?"

It was a little funny, but I wasn't joking in the way he meant. "No. What are they going to do?"

"I don't know. Dust for fingerprints. Look for DNA. I think they're going to do the stuff that cops do." He sounded a tiny bit exasperated.

"I think those are things the cops do on TV. I think in downtown Chicago, someone leaving a broken toy and a weird note in some chick's pathetically -easy -to -break -into vehicle won't get their whole crime scene unit out."

"At least there'd be a record of it."

"There is a record. It's just of a trunk being forced open."

He was silent for a moment. I stopped tapping the pen and waited. "Amanda, who would do that? Who would leave a note like that for you? And, more importantly, why?"

Now it was my turn to pause. I wasn't going to answer that. Not yet. Not before I got some other answers. Answering would require me to dig a lot deeper into my own past than I wanted to. Ever. I wasn't stupid. I realized I might have to think about certain things, but it wasn't going to be tonight. It wasn't going to be the day after I collected my mother's belongings. It wasn't going to be like this. "I have to think about it," I said, suddenly wanting more than anything to hang up the phone. Why the hell had I called him anyway?

Oh, yeah. Because he apparently was the only other person on the planet who had any interest in why or how my mother had killed herself.

"Okay. I think that's probably a good thing. Call me if you come up with anything. Or even if you don't."

I laughed. "Sure. I'm positive you're thrilled with getting crazy calls from the crazy daughter of your crazy dead patient in your off hours."

He didn't say anything for a few seconds. Then his voice came back, deep and rumbling over the phone. "You're not crazy. So call, okay? I want you to."

I felt the hot prick of tears start again. "Thanks." My voice sounded all weird and wobbly. Pathetic, much?

"You're welcome. Try to get some rest."

We hung up. I stood in the middle of the room, pinching the bridge of my nose for a few seconds. Then I pulled the stupid box back out, dug into it, and pulled out my mother's COGG necklace.

I carried it into my bedroom and set it carefully on my dresser as I opened up my jewelry box. Then I pulled out my COGG necklace. The one that Patrick Collier himself had fastened around my neck. I still remembered how he had rested his hands on my shoulders for a moment after fastening the clasp. His touch had been gentle. His fingers had been warm. But the sensation he had left behind was a tingling that had made all the hairs on my arm stand on end. It had made my breath come a little faster. It had made me lick my lips in anticipation, as if someone had promised me a hot fudge sundae.

My mother had been there. I had looked up and seen her, hands clasped under her chin, eyes glittering with happiness. She had no idea what she was witnessing. I hadn't really known what she was witnessing, either. I had been sixteen. Sixteen and stupid.

I remembered the pride I'd felt because Patrick had put the necklace on me himself. I remembered the thrill I'd felt because he'd touched me. I remembered feeling everyone's eyes on me and knowing that some of them were jealous of the attention I got from Patrick. I remembered loving their jealousy, loving the look in their eyes.

And I remembered other ways people had looked at me. I remembered dark eyes, filled with tears, begging me for help. Then I was filled with shame. Shame at what had come next. Shame at what it had done to my family. Shame at my own shortcomings, then and now.

I lifted the necklace up, letting it turn and sway in front of my eyes. Light glinted off its silver surface.

Then I balled it up in my fist and threw it at the wall as hard as I could.

CHAPTER
7

Monday, February 20

IT WAS A RELIEF WHEN the alarm went off and I realized it was Monday morning and I could go back to work. I liked work. Work made sense. There were machines to calibrate. Dilutions to make. Liquids to pipette. Things were measurable. Cause and effect became clear. It was clean and precise and made me feel like the world didn't have to be a place of dangerous and crazy chaos. The lab was my wheelhouse. My paint, as Dylan used to say when he played basketball. That's where the rituals that made me feel calm and safe happened.

After my little temper tantrum last night, I'd picked up both my necklace and my mother's and put them in the jewelry box where I never had to look at them again. I'd put Mom's box under my desk. When I got out of bed, I could pretend that none of it had ever happened, which was exactly what I did.

I snapped on the morning news while I ate my Wheaties. The talking head said a few things about the cold weather and how it was supposed to last for several days. Then she did a little promo for a piece coming up later about how to weatherproof your home.

Then she did one of those anchorperson things where her face suddenly became very serious. I had no idea how those people pull that off. Their faces must be made of rubber. "Notorious child killer Linda Framingham has committed suicide while in custody at the Elgin State Mental Hospital."

I nearly spit my Wheaties out on the counter.

"Ten years ago, Framingham, who was later diagnosed as suffering from bipolar disorder and severe postpartum depression, smothered her youngest child, three-year-old Jackson, with a pillow, then woke her teenaged daughter to help her kill her other son, shocking her Highland Park community. The daughter summoned police and Framingham was arrested. She was found Not Guilty by Reason of Insanity and has been incarcerated in Elgin since that time."

Please don't use my name. Please don't use Dylan's name. Please don't say our names, I silently begged the woman on the screen. Please.

"Family members blamed the influence of infamous Children of the Greater God cult leader, Patrick Collier, for Framingham's final break with sanity. No evidence was found to implicate Collier, although he was later jailed for mismanagement of funds. He is up for parole at the end of this month."

I let out the breath I'd been holding. They hadn't used my name or Dylan's. No one watching the newscast would connect us with Mom or COGG. At least, I didn't think they would. Mom had never taken Dad's last name, and that's what both Dylan and I used.

"Authorities are investigating the circumstances around Framingham's suicide," the anchorwoman said.

Yeah, sure they were. Just like they were investigating the break-in of my car.

I took another bite of cereal, but it tasted like cardboard. I dumped it down the sink and finished getting ready for work.

The lake effect had brought temperatures up a bit. Add the thousands of feet tramping through the Loop, and what had been ice was now slush. I decided to think of it as an improvement. About halfway to the L to go to work, my stomach let me know that skipping breakfast was not to its liking. I popped into the coffee shop by the LaSalle/Van Buren L stop to grab a muffin and a cup of coffee.

On my way in, I ran into Will Friedrichs, the CEO of Bellefountaine. He was hard to miss, as usual. He always looked like he'd stepped off a magazine cover. It made sense. A man who ran a cosmetics company ought to look damn good, after all. There were some shiny places on his forehead and nose that made a few of us wonder if he'd had some plastic surgery. I was about 90 percent certain he dyed his hair. Still, the overall package never failed to look good. "Will! What are you doing here?"

He looked even more surprised to see me than I was to see him. "Amanda?"

"One and the same." Someone jostled me from behind and I stepped into the shop to get out of the way. "What are you doing here?" I knew he didn't live down here. He was out in the suburbs; Winnetka, to be exact. He'd had us all out to his house for a barbecue back in July. His backyard was the size of the park down the street from my loft.

"Had an early -morning meeting with some guys," he said, waving his hand out toward the street.

I got it then. He'd been meeting with money guys. The rumor was that Bellefountaine was about to be purchased by a much bigger cosmetic company. It made sense that Will would need to be talking to financial whizzes. This kind of deal meant millions of dollars would change hands. Tens of millions, even. A person didn't make that kind of deal without consulting the kind of guys who worked around the Board of Trade.

"And you?" he asked.

"Oh, I live a few blocks away. I thought I'd stop here and get some coffee on my way to the lab."

"Excellent. I want you wellcaffeinated at work. How's everything going at the lab?" He laughed and rubbed his hands together. One more thing I liked about Will: he kept in touch with what was happening in the labs. He kept his fingers on the pulse of the products we were bringing to life.

"Great. Terrific, even. I've got one set of numbers for the Cover Me tests that don't seem quite right, but other than that, good."

"What kind of not right?" His voice sounded concerned, but his forehead didn't budge. Had to be Botox. I didn't blame him for being concerned, even if he couldn't make the appropriate facial expressions. Cover Me was the product that was driving the interest in buying our shop. It wouldn't come out for another six to nine months or so, but when it did, it was going to be a bombshell. One of the rumors I'd heard was that Revlon wanted to buy us before Cover Me rolled out so it could be their baby from the get -go.

Cover Me started as an anti-aging product. Not exactly revolutionary. There really isn't a cosmetic company out there that isn't trying to help Baby Boomers look more baby and less boom. Even women in their thirties worry about wrinkles. Then partway through our first set of tests on the product, we noticed that Cover Me seemed to actually soften the synthetic skin we were testing it on. Not just make it soft, but actually remove ridges.

We decided to see what would happen if we put it on scar tissue. The results were nearly miraculous. Cover Me reduced ridging and puckering of scar tissue by nearly 80 percent.

I'll never forget the meeting where we showed our findings to Will. Gobsmacked is the word I think best described his expression. They were gobsmacked - worthy findings.

Facial trauma is psychologically devastating. Whether it's from a birth defect or an injury, your face is what you present to the world. If it's jacked up, you feel jacked up. All the time. People with facial trauma have been shown to have more depression and more anxiety than people with other kinds of scarring. The idea that I could be a part of developing a product that could help reduce that depression and anxiety for so many people made me feel like a Goddamn super hero. It's bad enough to walk around in the world with scars no one can see; to have to do it with all the scars being basically the first thing anybody ever sees about you? Devastating.

"I'm not sure," I said. "That's the thing. I'll figure it out, though, and then we'll fix it." I smiled. I would, too. That was what I was good at. That was what Will paid me for.

"You keep me posted on how that goes, okay?" Then he patted me on the back and left the coffee shop.

I ordered a lemon poppyseed muffin and a skinny vanilla latte and turned toward the door. As I did, I saw the back of a blonde woman leaving the shop. She turned and walked past the plate glass window at the front of the shop. Something about her profile was familiar. High cheekbones. Slightly pointed chin. Freckles. Then it hit me: it was the nursing assistant from Elgin, the one who'd brought me the box of my mother's belongings. I elbowed my way through the crowd, trying to catch her. Maybe she would know who put those photos and articles in my mother's room. By the time I got to the sidewalk, though, she was nowhere to be seen. I wondered what she'd been doing here, so many miles away from Elgin, but I was pretty sure it was her. Maybe I'd call the hospital and ask her.

I headed for the L along with a few hundred or more of my fellow Chicagoans. I missed making the light at the corner of Van Buren and Financial Place by a few steps and stopped at the curb. I let my mind wander. If it wanted to bounce around like a particle in a Brownian motion demonstration, so be it. I gave it free rein. I hoped I'd be better able to focus when I got to the lab if I let my thoughts bounce now.

And bounce they did. Mom. Dylan. Mom again. The necklaces in my jewelry box. The photo of Jackson in the box of Mom's belongings. Dr. Ashmore...Sam. Sam's blue eyes. Tear-filled brown eyes. Patrick Collier. Mom again.

I wasn't really paying attention to who else might be walking with me. Standing in a crowd of strangers waiting for the little walking man was beyond familiar and, frankly, comforting. Just because I was a loner didn't mean I always wanted to be alone.

What wasn't familiar was feeling of hands at the small of my back shoving me off the curb directly in the path of a Yellow Cab intent on making the light.

I'd always heard people talking about how time seemed to stand still at the moment of an accident, everything decelerating into a slow motion movie. That's not how it happened for me. At least not that morning. One second I felt those hands at the small of my back, and the next I was standing on the sidewalk with a man clutching the back of my coat and asking if I was okay while I stared at the flattened remains of my skinny vanilla latte in the street.

"What happened?" the man who saved me asked. "Did you lose your balance?"

I didn't have an answer. Even if I had, I wasn't sure I would be able to speak. My heart beat at a frantic pace and my breath came in pants. I was damn glad I'd gone to the bathroom before I left home because otherwise I might have needed to go back to change. "I'm not sure," I finally gasped out. "It felt like someone pushed me."

A knot of people had formed around us. Everyone looked around at everyone else. I looked, too. Not one face was at all familiar.

"No," the man said, shaking his head. He let go of my coat and straightened his own and then straightened his tie, too. "Who would do something like that?"

"I don't know. I'm not sure." My heart slowed down, but my body started to shake.

"You're upset," a woman said, patting my shoulder. "It was scary. You're probably a little bit in shock, but you're fine. You're okay."

By now the light had changed again and more people were surging toward the crosswalk, trying to flow past our group.

"We should walk or we will get shoved into the street," someone said. There were murmurs of agreement from a few.

We all started to cross. On the other side, I grabbed the arm of the man who had pulled me back from the curb. "Thank you," I said. "I think you might have saved my life."

He waved me away. "All in a day's work," he said and laughed, then turned to walk down Van Buren away from me.

I'd stopped shaking by the time I got to work, although I apparently still didn't look good based on Yolanda's "You okay, girl? If you're sick, go home. I don't need any of your bugs getting on me."

I smiled. "No bugs," I said. "Just a near -death experience on my way to work."

"Well, if that's all it was," she said, waving me in.

I dropped my bag and coat at my desk and went to replace the coffee I'd lost with some from the staff kitchen on our floor. Sara walked in right ahead of me. I looked at the amount of coffee in the pot. There was only enough for one of us. I sighed.

"Go ahead," she said. "I'll make a fresh pot."

"You sure?" I asked, already reaching for a mug. I wasn't proud and I was a little desperate.

"Yeah. You look like you need it. Tough weekend?" She emptied the grounds from the coffeemaker as soon as I poured my mug full. "You seemed upset on Friday."

"I got some bad news," I said, rummaging in the refrigerator for some cream. "I'll be okay."

"I'm sorry to hear that. Anything I can do to help?" She filled the pot with fresh water from the cooler.

I straightened up clutching something French vanillaflavored. "You already let me take the last cup of coffee. I'm not sure it gets better than that."

She laughed and I left to go to my lab.

Promises to Will Friedrichs and additional coffee aside, I wasn't making much progress on figuring out what was wrong with my numbers an hour later. My mind kept flitting back to my mother and to the mangled Spiderman in the trunk of my car and to everything that happened before my mother's arrest. It had been twelve years since my father left us for younger greener pastures, eleven since my mother got involved with Children of the Greater God, and ten since she was committed to Elgin.

I didn't think it was a coincidence that my mother had been goaded into committing suicide or that I was receiving threats right when Patrick Collier was up for parole, but I couldn't figure out why. Why now? My mother or I could have come forward with our last bits of damning information any time in the past decade, but we hadn't. Neither of us had rocked the boat in any way, so why now?

Did it matter? I supposed not. Explaining to Patrick Collier's followers that their timing was illogical would not make my mother less dead or recapitate Spidey.

I looked back at my columns and columns of numbers. They danced in front of my eyes. Damn them. Just when I really needed them to soothe me, they decided to stop making sense. I slammed down the pen I'd been using to tick down the rows as Jesse Garcia came into the lab. "You okay?" he asked.

I pressed my lips together in what I hoped passed for a smile. "Fine. Thanks. Just a little frustrated."

"I wanted to come by and see if you were okay after Friday night." He looked a little uncomfortable. "You seemed upset."

That was a powerful understatement. "I'm okay. I had some bad news about a family member." I took a sip of coffee. The office machine didn't make anything near as nice as what I'd lost on the street this morning, but it was drinkable. Barely. Someone must have put in too much grounds this morning, it was more bitter than usual and long gone cold.

He pulled up a chair and sat down. Great. It was going to be a long conversation. "Anything I can do to help?"

I looked into those big brown eyes and felt myself leaning toward him. Would a little hanky panky be such a bad thing? It would feel good. It would be distracting. Then I gave myself a mental kick. Don't fish off the company pier. My dad used to say that all the time before he started screwing his marketing assistant. In retrospect, he may have been protesting a bit too much. "Thanks, but I've got it under control."

"No doubt." He leaned over and puts his hand on mine. "But sometimes it's okay to lean on someone else."

I stared at his hand on mine. This after the unsolicited hug from Sara on Friday? Had someone stuck a giant Touch Me sign on my back? I slid my hand out from underneath his. "Thanks, but I'm fine."

He sighed. "If you change your mind, you know where to find me."

I nodded. "Sure do." Jesse had given me his cell phone number about four times in the past three months. Just in case. As if to prove a point, my cell phone rang just then. I checked the display. What do you know, it was Dr. Ashmore. I gave Jesse a smile I hoped looked apologetic and not relieved and said, "I need to get this."I swiveled my chair away from him and picked up.

"Hi, Amanda. How are you?" I decided I liked his voice. He didn't use that weird, plummy, overly mellow, FM DJ voice that some shrinks used. No vocal fry, either. Behind me, I heard Jesse leaving the lab and sighed a little in relief. It wasn't that I didn't find Jesse attractive. I did. It was just that the attraction repelled me at the same time.

"Fine, thanks. You?" I said in response to Ashmore's question. It was almost as automatic as breathing.

"Really?"

Oh. He actually wanted to know. Didn't change anything. "I'm fine. Really. I was upset last night. I'm sorry I yelled at you. But I'm fine now."

"Good." He didn't sound convinced, but that was his problem, wasn't it? "I wanted to let you know that I found out who packed up your mother's room."

I sat up straighter. "Yeah?"

"Remember the nursing assistant who brought the box to my office?"

"Sure. Lori? Leslie?" The woman whose profile I was sure I saw out of the coffee shop window.

"Lois. Lois Brower."

"Great. Did you get a chance to talk to her?"

"Unfortunately, she's not scheduled to be back on duty until Wednesday. She's relatively new so she works the weekends and gets a couple of weekdays off."

"Oh." I couldn't help but be disappointed. Knowing where those things came from would definitely be our first step in figuring out what had happened to my mom. And maybe to figuring out who exactly was leaving mutilated tiny superhero figures in my car. "Do you think we could call her?"

"I had the same thought. I tried the number we have listed for her, but it's been disconnected."

"That's weird."

"Yes and no. Nursing assistants don't get paid a lot. We've had more than a few staff members with financial problems here and there. We try to help out if we can, but they have to come to us. Sometimes they're too embarrassed to reach out. I'm sure it's something like that. I have a note on my desk to look for her first thing on Wednesday."

"Okay." I sighed. Wednesday seemed far away right now and his desk was practically a superfund site, but there didn't seem to be much else we could do.

"I wanted you to know that I wasn't ignoring the situation. I'm going to look into it." Ah, earnestness. It was kind of sweet.

"Thanks, doc. I appreciate it."

"It's Sam, remember?"

"Thanks, Sam."

"Talk to you Wednesday."

"You bet."

We hung up and I turned back around, surprised to still find Jesse sitting there.

"Everything okay?" he asked again.

"Fine. Totally fine. I just want to go over these results again." I gestured toward the papers on my desk.

"Yeah. Sure. Got it. Let me know if you need anything." He stood and left.

I took another gulp of cold coffee and went back to my numbers. Finally, something clicked. I flipped from one set of data to another and realized that while the numbers weren't the same, the relationship between them was a little too exact. In science, we're all about reproducible results. If you can't make it happen the same way more than once, it could be a fluke or maybe someone had done something wrong or read something wrong. But replicated results weren't the same thing as identical results. Life was imprecise and sometimes science was, too. The data should be within a defined margin of error, but not exactly the same.

I started plugging numbers into my calculator. It didn't take more than ten minutes to realize that I'd been right. The relationship between the numbers was too consistent, too exact, too identical to be natural. I'd found it. I'd found what was wrong with the numbers. Now I just had to figure out why someone had messed with the data. There were lots of reasons why. First and foremost was plain laziness. Why run the experiment when you can dry lab it, our phrase for faking results? It's faster, easier, and certainly less expensive. If you're already pretty sure what your results will be, why not? The answer to that question happens to be that whole scientific ethics thing. It's just plain unethical to do that.

Another reason could be that whoever ran that particular experiment screwed up. Maybe something went wrong. They forgot to turn something off or on at the right time. They didn't mix something correctly. Whatever. Dozens of things can go wrong. It could be very tempting to put in the numbers you thought you were supposed to get rather than rerunning something that could take several days.

Finally, well finally, there was something worse. Someone could be intentionally trying to mislead whoever was reading the report. That idea froze me.

At first I thought the tingling sensation in my fingers and toes was due to the excitement of finally figuring out what was wrong with the data in front of me. Within minutes, however, I was shivering even though sweat beaded on my forehead. Something wasn't right. I needed help. I tried to stand, but my legs were numb and rubbery. My knees buckled beneath me.

I managed to pick up the phone and call Yolanda at the reception desk before I collapsed to the floor.

I woke feeling woozy and confused. My arm throbbed. My head pounded. My stomach clenched and unclenched. Whatever I was lying on was hard and stiff and unforgiving. I smelled plastic. I resisted opening my eyes. I could see through the lids that the lights wherever I was were much too bright.

Finally my curiosity won out. I cracked one eyelid open. Putty-colored rolling drawers. A rolling tray with a fake wood top. Linoleum. An ugly curtain hanging from a metal track.

And Dr. Sam Ashmore.

"Hey there," he said, leaning forward on the plastic chair where he sat, some kind of journal folded over in his lap. He had on khaki pants and a button - down dress shirt. No tie. Brown dress shoes and argyle socks. Who wore argyle anymore?

"Hospital?" I asked, my voice frog-like and croaking from my dry throat.

"Yeah. Rush Presbyterian." He cocked his head to one side. "Do you know what happened?"

I cast back through my memories. The newscast about Mom's suicide. Getting the muffin. Losing it and my latte in the street. Getting to work. Then pain.

"I'm not sure," I said. Not wanting to say out loud what I was thinking. It was too ridiculous. Too bizarre. It made me sound too crazy.

"They think you somehow ingested some poison." Sam said the words slowly but softly. It sounded reassuringly medical.

"What kind of poison?" I asked.

"They're still running tests." He reached over and took my hand. "Do you know what kind?"

I was momentarily confused. How should I know? The only way I would know was if I somehow took it on purpose, which was when it hit me that he was asking if I was the poisoned apple that hadn't fallen far from the batshit crazy tree. He was asking if I'd tried to kill myself. "No," I said. "I have no idea."

He nodded and leaned back in his chair.

"Why exactly are you here?" I asked. Since when did the hospital call your dead mother's shrink when you wound up in the emergency room?

"Apparently you never filled in the emergency contact information at work. They found my card in your wallet and called." He rolled up the journal he'd been reading and tapped it on his knee. "Is there someone you'd like me to call?"

I pretended to think about it so I wouldn't seem totally lame and pathetic, like maybe I had a long list of friends that I could call on in case of emergency. I didn't. I didn't really do friendship. Friendship meant sharing, and anything I had to share was pretty nasty. Dad would come if I called. I wasn't sure that was an improvement on handling it myself, though. "Not really. Do you know when I'm going to be released?"

"They're finding a room for you now. Rumor has it that they're going to keep you overnight for observation." He glanced up at the clock. "It shouldn't be much longer."

"Terrific." I glanced around. Was my purse here? My clothes? I'd need something besides the hospital gown I was wearing to get home in later. I'd need money for a cab. I was a good problem solver. I'd figure it out. I had other more pressing matters on my mind now. "Sam?"

"Yes." He leaned forward to take my hand again. "What is it, Amanda?"

"Sam, I think someone might be trying to kill me."

CHAPTER
8

THE WORDS SOUNDED RIDICULOUS, MELODRAMATIC, delusional. I couldn't not say them, though. I had to tell someone. I had to get help.

Sam looked down at my hand in his and then back up again. "Amanda, are you sure? Couldn't this have been an accident? A slip-up in the lab? Carelessness of some kind by someone?"

I slid my hand out of his grasp. I'd known he would probably react that way. Any sane person would. It still disappointed me. Emotions were so irrational; no wonder I preferred numbers. "Of course it could be. And whoever pushed me out into traffic this morning might have just been clumsy, and whoever broke into the trunk of my car might have just been playing a prank."

"Tell me about this morning," he said, brows furrowed.

I told him about feeling the hands at my lower back and about how the only reason I hadn't landed flat on my face in front of a speeding vehicle was because of the businessman with fast reflexes who had been standing next to me. "Oh, also, I thought I saw Lois Brower."

He shook his head. "Where? When you were pushed?"

"No. A few minutes before. Right as I was leaving the coffee shop. I could have sworn I saw her out on the sidewalk. She was gone by the time I got out there, though."

He leaned back in his chair, nodding a little to himself. Finally, he said, "Then we'd better tell the doctor to call the police."

Shortly after I'd been moved out of the emergency area and into a room, the police showed up in the person of Detective Afano Pagoa. Or at least that's what it said on the card he gave me. He was huge. Tall with arms that looked like they were going to burst the seams of his suit jacket. His hair was cut so close to his scalp, I could see the brown skin shining through. He dwarfed the chair he pulled to my bedside. After he introduced himself, he turned to Sam. "And you are?"

"Dr. Sam Ashmore." He held out his hand to shake.

Pagoa looked at the hand before taking it. Clearly he was a cautious guy. I wasn't sure if that was good news for me or not. "What relation are you to Miss Sinclair?" he asked.

"A friend," Sam said without hesitation. I felt a little heat on my cheeks. I wasn't sure if I could have answered that quickly and with that much confidence. Dead mother's shrink would definitely have started the interview rolling in some interesting directions, though.

"Why do you think someone might be trying to murder you, Miss Sinclair?" Pagoa asked.

So much for the pleasantries. I glanced over at the IV running saline into my arm and then back at him. My mental "duh" echoed loudly through the room.

"Was there something besides what brought you here today that makes you think someone is trying to hurt you?" He sighed as if the question made him tired.

I told him about being pushed into the street on my way to work and the black SUV that had nearly run me over by the parking garage.

Then I told him about Spidey.

His eyebrows went up on that. "Do you still have the toy and the note?"

I nodded. "They're at my apartment."

"Did you report this?"

"Sort of. I reported that someone broke into my car. At the time, I thought the Spiderman toy was somebody's idea of a bad joke." At the time, no one had tried to shove me in front of a speeding taxi cab or poisoned me.

"A joke threatening you? What kind of joke would that be?" he asked, making notes on a little pad he'd pulled out of his breast pocket.

"I didn't say it was a funny joke." Pagoa shot me a look and I decided to try to curb my tendency toward irreverence. Something about authority figures brought out the sarcasm in me. I needed Pagoa to take me seriously. To have him do that, I would have to answer seriously.

"Why would someone want to kill you?" he asked once more.

I plucked at the scratchy blanket that covered me. "My mother is Linda Framingham."

"And?" By the look on his face, he had no idea what my mother's name meant.

"And I think this is somehow related to Patrick Collier of Children of the Greater God being released from prison." There. It was out in the open.

A wave of recognition washed over his face. The stages of it washed over his face. Yes, that Linda Framingham. I was that Amanda. That daughter. That walking stack of damaged goods.

"It was my understanding that your mother committed suicide," he said.

"I think she was driven to it. I found a picture of my brother and a news article about Collier's upcoming release in her effects." I didn't look over at Sam as I said that. It was still his institution that had somehow not safeguarded my mother.

Detective Pagoa's pen hovered over his notepad. "You think someone slipped those items to your mother in an attempt to make her kill herself?"

I nodded. It sounded stupid when he said it like that. Maybe it was stupid. But someone had put those things in my mother's belongings, someone who didn't wish her well, and now she was dead. Just because it wasn't exactly cause and effect didn't mean the events were unrelated.

"What did the medical examiner rule?" he asked.

"There isn't a ruling yet," Sam said.

Pagoa nodded and flipped his pad shut. "You're here overnight?"

"Yes. That's what I heard."

"Okay. I'm going to assume you're safe here. When you're released, call me and I'll meet you at your apartment to pick up the toy and the note. You can show me where the garage is, too." He stood to leave. At the door to the room, Pagoa turned around. "Is there a reason that the cult would want to harm you and your mother?"

I shrugged. "Revenge, possibly. It was because of my mother that the authorities started investigating Collier and COGG. They might never have found out how he was mishandling money if my mother hadn't done what she did." I still couldn't say it, couldn't force the words from my mouth: If my mother hadn't murdered my brother. If she hadn't expected me to help her kill again.

Pagoa nodded. "I remember." Then he was gone, moving nearly without sound despite his size.

I let my head drop back on the pillows and shut my eyes.

"Do you need anything? Painkillers? Water?" Sam asked.

"No. Thank you. I'm fine." I opened my eyes and turned to look at him. Behind him I could see the window with its scenic view of more hospital rooftop. The sky had turned nearly black. He'd spent the whole day by my bedside. "I'm so sorry to have wasted your entire day. You should go."

"I don't think my day has been wasted." He held up the stack of journals. "I haven't been this caught up on my reading since I started at Elgin."

He was a nice man, trying to make me feel not guilty for the circumstances that had him sitting by my bedside for hours. Nice should only have to stretch so far, though. "Go," I said. "I'm fine."

He rested his hand on my arm. "There's no place I need to be."

Before I could argue with that, Sara, Jesse, and Anna came through the door in a crinkling bustle of cellophane-wrapped flowers and Mylar balloons. Sara leaned over to give me a quick hug, her coat chill against my too warm cheek. The scent of bus exhaust and snow hung around her. She smelled like the city, like anonymity, like safety. I found myself clutching her back. My world had truly gone topsy-turvy.

"You poor thing," she said. "Everyone was so worried."

"Did anyone else get sick?" I asked. Maybe Pagoa was right. Maybe it was all a mistake. I'd had only a few bites of cereal and a cup of office coffee today, and I wasn't the only one to drink from that pot.

"Nobody else," Anna said. She held up the balloon bouquet. "This is from everyone at the lab. Everybody wanted to come to see you, but we thought that might be too overwhelming."

There were at least fifteen of us that worked in the lab. The room was crowded with four visitors. "Thank you. That's very nice."

"I brought you these," Sara said, plunking down a stack of magazines on my tray table. "Nothing but gossip and fashion. No science. No politics. No news."

I smiled. "Thanks." I had no idea what might make her think I'd find gossip or fashion diverting, but it was a nice gesture.

Jesse had said nothing since walking in the door. He'd been too busy staring at Sam. "Who's your friend?" he finally asked.

Sam stood and extended his hand. "Sam Ashmore."

They shook and there was a general murmuring of names. Sam picked up his stack of journals, slid them into his briefcase, and shouldered into his coat. "I'll call you tomorrow, Amanda," he said. "Let me know if you need anything."

"Thank you for everything," I said. It was woefully inadequate, but I didn't know what else to say, especially with my coworkers watching.

"You're welcome." He nodded to the others and slipped out the door.

"Well, aren't you the dark horse," Anna said, taking Sam's seat.

"What?" I asked.

"You're always so…self-contained. I didn't know there was someone in your life. Especially not someone who looked like that." She grinned. "Have you been dating long?"

I shook my head. "We're not dating. Sam is…" And there it was again. What should I call him? My dead mother's shrink. Kind of a conversation stopper. Or worse, a conversation starter that would take us all places we didn't want to go. "Sam is just a friend."

Sara sighed. "Too bad. He's cute."

Jesse glared at her. "If you like the tweedy professortype."

"Tweedy professor has its place." Sara grinned. "I always thought the Professor was the hunkiest character on Gilligan's Island."

Anna laughed. "He didn't exactly have a lot of competition, Sara. There wasn't a lot of point to marrying for money on an island like that, so count out Thurston Howell."

"Plus he was already married," Sara pointed out.

"And Skipper?" Anna shuddered. "Ew!"

Jesse finally smiled. "Poor Gilligan. He's not even in the running."

I stayed silent and let it wash over me, this good-humored bickering among my coworkers. So surface. So easy. No wonder I liked going to the lab. Then Sara was brushing my hair off my face. I jumped, startled.

"Sorry," she said. "You dozed off there for a second. You must need to rest. Is there anything we can do for you before we go?"

"There is, but it's a pretty huge favor," I said, not sure I even wanted to ask, but equally unsure what I would wear home if I didn't.

"Anything," Jesse said, stepping forward.

"They're going to release me tomorrow and I don't have any clothes." I gestured at the clear bag marked Patient's Belongings that hung in the corner. "Most of them were ruined."

"Are your keys in your purse?" Anna asked.

I nodded.

"No problem, then. We'll stop by your place tonight, pick up some things." She crossed the room and retrieved the bag, fishing my purse out and handing it to me.

I hesitated. I'd planned on giving them money and asking them to pick something up for me. "There's a Target on Jackson. That would be closer." I pulled two twenties out of my wallet. That would be enough for a pair of sweats and a T-shirt, a pair of socks.

"Don't be silly," Anna said. "If we go to your place, we can get you a jacket and shoes and even your own toothbrush."

"But it's farther and there's no parking. It's already late." I had a long list of reasons to give them, although I had no intention of giving them the real reason.

"It's barely six o'clock." Anna frowned. "Let us do this for you, Amanda. Let us help."

She said it as if I would be doing them the favor. My limbs felt so heavy. I didn't have the energy to argue. "If you really think so…" My voice trailed off.

"Of course we do. Now tell us where everything is." Sara pulled out her phone and looked at me expectantly.

I told them where to find my clothes, my toothbrush, my fleece jacket. "That wasn't so hard, was it?" Anna teased.

It was, though. It was awful. They would be in my loft. Their hands would be in my closets and my drawers. None of my secrets would be safe.

I looked at their faces. Their open, shining faces. All three looked pleased with themselves for helping me, and I stopped fighting it at all. I handed over my keys.

"Thank you," was all I could manage to say before I felt my eyes starting to close again.

CHAPTER

9

Tuesday, February 21

I'D MANAGED TO CLEAN myself up a little bit before Sara showed up the next morning. "I think I got everything," she said, plopping an overnight bag down on a chair. "Your place is awesome. It wasn't exactly what I was expecting."

I arched my eyebrows. "What kind of place did you think I'd live in?"

"Not something that warm, I guess. Maybe more steel and glass and less exposed brick and wood." She sat down on the edge of the bed. "How are you feeling?"

"Better," I said, trying to sit up a little straighter. The nausea was gone and so were the tingling sensations in my hands and feet. My throat was still a little raw, but otherwise I felt intact. "The nurse said the doctor would be by before ten to release me."

"You have a ride home?" she asked. "I could zip back here. No problem."

I faltered. Sara was offering to leave work to give me a ride home. I had somehow inadvertently made a friend. What I knew that she didn't was the false pretenses under which that friendship was made. Sara thought the Amanda she saw at work—the person who smiled at people in the hallway and always made a fresh pot of coffee when she'd had the last of the pot and was careful with her tone in meetings and emails -—was the whole sum of me. She saw Work Amanda. She didn't realize that there was a whole separate Amanda with a whole separate life and, more importantly, a whole separate past.

I wanted to let her see the Other Amanda, to not keep everything so rigidly separate. It would be nice to have a friend. Someone to talk to. Someone to watch movies with. Someone to go shopping with. It took energy and discipline to keep my life in neat tidy boxes, and I was tired. But the second she saw what was in that other box? Well, I wouldn't blame her if she ran away and took a long hot shower to make sure all the Other Amanda cooties were off her.

"I've got it covered," I said. "You've already done so much. I really appreciate it."

"You're sure?" she asked, her brow furrowed a bit.

"Totally. A friend is coming to pick me up." No need to explain that by "friend," I meant "police detective." That would be a peek inside the box. "Really, thank you so much for everything."

Sara slid her hand from mine and waved it at me. "Girl, it was nothing. Barely even out of my way. It was like a field trip for Jesse and Anna and me. We all wanted to do something. You scared the bejeesus out of us, you know."

"I scared it out of me, too," I admitted. At least, someone had.

After Sara left, I opened the bag she'd packed for me. For someone who had never been inside my apartment, she'd done a pretty good job of getting me what I needed. Toothbrush, toothpaste, hairbrush, even a wand of mascara and a tube of lip gloss, not that that would help much at the moment. My reflection told me I clearly wasn't going to win any beauty contests today. The shadows under my eyes were deep and purple, my skin pale, my lips cracked and bloodless. I pulled my hair back into a ponytail, pulled on the clothes Sara had brought, and waited for Detective Pagoa.

He showed up about twenty minutes after Dr. Mullins came by to release me. She looked nearly as tired as I felt, but less battered. Her blonde hair was twisted up in a messy bun and she had a pair of black half-glasses that rode low on her nose. She was definitely rocking the white jacket, though. Maybe she had hers tailored. I felt particularly unkempt sitting cross-legged in front of her on my hospital bed.

"So do you have any idea how you managed to get such a high level of salicylate in your bloodstream?" she asked, glanced at my chart.

"Salicylate? You mean aspirin?" I pulled my knees up to my chest and wrapped my arms around them.

She glanced up, eyes slightly narrowed, and made a note on the chart. "Yes. Aspirin."

I shook my head. "No. No idea."

She shut the chart and looked at me for a moment before speaking. "Amanda, are you having any thoughts about harming yourself?"

"No," I said firmly. "I'm not. I didn't do this."

I'd known the question was coming.

Nine years ago, though, no one had seen it coming. It had happened more than a year after that night, a year after I'd sat in the hallway outside Jackson's room rocking and crying, a year after the police had dragged my mother out the door as she screamed at me. Everyone thought the worst was over.

Maybe it was. Maybe that's why I couldn't handle it. Every day I woke up and brushed my teeth and showered and put on clothes. Every day Dylan and I went to school. Every day I came back to my father's house and did my homework and ate dinner.

Jackson would never have another day. He would never zoom down the hallway, arms outstretched, pretending to be Spiderman. He would never climb another tree or rocket down another slide or eat another ice cream sundae.

My mother might never, either. She spent every day locked up in Elgin, staring at a wall. I didn't know if she'd ever speak again and, if she did, if it would be to scream those same hateful words at me. Spiteful little slut. Traitorous whore. Demon child.

Even Patrick Collier's circumstances had changed. I'd watched on the news as they'd walked him out of the COGG compound, hands cuffed behind his back, head bowed. What would he say to me now? Knowing him, it would be words of forgiveness, offers to pray for my soul. The shame would be worse than the horrible names my mother had called me.

Dad and Jessica went to work. Dylan and I went to school. Everything was normal. At least, it appeared normal.

I didn't go off the rails completely. Maybe that's why no one saw it coming or realized how twisted and broken I was inside. Before Jackson's death, I'd made a real show of my pain. I'd gotten drunk, skipped school, stolen pills, slept with pretty much any boy who'd have me. Everyone had known that something was wrong, though they didn't know what. I couldn't bear to tell them. We were all clear on the fact that something wasn't right, though.

Afterwards, though, everyone seemed to know what was wrong. I was the girl whose mother had killed her brother. I was the girl who'd been mixed up with the creepy cult. Once that had been cleared up, everything was fine, right? Some people even seemed to think I was some sort of hero for calling the police that night. They said I'd saved Dylan. Maybe I had. I wasn't a hero, though. Heroes' mothers don't assume they'll help kill their brother, and Mom had been completely, confidently sure that night that I would get up from my bed and hold Dylan down while she suffocated him with a pillow.

Mom had known what was in that Other Amanda box. Mom could see the sick and twisted parts of me that I kept squirreled away, hidden from everyone.

I'd known, though. Whoever said that ignorance is bliss was no dummy. I couldn't live with who I was, what I'd done. At eighteen, I didn't have the skill to keep that box locked up, hadn't yet had years of practice in keeping it hidden away even from myself.

So one night when Dad and Jessica were at the movies and Dylan was at a basketball game, I ran a nice warm bath, washed down all the painkillers that were leftover from when I had my wisdom teeth out with a halfbottle of Chardonnay from the back of the refrigerator, climbed into the tub, and took a razor blade to the insides of my wrists.

Yeah. There's a reason I always wear long-sleeved T-shirts. The scars were fainter these days, but someone who knew what they were looking at would spot them in a second.

At the time I'd felt as if I was letting all the evil out of me to run into the swirling waters of the bathtub. The pills and the booze and the warm water slowed everything down so I no longer felt like my inside were spinning so fast that little pieces of me might go flying through the air at any moment. Darkness crept in from the corners of my vision. Not a scary darkness. Not a deep pit in the cold hard ground in the middle of the night. Something softer, velvety even.

I would have been successful if Dad hadn't sucked so much at picking movies. Why he'd thought that Jessica would enjoy watching Javier Bardem in a bad hairdo wreak havoc through Texas was anyone's guess. The point was, however, that at some point in No Country for Old Men Jessica had stood up and walked out of the theater. She'd marched to the car with Dad apologizing behind her and demanded to be taken home, where she no doubt intended on drinking the halfbottle of Chardonnay I had already helped myself to.

I really don't know what happened next. I've been told, but I was far enough gone to not really experience the ambulance, the emergency room, the stitches, the gastric lavage. Just as well. I doubt it was pleasant.

I did remember, however, the locked ward. I remembered it vividly and had no intention of ever going back there.

A practiced eye wouldn't miss the scars on the insides of my arms, but I was pretty adept at keeping those covered. But my medical chart? Hard to cover that up.

I looked up at Dr. Mullins, with her tired eyes and her erect posture, and said, "That was a long time ago. This is nothing like that. I promise you, I did not try to hurt myself and I will not try to hurt myself."

She sighed. "I can get you someone to talk to. You don't have to go through whatever you're going through alone."

"I'm fine," I lied. "Completely fine."

She glanced pointedly at my IV line as I had to Detective Pagoa, which turned out to be his cue to walk into my room.

A look passed between them. It didn't really have to do with me. Just two professionals giving each other a quick once-over.

"I'm here to take Ms. Sinclair home," Detective Pagoa said. "Is she ready?"

Dr. Mullins glanced over at me. "The nurse will be here to take out her IV in a minute." She handed me a sheaf of papers mostly covered with type tiny enough to make my head ache. She hesitated for a second or two then pulled out her card and handed it to me as well. "If you change your mind, call my office. Okay?"

I took the card, running my thumb over its raised print. "Okay."

Then she was gone. She must have told the nurse to step on it because she was in there in record time to pull out my various lines, plop me in a wheelchair, and steer me to the curb, where Pagoa's Ford Taurus awaited us.

Neither of us said anything as I buckled myself in and he pulled away from the curb. I finally broke the silence. "You're going to want to take the Congress Parkway exit."

He gave me a second of side eye. "I know where you live."

"Is that supposed to make me feel better?" Because it didn't. It made me feel itchy.

"No. It's supposed to let you know that you don't need to give me directions," he said, thick hands resting at ten and two on the wheel.

I sank down a little in my seat and looked out the window. The gray clouds had cleared and the sky was a blue that made my eyeballs ache, light and crisp and sharp. The trees held their empty limbs upward like supplicants. Another couple of months and they'd be covered with green buds, the promise of life renewing. Not in February, though. Nothing bloomed in February in Chicago. I tapped my fingers in rhythm with the passing dotted white lines.

"Tell me again what you ate on Monday morning," Pagoa said.

We'd been over it at least twice already. I didn't think I was going to suddenly remember having downed an entire bottle of aspirin somewhere between waking up at home and waking up at the hospital.

"I had some cereal at home. I stopped at the coffee shop to get a latte and a muffin."

"Did you notice who served you the latte?" Pagoa asked.

"No. But I didn't really get to drink it, either. I spilled it when I was shoved at the intersection." That made it a moot point, in my opinion.

"But you took a few sips, right?" he asked.

"Yes. A few sips."

"And the muffin?"

"Lemon poppyseed," I said.

That earned me another bit of side eye. "Did you eat that or drop it, too?"

"I'm afraid it was also a casualty, although I had broken off one bite." It had actually turned my stomach a little to see that muffin squashed in the road. For a second I had imagined it was me flattened there on the asphalt.

"So nothing appreciable." He glanced over his shoulder and changed lanes. "What about once you got to work?"

"Coffee," I said. "I took the last of what was in the pot and Sara made a fresh one."

"So who else drank the same coffee as you did?"

"No idea. Whoever wanted some. There's pretty much always a pot going in the staff kitchen." Sometimes I thought the whole place ran on caffeine.

"Who has access to the kitchen?" he asked.

"Everyone. It's for the staff. We all use it." I paused. "Was it in my coffee?"

"We don't know. You dropped the mug when you passed out. Someone cleaned it up before we got there."

Knowing the Bellefountaine custodial staff, it had been cleaned up before the ambulance got me to the hospital. They liked for the facility to be kept clean. "But no one else got sick," I said.

"Nope. You were the only one."

We let that hang in the air between us. If the salicylate had been in my coffee, someone went to some lengths to make sure that I had been the only one to drink it.

Pagoa pulled off at the Congress Parkway exit and turned right onto Wells. He did a U turn where my street dead-ended and parked in front of the building. "You're not worried about getting a ticket?"

"Nope," he said, opening his door and getting out.

I couldn't decide if Detective Pagoa was a man of few words or if he really didn't like me. Maybe it was both. I opened my own door and got out with my purse, ducking into the back seat for my balloons and flowers. Up the street I saw a flicker of movement. My new homeless friend started to emerge from his favorite alcove. Our eyes met, then he glanced at Pagoa and back to me. I shook my head the tiniest bit and he ducked back out of sight.

Pagoa waited wordlessly while I punched in the code to open the front door of the building, then followed me to the elevator, up to the eighth floor, and to my loft. I opened the door. It occurred to me as he followed me in that I'd had more people through my home in the last three days than I had had in the last three months. More, probably. Maybe more than I'd ever had there. I didn't entertain much.

I deposited the flowers on the table then hung up my jacket and dropped my bags and went to my desk, where headless Spidey still resided in his paper bag. I handed it over to Mr. Chatty Cathy. He opened it, glanced inside, and nodded. "Can I see the other items? The ones you found in your mother's stuff?"

I froze. I didn't want to show him her things. It felt too invasive. I couldn't exactly expect him to listen to me if I didn't, though. I pulled the box out from under my desk and lifted it onto the table. I took off the top and sifted through for the news articles about Jackson's death and Collier's upcoming release.

"May I take these?" he asked.

I nodded. "Her doctor has the picture of my brother, but it was in this box, too."

"And you think that would be enough to make her kill herself?" he asked, still looking over the clippings.

I sat down at the table, unable to hold the weariness at bay any longer. "Possibly. If nothing else, it could have sent her down some mental pathways that would lead there eventually. She didn't do well taking about Jackson or Collier."

He glanced at the watercolors that rested on top of the other items. "Nice paintings," he said.

"She was very talented." I lifted out the one of the still lifes. She explained to me once why she always put something that was decaying in her compositions. It had to do with the transience of all things, reminders of how all things must pass. When I told her it was morbid, she disagreed. She talked about the cycle of life and the necessity of opposites. I'd probably been about ten when we had that conversation. I hadn't understood a word of what she was saying. I did now. There's no light without the darkness.

"Is there anything else?" he asked. "Anything else that might point at Collier and Children of the Greater God?"

I shook my head. "No. At least not yet."

"You expect more?" He cocked his head.

"I don't think they've gotten whatever it is they want yet."

CHAPTER

10

AFTER PAGOA LEFT, I MADE myself a bowl of soup and curled up on the couch under an afghan. I was trying to decide between taking a nap and watching TV when my cell phone chirped. It was Sam.

Sam: *How's it going?*

Me: *Good. Am home.*

Sam: *Alone?*

Me: *Pagoa gave me a ride. He's gone now.* I TOLD HIM YOU HAVE THE PHOTO OF JACKSON.

Sam: OK. *U OK? Need anything?*

Me: *No. Just tired.*

Sam: *May I stop by tonight to check on you?*

I let that one sit for a while. At this rate, I was going to have to install a revolving door on the place. Before you knew it, I'd be having cocktail parties and barbecues up on the roof. On the other hand, the apartment was very quiet.

Me: *Sure.*

Sam: *Good. See you* LATER.

I pulled the afghan up over my shoulders and started to drift off when the phone actually rang. I jumped. No one calls anyone anymore. People text or email or message. The caller ID said the call was from Bellefountaine. I picked up.

"Amanda, please tell me you're all right." It was Will Friedrichs. Wow. I didn't think I'd ever had the CEO call me for phoning in sick.

"I'm fine. Or I will be. I just need a day or so to recover." Beyond feeling like the idea of eating anything other than soup wasn't going to happen for another a week or so and like I could sleep for eighteen hours solid, I was fine.

"You take all the time you need. All of it. We will get along fine here and your spot will be waiting for you when you get back." I could see him in mind's eye. Dark and intense, like always. Whatever was in front of him had his full focus for that moment. I could practically feel his energy humming through the phone line.

"Thanks. I'm sure I'll be back in by Thursday at the latest."

"Don't rush it, Amanda. I'm serious. There's nothing more important than your health. Nothing."

"Thanks, Will. I really appreciate it." I didn't think many CEOs would take the time to reassure an employee like that. I was lucky to work for

Bellefountaine for so many reasons. Interesting work. Good ethics. A great boss.

"We'll reassign the QC on that FDA report to someone else. Don't you worry about it."

I sat up so fast I almost choked on my own spit. "No. Don't do that. I was getting somewhere with it. Really." I hadn't thought about it at all until Will brought it up. The numbers. I'd figured out what was wrong with the numbers. Something was going right in my life.

"If you're sure," he said, sounding wary.

"Totally sure. A hundred percent. Someone else would be starting from scratch." Someone else might not notice where the number sequences became too consistent. Or be willing to look into that the way that I would. Cover Me was going to be a great product. Better than great, revolutionary. I wanted its path through FDA approval to go as smoothly as possible. The last thing I wanted was for someone at a federal agency to catch some weird number discrepancy in a chart and kick it back to us.

"True, but I don't want you coming back too soon. Okay?"

"Got it."

We said good-bye and I hung up the phone. I struggled out of my afghan cocoon and went to retrieve my laptop. I remembered a glimmer of what I'd hit on right before I'd felt my hands and feet start to tingle. I wanted to check it out and see if it was what I thought it was. A set of numbers that were too consistent, whose mathematical relationship to each other was too predictable, too exact.

A flurry of panic went through me when I couldn't find my laptop. I always put my briefcase on my desk when I got home, but it wasn't there. Then I remembered that it must still be at work. Whoever had bundled up my stuff to send with me to the hospital—I suspected Sara—had included my purse but not my briefcase.

Then she'd been here, too. I turned slowly around surveying my domain. What had she seen? What had she thought about what she'd seen? I felt the blood slowly drain from my face. Would she have gone through my things? I grabbed onto the back of my desk chair. Would she have looked through my mother's things?

I didn't think I could bear that. At work, I was Amanda Sinclair, lab technician. I wasn't Linda Framingham's daughter or Jackson's sister. I loved it. I loved the work and I loved being known only as the person who did that work. If Sara had gotten nosey and gone through my things and figured out who I was...I couldn't handle it. I wouldn't be able to go back. I knew all too well what it was like to walk among people who knew who such things about me. The whispers. The stares. The pity.

I glanced under the desk at the box of my mother's belongings. Had it seemed undisturbed when I'd pulled it out to show Pagoa? I couldn't remember. I shut my eyes and tried to visualize it but got nothing.

Why hadn't I checked it? I went into my bedroom. Sara would have had to come in here to get my clothes. It wasn't a big room and the wall that separated it from the living area didn't go all the way to the ceiling. My bed looked as it had when I'd left to go to work on Monday morning. The gray comforter pulled up. The pillows propped against the headboard. Sara hadn't been doing a Goldilocks thing and slept in my bed.

I returned to the couch and tunneled back under my afghan. My resolve stiffened. I'd go back to work tomorrow. No question about it.

I was more popular that afternoon than I'd been possibly ever. In addition to the texts from Sam and the call from Will, Sara texted to see if I'd like her to bring dinner over. I declined but told her I'd see her at work the next day, which prompted another flurry of texts about being careful and not rushing.

Then around three the intercom for the door buzzed. I clicked on the television to channel 28, which had running footage of the front door. A dude with a baseball cap and a bouquet of flowers stood in the foyer.

My finger hovered over the button that would buzz him in. I couldn't think of a single soul who would be sending me a bouquet today. The folks at work got me flowers yesterday. On the other hand, pretending to be a delivery guy seemed like a pretty slick way to be let into a secure building. Someone had managed to get into Bellefountaine's lab to lace my coffee with something nasty. Had whoever done that pretended to deliver flowers to the office? Or lab supplies? Or paper towels for the bathroom?

I hit the intercom button. "You can leave those down there."

"What?" He cupped a hand around his ear. "I can't hear you."

"Leave them. I'll pick them up later," I yelled.

He looked at the outer door and then up into the camera. "It's three degrees out, lady. They won't last."

Now I definitely didn't want him up by my apartment or in the building. He wanted in a little too bad. I pulled out my phone and snapped a photo of his face on the television just in case. "What's it to you?" I asked.

He shrugged and set the vase down in the corner. "Suit yourself."

I was pretty sure I heard him mutter another word as he went out the door. I didn't care.

I hung up the phone, my heart beating faster. Were the flowers a ruse to get in my building? To get in my apartment? What would he have done if I'd let him in?

I left the lobby camera on and watched people come in and out of the building. No one touched the flowers except one Chihuahua who started to lift his leg on the vase before the dog walker pulled him away. Finally I drifted off watching the front door of my building as if it were a reality show.

Sam showed up at seven with take-out bags in his hands. "Do you think you can bring up that bouquet in the corner?" I asked over the intercom.

He glanced down at the flowers. "Are you sure? They look a little worse for the wear."

"If you can," I said.

He stooped to scoop them up and I buzzed him in then went to the front door of the apartment to wait. He came in, a chill wafting from his coat, hands full of food and flowers. I took the cold vase from him and set it on the kitchen counter. I brushed my hands off on my pants although I didn't think there was anything on them.

"You should call the florist. The delivery guy shouldn't have left them in the foyer like that. They're a mess." Sam set the take-out bags next to the flowers on the counter. He hung up his coat on the rack next to mine. I couldn't decide if it felt comforting or intrusive to have him know where to stow his things. I settled on weird. It felt weird. Everything felt weird. Apparently weird was the new normal.

"I made him leave them there." I stared at the flowers, at the little envelope propped among the baby's breath.

He paused for a fraction of a second as he pulled cartons out of the bag. I smelled soup, warm and chickeny. My stomach growled. "I didn't know who they were from or who was delivering them or, well, anything," I continued, realizing how paranoid it sounded as it came out of my mouth.

Instead of chiding me, however, Sam nodded. "Smart. Probably not a good idea to let anyone or anything into the apartment without knowing. At least not until the cops figure out what's going on."

I swallowed against the prickling I felt in my throat. It was good to know someone was worried about me, that someone was on my side.

He pointed at the card. "Want me to look?"

I nodded. I wasn't sure I could take the visceral kick of opening it to find another threat, some kind of floral card version of the decapitated Spiderman, or another photo of Jackson like the one in my mother's belongings.

He plucked the card from its pronged holder and ripped the envelope open. There was a slight tightening of his jaw as he read it.

"What is it?" I asked, my voice a little higher than its usual pitch.

Wordlessly he handed it to me.

Get Well Soon. We Miss You! Jesse

I sagged against the counter. Just Jesse. Just flowers. Just a stupid little note from a coworker with a crush. I put the card in the trash and then looked at the flowers. They were wilted and limp and I wasn't 100 percent certain that the Chihuahua hadn't peed on them on his way back in because I'd dozed off. Poor Jesse. He'd tried to do something sweet and had instead turned me into a paranoid mess for half the afternoon. I dumped the flowers in the garbage with the card and rinsed the vase out.

Sam whistled as he dished chicken soup and matzoh balls into bowls. "My mother calls this Jewish penicillin. Of course, she makes her own."

Even on her best days, my mother hadn't been a soup-making kind of mom. "That sounds nice."

He nodded. "I wasn't sure if you'd be ready for much else, but I figured if you didn't want a bagel you could put them in the freezer." He opened the other bag and set out bagels and cream cheese.

My stomach let out another loud growl.

"Borborygmus," he said.

"Excuse me?" I ate a spoonful of soup and felt like I could feel the life returning to my body.

"It's the technical term for stomach growling." He busied himself slicing a bagel and spreading it with cream cheese.

"Good to know." I ate more soup. "So are both your parents still alive?"

He nodded, but slowly, like he was being cautious.

"They still married to each other?"

He nodded again.

"Alcoholics?"

He shook his head.

"Abusive?"

He shook his head again.

"I thought shrinks went into psychiatry to try to fix their own crazy." The soup was really good, but the matzoh balls were like heaven. Soft. Fluffy. But with a tiny bit of bite to them.

"Stereotypes can steer you wrong sometimes," he said through a mouthful.

The food was so good and felt so nourishing, I had to keep reminding myself to take it slow. Then unbidden, another thought ran through my head. A memory of someone else trying not to cram food into his mouth even though he was so hungry it hurt. Laughing at how good it all tasted through a half-full mouth. Black hair matted and dirty. Brown eyes that shone with gratitude.

Marcus. I was going to have to face what happened to Marcus sooner rather than later. I'd managed to tuck it away in a compartment like all the other things for a decade now, but I was beginning to think that everything that was happening now was tied to him. Someone wanted that secret to stay buried. Maybe that was reason enough to uncover it now. The thought was like a stab to my gut.

I'd found him at the bus station on Harrison. It was one of the regular places we went. Me and Celeste and Brandon and Ryan. The A Team, Patrick used to call us. The cream of the crop. We all stood a little taller when he said things like that. We all lived for the light and warmth of his praise.

Together we looked like one of those United Colors of Benneton ads. Celeste with her mocha skin and braids. Brandon with his slanted almond eyes and golden skin. Ryan with his jet black hair and melting brown eyes. And then me, the white girl.

Patrick said it was easier for kids to relate to someone who looked like them. Black kids were more comfortable talking to other black kids. Asian kids were more comfortable talking to other Asian kids. White kids, Latino kids, they all would connect better with someone who looked like them. Since the first step was the connection, why not make it easier?

But even though Marcus was Latino—Mexican, to be specific—it wasn't Puerto Rican Ryan he'd connected with that night. It was me.

"Hey," Sam said. "You look like you're a million miles away. You okay?"

I shook myself and the memory away. I hadn't thought about Marcus in years. Not really. Nightmares don't count. I took another bite of soup. "Totally fine. This is delicious. Thank you so much for bringing it." It wouldn't have killed me to eat another can of soup for dinner, but this was much better.

"No problem." He pushed his plate away and leaned back in his chair. "There's something else I need to tell you."

I set my spoon down. "Okay." In my experience, those words weren't usually followed by anything good. It was rare that the something that needed to be told was that you'd won the lottery, or were getting a promotion, or even that the person had brought ice cream for dessert.

"I decided to stop by Lois Brower's home to ask her about the things you found in your mother's belongings."

I leaned forward. "Great. What did she say?"

He shook his head. "She didn't say anything. Her address doesn't exist."

"What do you mean it doesn't exist?"

"I mean, that there is no 375 Balboa Drive in Chicago. There's a 373 and a 377, but no 375. There's not even an empty lot there." He rocked onto the back legs of the chair.

That made no sense. "Why would she give you a phony address?"

He shook his head. "No idea. I intend to ask her tomorrow. She's scheduled for a shift at seven."

I chewed on the edge of my thumb. A disconnected phone and a nonexistent address. It felt ominous. Weird. Maybe it meant nothing, though. Sam thought the disconnected number could just be a sign of financial trouble. Maybe the fake address was part of that, too. Maybe the poor thing lived in her car or at a shelter. Or maybe not. "You'll let me know what she says?"

"Of course."

After the soup was gone, Sam cleared the table while I put the dishes in the dishwasher. Then the air went awkward between us.

"I, uh, guess I should go now," he said, reaching for his coat.

I hesitated, then nodded. "Yeah. I should turn in early."

"Okay, then. I'll check in with you tomorrow again, if that's okay."

I nodded again. "Let me know what Lois Brower has to say."

"Absolutely."

I walked him to the door.

"Amanda," he said, his hand on the door knob.

"Yes?"

He pressed his lips together for a moment, his blue eyes looking into mine, and then said, "Be careful."

"Always," I said.

Then he was gone.

CHAPTER

11

Wednesday, February 22

WEDNESDAY MORNING WHEN I GOT into work, Yolanda launched from behind her desk and wrapped her arms around me. "I'm so glad you're okay!" Then she grabbed me by the shoulders and held me at arm's length. "Should you be here? Shouldn't you be resting?"

That pretty much set the pattern for the rest of the day. Everyone was thrilled to see me, everyone thought I should be at home, everyone somehow thought it was okay to touch me. The unsolicited hugs were nearly as bad as getting poisoned. Well, not really. I still wasn't thrilled, though. What's more, they were probably right. Getting to the lab had nearly exhausted me. I couldn't stay home alone another day, though. I just couldn't.

If Sara had gone through my things while she'd been in my apartment and figured out who I was, she gave no sign of it. There was concern in her eyes, but none of the other things I'd become accustomed to people thinking once they found out I was the daughter of notorious child-killer Linda Framingham, the very special daughter who had called the police rather than kill her brother. Total hero material, right?

Once I navigated the maze of well-wishers and made it to my desk, I was amazed at the amount of work that had built up from only two days of being away. I spent most of the morning wading through my email inbox.

I took a break for lunch at about twelvethirty. I had leftover soup from the batch Sam had brought the night before and went to heat it up in the staff kitchen's microwave.

Jesse stopped me as I left the lab. "Hey. I was wondering if you wanted to go out for lunch."

I held up the bag. "Brought my own. I'm probably not ready for anything more adventurous than soup."

He nodded. "Okay. Let me know if I can bring back anything for you. You have my cell."

"Thanks." The kitchen was uncharacteristically messy. Coffee grounds were scattered over the counter and there was a sticky spot on the floor. The inside of the microwave looked like someone had exploded a science project in it. I wiped it out as best I could with a damp paper towel and put my soup in to heat up.

"Nasty," Melinda said as she came in with her own Tupperwared lunch.

"What's going on? It's always so clean in here. If Will sees this, he'll freak." The microwave dinged and I took the soup out and stirred it, stepping aside so Melinda could warm up what looked like some homemade lasagna. My stomach growled.

"I heard the janitorial staff was short this week. Somebody didn't show up and they're scrambling to replace him. You know how it is, though. There's all those background checks that everyone has to go through. It takes a few days." She pulled out her lasagna. It smelled amazing.

I went back to the lab before I decided to knock her Tupperware out of her hands and run off with her lunch. Soup might be good for a wary stomach, but lasagna was solace to the soul. I went back to my office with my soup. Another day, another season, we might have both been heading up to the rooftop garden Will had put on top of the building. In spring and summer, it was glorious. Right now you could get frostbite just opening the door.

It was nearly the end of the day before I could return to the report for the FDA on Cover Me. I flipped through until I found the page with the charts I'd been focusing on right before all hell had broken loose on Monday.

I started plugging numbers into my calculator. Sure enough, it was exactly as I had suspected. The base numbers seemed random within a range, but then their progressions were identical. Too identical. The results indicated our original tests were more reproducible than anything in nature could possibly be.

The numbers had come from an Ames test we'd run on the component parts of Cover Me to see if anything we were putting into our product was mutagenic and at what concentration it became that way. At Bellefountaine, we used the fluctuation method with ninety-six well plates rather than the old-fashioned agar plates. We'd tested the component parts in six different strengths. Or, at least, that's what we said we'd done in the report. I wasn't so sure we actually had. Those numbers weren't real. There were reasons someone might put fake numbers into a report like this. Maybe something had gone wrong while they were running it and they didn't want to start over so they decided to fudge it.

The only thing that made sense was to run the tests again. Even if there was nothing wrong, I wanted numbers I could count on in that report. After all, I stood to make some decent money, too, if all our stock options suddenly became worthwhile.

I leaned back in my chair and pinched my nose to stop the headache I could feel forming behind my right eye.

"You okay?" Jesse asked from the doorway.

I sat up straight and smiled. "Fine. Just a little tired."

"Then it's time to go home. Come on. Pack up and I'll walk you to the L. Or better yet, put you in a cab."

"Jesse, I'm fine. I don't need help getting to the L." He was right, though. It was time to go home. I could start running the new Ames tests Thursday morning.

He shifted from one foot to the other. "I think maybe you do," he finally said. "You drank or ate something that could have killed you on Monday. Unless you took it yourself—"

"I did not take it myself," I interrupted him.

He held up his hand to stop me before I could go on. "If you didn't take it yourself, somebody poisoned you, Amanda."

I sank back in my chair.

"I don't know who would want to harm you or why, but I know you got a phone call on Friday night that made you go from festive to freaked in about ten seconds. Maybe this has to do with that. Maybe it doesn't. You didn't want to talk about it then. Maybe you want to talk about it now?" He paused, big puppy dog brown eyes hopeful.

I shook my head.

"Whether you want to talk or not, the least I can do is make sure you start out on your trip home safely." He crossed his arms over his chest. I wondered if he knew how much it made his biceps bulge.

I thought about those hard hands on the small of my back as the taxi rushed toward me. Maybe a companion on the streets wouldn't be such a bad thing. "Thanks," I said. "That would be nice."

He blew out a breath like he'd been swimming underwater for a couple of laps. "Great. I'll get my coat."

We walked out the doors of Bellefountaine together. The sun was low on the horizon. Our shadows stretched out in front of us. I pulled my hat down more firmly over my ears as the chill worked its way up from the soles of my boots through my spine.

"Cab?" Jesse asked.

I shook my head. "With traffic at this time of day, it's actually faster to take the L."

"Okay, then." He took my hand and tucked it into the crook of his arm and headed for the tracks. I didn't let go until I got on my train.

I decided to take the extra minutes to transfer to the Blue Line and get myself a block closer to home. LaSalle is an underground station, creepy on its best days with its burrow-like feeling, and the concrete tunnels added dampness to the cold from the weather. In the summer, it actually felt good, kind of like a swampcooler. When it was ten degrees out, it was just creepy and cold. I emerged onto Congress Parkway and turned south to go home at the intersection with Wells.

I felt the first prickle of unease less than a block from the station, that uncomfortable feeling that someone was watching. I glanced behind me. Nothing. Well, not nothing. People everywhere. People packed the Loop at this time of day. A sea of people swarmed along the sidewalk. I pulled the collar of my coat up and turned back toward home.

The farther south I headed, the thinner the crowds became. By the time I reached the corner of Polk I was alone. I was also only a half block from my apartment. I glanced behind me one last time as I waited for the walk signal. The homeless guy—I was starting to think of him as my homeless guy—stood about ten yards back. He nodded at me, then made a shooing gesture, like he was sending me home. I had no idea how long he had been following me. He could have been in the crowd when I'd come out of the L station or maybe he'd fallen in behind me when I'd turned onto the block. My heart thumped. He made the shooing gesture again. I turned. The light had changed. I didn't wait or question him. I went.

It didn't strike me as good news that a homeless guy had become obsessed with me. Could he have followed me on Monday? Could it have been his hands I'd felt at the small of my back? I quickened my pace, glancing behind myself every few steps. Homeless Dude stayed where he was. At least he wasn't chasing me. I opened the outer door of my building and slammed it behind me. I got into the elevator, grateful for once that a neighbor clearly just back from a dog walk with her West Highland Terrier stuck an arm into the car as the doors were closing and got on with me. I wasn't sure I wanted to be alone. The dog looked up at me and yipped.

"Sorry," she said to me and then to the dog, "Quiet, Edwina."

"No problem," I said. The dog looked at me again as if I was somehow at fault for it getting in trouble. Even the animal kingdom was turning against me. The woman and her dog got out on the fifth floor. I rode the rest of the way to the eighth by myself.

I hurried down the hall and let myself into the apartment, shut the door behind me, leaned back against it, and let the safety of home wash over me. I slipped out of my coat and boots and padded into the apartment. I'd heard other single women talk about how hard it was to come home to an empty apartment or house night after night. To me, it was like rubbing salve on skin that had been roughened by brushing against other people all day long. The silence was like a blanket of peace I could pull over myself. The stillness was like a drink of cold water on a hot day. Which all might go a long way in explaining why I wasn't thrilled when the intercom buzzed. I flicked on the television to see Sam standing in the foyer holding aloft bags of what had to be take-out food.

I buzzed him in and then went to the apartment door and leaned against the jamb waiting for him.

"I wasn't expecting you," I said as he came within speaking distance.

He tilted his head. "I probably should have called first."

I considered responding with a You think? but whatever he had in those take-out bags smelled way too good. I stepped back and let him in the apartment.

"I thought you might be ready for macaroni and cheese." He shrugged out of his coat and started pulling dishes out of the cabinets in the kitchen.

I watched, wordless, wondering when he'd become so comfortable in my kitchen, in my life. I wasn't sure how I felt about it. The heels of my mother's death didn't exactly feel like the right time to start something with someone or anything with anyone for that matter. Yet, that food definitely smelled good. We sat down at the table.

"Lois Brower didn't come to work today," he announced as he dished out the mac and cheese.

"Did she call in?" I wasn't surprised. Maybe a little disappointed, but not surprised. The disconnected phone and the fake address were too much of a coincidence. But if Lois Brower had been the person to sneak a photo of my brother into my mother's room, the big question was why? Who was she? Why would she do something like that?

"Nope." He took a bite of food. "Just didn't show up. I asked around some more. No one seems to know much about her. She was friendly, but somehow never really divulged much about herself."

"So a dead end." I pushed the food around on my plate.

"At least for now," Sam agreed.

I was disappointed. There had to be some kind of connection, though. She would have to have a reason for doing that to my mother, and I could only think of one.

"How thoroughly do you vet the people that you hire at the medical center?" I asked.

"Very. We don't hire anyone with a criminal record. We double-check all references."

I'd figured that. "But you don't check for, say, what ties they might have to different churches, do you?"

"Well, no. That would be illegal. We don't discriminate on the basis of religion. Or race. Or sexual preference. Or gender. What exactly are you thinking, Amanda?"

I started tapping again. "I'm thinking that it would be easy for someone who was part of, say, the Children of the Greater God to get hired at Elgin and no one would ever know."

"Yes, but why? What could they possibly want with your mother or with you? What are you not telling me, Amanda?"

"I did tell you. Patrick Collier is coming up for parole. His followers are still here. They're still active. Hell, they still have an actual physical church." It was out towards Lockport. I hadn't been there in years. Not since two weeks before Jackson died, in fact. I didn't know if it was the same sprawling compound it had been when I'd spent every weekend, evening, and free moment there or if it had changed entirely. I didn't want to know.

"Do you know something that would keep Collier from getting his parole? Did your mother know something? Is that what you're trying to say here?"

I couldn't help it. "Of course we know something. We know that he took a mentally unstable woman and threw her so far off her rocker that she killed one son and woke up her daughter in the middle of the night to ask for her help in killing the other son. What more do we have to know than that?"

His voice was maddeningly calm. "I know that, Amanda. Everyone knows that. That's my point—that information is out in the world. There would be no reason to silence your mother or you to keep you from talking about it."

That took the wind out of my sails. I wasn't exactly becalmed, but I wasn't racing through the storm, either. "I see your point," I replied, lowering my decibel level quite a bit.

"Is there something else, Amanda? Something that you haven't told the authorities? Something that would hurt Collier getting parole?"

I decided to change the topic. "You know," I said, taking a small bite. I almost sighed at the creamy cheesiness. "You probably could have told me about Lois Brower over the phone."

A faint flush crept up his cheeks. "I know."

"And yet…" I gestured at the table.

"I wanted to check on you as well as tell you about Brower not showing up for work," he said.

"Bringing dinner seemed like a good way to accomplish both."

I nodded slowly. "Check on me?" I asked.

The flush got redder. "I didn't protect your mother the way I should have. Whatever happened, however it happened, it happened on my watch."

I set my fork down. "So this is all about your honor and ethics?"

He shifted, uncomfortable. "Mainly."

"Mainly?"

He extended his hand across the table toward me. "I don't want anyone else in your family to be hurt on my watch."

"You might be a little late for that," I said, but I found myself reaching across and taking his hand.

I don't know what might have happened from there if the intercom hadn't buzzed again. I flipped on the television. Detective Pagoa stood like a mountain outside my building's door. I glanced over at Sam.

"Are you going to let him in?" he asked.

I buzzed him in.

"Sorry to interrupt your dinner," Pagoa said when he came in. It didn't sound sincere to me.

I sat down in my chair and gestured toward one for him.

"That's okay," he said, looming over us. "Been sitting all day."

"So how can we help you?" I asked.

He glanced over at Sam. "Is now a good time to talk?"

"Yes," I said. "It's fine."

"I think I should start with your mother. The medical examiner has finished her investigation and has ruled your mother's death a suicide," Pagoa said.

I bowed my head. I wasn't surprised. What else were they going to conclude? "What about the idea that someone might have driven her to take her own life?" I asked.

Pagoa heaved a sigh, which made his massive shoulders rise and fall like rocks resettling after an avalanche. "That would be more of an issue with the institution at Elgin. It's not a police matter. Sending someone a photograph or a news article does not rise to the level of harassment." He looked pointedly at Sam.

Again, I felt no surprise. Anger? You bet. I wasn't sure at whom to direct it, but I felt the red starting to rise up behind my eyes. "Okay, then. Will I be able to see the autopsy report?"

"Of course." Pagoa paused. "Then we come to the matter of what happened to you on Monday."

I tucked my hands under my thighs to keep from shredding my napkin into tiny pieces.

"The timing of you succumbing to the poison points to you having ingested something at work," he continued.

I nodded. I knew that.

"But the only thing you ate or drank was coffee from a communal pot, and no one else got sick. We were unable to test the pot. It had been thoroughly cleaned before anyone realized it could be evidence. Same with the mug you had been drinking out of."

Stupid Bellefountaine custodial staff. Too bad it hadn't happened later in the week when that one janitor quit.

"So without knowing where the poison came from, it's hard to figure out who did it," I said.

Pagoa went very still. "Ms. Sinclair, if there is anything else you need to tell me, now is the time to do it."

I looked up at him, confused. "I'm not sure what else I could tell you. I didn't go anywhere else or do anything else that day."

"I'm aware." He pulled out the chair and sat down. "Sometimes we do something or say something and it seems like we can't take it back. It starts a chain of events that feels like an unstoppable train. I'm telling you that it's okay. We can stop the train. In fact, I'm hoping we can stop it before it goes any further."

"A train? I don't think I understand." He was getting at something, but I wasn't sure what.

He rubbed at his forehead with his thumb, eyes squinched shut for a moment. Then he took a deep breath and looked straight at me. "Miss Sinclair, if you ingested that salicylate yourself, please tell me now. It is a crime to file a false police report, but we can let this go with a conversation between the two of us right now. If you persist in your claims that agents of the Children of the Greater God are trying to kill you, well...I'm not sure how long I can protect you."

I sat there, stunned. "You're suggesting that I poisoned myself and for some reason decide to blame COGG?"

"Everyone is aware that you and your family have always held Patrick Collier responsible for what happened to your little brother. I'm sure it's devastating to have Collier leaving prison, especially with your mother's suicide. We're also aware of some of your previous...difficulties." Maybe it was my imagination, but I could have sworn he glanced at my wrists. "Maybe things came together and it seemed easiest to try to blame Collier."

I pushed my chair back and stood. "I think I'd like you to leave now, Detective Pagoa."

He stood as well, towering over me. "Certainly, but please think about what I said. Right now we have no leads to follow, but your case will remain open. I could close it out with a word from you and there would be no reason for us to pursue a false -report case against you."

I clenched my hands into fists at my sides to keep myself under control. "Listen to these words: I did not poison myself. I don't believe that my mother killed herself, at least not without some prompting. I think when the truth eventually comes out about all of this—if it ever comes out—you'll regret making these kinds of allegations."

Pagoa held his hands up, palms out. "Let me know if you change your mind. I'll see myself out."

I followed him down the hallway anyway, throwing the dead bolt as soon as the door shut behind him. I leaned my forehead against the door. The last words Patrick Collier ever directly spoke to me echoed in my head: You can tell anyone you want to tell, Sister Amanda. No one is going to believe you.

He'd been so right.

From behind me, Sam said, "Wanna talk about it?"

I shook my head.

The warm weight of his hand fell on my shoulder. "How can I help?"

Tears welled behind my closed eyelids. I didn't trust myself to speak.

"I could make you some hot tea," he suggested.

A laugh burbled up in my throat and escaped. What on earth would hot tea help? On the other hand, what would it hurt?

"I could put whiskey in it," he offered.

I turned, brushing at my face with the back of my hand in case any stray tears had escaped. "I appreciate the offer, but I think maybe I need to be by myself for the moment."

He frowned. "Are you sure?"

I straightened and tugged down my shirt. Fake it till you make it. "Yeah. I am. It's the end of the whole thing anyway, right?"

"Possibly," he said.

"See?" I brushed past him and walked down the hall to the dining room and started picking up the dishes. My plate of warm cheesy comfort food now looked like a congealed glutinous mess. Somehow my appetite was gone. "I'm fine."

"Mmhmm." He leaned against the kitchen counter and crossed his arms over his chest. "What about COGG? Aren't you worried about them?"

I scraped the plates into the garbage. "It's clear they don't have to worry about me. If they realize that it doesn't matter if I talk or not since no one is going to believe me, then there's no reason to threaten me, is there?"

"You make it sound so rational."

I shrugged as I put dishes in the dishwasher. "It is. Besides, what more is there to look at? Even if Pagoa believed me, I don't see what other investigative avenues he has open to him." I shut the dishwasher. "I'm fine. I mean, of course I'm a little upset, but it's kind of a relief to say it's over. I really just want to crawl into bed with a book and get a good night's sleep."

Sam nodded slowly, as if thinking over my words. "All right then. I'll go." He picked up his coat and started putting it on. "You'll call me if you need anything?"

"Of course." I didn't look him in the eye. I knew I wouldn't be calling him. He probably knew, too. Whatever might have been starting between us was over.

After Sam left, I did exactly what I'd told him I was going to do. I cuddled up in my bed with a hot cup of tea (after all, what could it hurt?), a romance about a brave young woman fighting for her home with a hunky guy in a kilt by her side, and let myself drift.

My cell phone buzzed me awake at elevenfifteen. There was a text from Dylan. It said: What the hell, Amanda? followed by a photo of a COGG necklace hanging from a doorknob. Then another text from him: This was hanging on my dorm room door.

I stared at the photo, then got up and opened my jewelry box. Only one necklace lay inside.

CHAPTER
12

Thursday, February 23

WHEN THE ALARM WENT OFF the next morning, I thought about calling in sick. After all, everyone had told me I had come back too soon. No one would blame me for taking another day.

Then I considered spending the day alone in the apartment someone else had been in—someone who had, as far as I could tell, disturbed nothing except for taking one of the COGG necklaces from my jewelry box, someone who had known where to find that necklace and what it had meant and exactly how much it would chill me to find out it had been hung on my brother's dorm room doorknob.

But someone had been in my apartment, someone I knew, someone I'd invited in. Sara had come to get my things when I was in the hospital. I'd given her the key myself, and who knew what she'd done when I wasn't here? And she'd been the one standing by the coffee pot when I'd walked into the kitchen Monday morning.

But why? It made no sense. None at all.

Dylan and I had talked for over an hour after he texted me the photo of the necklace. Anybody could have left the necklace on his doorknob. Sure, the dorms were locked, but residents were notoriously bad about letting in anyone who asked and propping doors open. It wouldn't have taken Ethan Hunt to get in. No one remembered seeing anyone hang the necklace on the doorknob, but Dylan didn't want to press anyone too hard. He didn't want anyone to take particular notice, to wonder why he was so upset, to ask what the necklace might mean.

I didn't blame him. I shared the same horror of anyone connecting me to COGG and, from there, to our mother.

"I don't get it, Amanda," he said. "Why would COGG bother with us? What's the point?"

"I don't really know." I had some suspicions, but that's all they were. Dylan didn't need to know what I suspected, just like he didn't need to know about my near -misses or my suspicions about how Mom died. Mom had been right about one thing the night she'd killed Jackson: Dylan was still an innocent. I would do everything in my power to protect that.

"I don't like it," he said.

I laughed. "You think I do?"

He sighed. "No, Amanda. I don't."

"Stash the necklace somewhere or, better yet, pitch it. Get rid of it. Then get some sleep." I laid back on my own pillows wondering if I was going to get any with my mind racing like it was.

"Okay. I will." He paused. "You're sure I should pitch it? What if we need it? For, like, evidence of something."

"I can't imagine what it would prove."

We finally said good night with promises to get together for dinner some time soon and hung up.

True to form, I did sleep. I dreamed about cold, damp earth, about decaying leaves, about insects crawling through mud, about hands outstretched, about pleading eyes. I woke tangled in the sheets as if I'd been wrestling throughout the night and feeling like I hadn't actually rested.

I stood under the shower, face up, letting the hot water stream around me, washing away the dreams of the night before. There wasn't enough hot water in Chicago to wash away the humiliation I felt about Pagoa's visit. I'd have to live with that.

I ate my cereal and drank my coffee. I didn't turn on the news. I felt almost human when I stepped out onto the sidewalk and slammed into the frigid cold air. I stopped for a second, willing myself to let my shoulders down, to let the tension out. It didn't mean I wouldn't feel like the inside of my nostrils had frozen, but at least I wouldn't shake.

I settled my bag on my shoulder and walked toward the L station, relieved to see that my homeless friend/stalker wasn't asleep in the doorway down the block. I didn't think anyone could survive sleeping rough in this cold. I hoped he'd gotten into a shelter or someplace else warm.

The sun was up, but its rays were weak, barely penetrating the cloud cover. The air was sharp and tinged with the smells of diesel fuel and the river. I smiled. It might not be pretty, but it was home.

It felt normal to be at work. All the hugging was apparently behind me. Even the kitchen was back to its usual tidy order. I hesitated at the coffeemaker and decided it was okay to be a little gun shy. I was sufficiently caffeinated for the moment anyway. I could get another cup at lunchtime, one from an anonymous and overpriced barista at the Starbucks down the street, perhaps.

The lab was busy already. Sara and Jesse and Anna milled around, setting up samples, running gels, answering emails. I made my way to the alcove where my desk sat and dumped my stuff.

I reviewed protocols and started the process of running the Ames test on the Cover Me components again. I went to the supply racks and pulled several Ames test kits and started setting up the buffer, the mutated Salmonella bacteria, the histidine, the well plates, and everything else on my bench area of the lab. For the next several hours, I mixed, made dilutions, incubated, and transferred substances into my well plates.

Jesse knocked on the wall by my desk. "Lunch?" he asked.

I looked at the clock. I hadn't realized how late it had gotten. Time flies when you're looking for carcinogens, I guess. I thought regretfully of the mac and cheese I had so unceremoniously scraped into the garbage the night before. "Sure." I stood up and went for my coat.

He frowned, looking at my bench. "What are you doing, anyway?"

"Double-checking some of the results in the report." I shrugged into my coat and picked up my scarf.

"Why? Those tests were run and run and run again." He leaned against the counter.

I shrugged. I wasn't ready to share what I'd found. Accusing someone of falsifying results was a serious step. I wanted to be sure I had all the information I needed before I even thought about it. "I like to be thorough."

He snorted. "That's true, but all the way back to the Ames?"

I sang a little line about the beginning being a very good place to start.

Now he looked really confused. "What?"

"Not a fan of *The* Sound of Music, then?" I asked.

He shook his head. "Musicals are not really my thing."

145

Poor Jesse. He didn't even realize that was another strike against him.

Sara and Melinda joined us. Anna was running something that she wanted to keep an eye on, so we told her we'd bring her back a sandwich. The four of us checked out with Yolanda and then stepped outside. Sara clapped her hands over her ears. "Oh, man. Is winter ever going to be over? I feel like I'm never going to be warm again."

Melinda wrapped her scarf around the lower part of her face. "I need a week of tropical sunshine. Minimum."

We walked toward the deli two blocks over. "Doesn't the cold bother you, Amanda?" Jesse asked, falling in step next to me as Melinda and Sara discussed the relative merits of Belize and Costa Rica for their tropical vacations.

I shrugged. "There's nothing really I can do about it."

He laughed. "Very pragmatic. I expected nothing else." After a few more steps, he asked, "You grew up around here, right? Have you ever thought about living any place else?"

I had. Especially that last year or so of high school when my infamy was still so much in the forefront of everyone's minds and my mom still hit the news headlines as she made her way through the court system. I'd thought about it a lot. Almost obsessively.

Then Dad and Jessica had made it clear that if I wanted them to pay for college, I was going to go some place nearby. They said things about keeping an eye on me, which I knew was code for making sure I didn't try to off myself again. By the time I was done with my degree, I'd realized that no one else was going to help out with Mom. I needed to stay close so I could get to Elgin when I was needed.

Now that was done. Mom was dead. There was nothing to keep me in Chicago anymore, or even in Illinois. I could go anywhere. It hit me like I'd run full force into a brick wall, and I actually stopped walking for a second.

Jesse stopped a step or two ahead of me and turned. "You okay?"

"Yeah," I said. "Totally okay."

We walked into the deli. It was like walking into a steam room, but a particularly yummy -smelling steam room. We all started peeling off hats and scarves and gloves. I ordered a pastrami and a large coffee.

"Can't blame you for not trusting the office coffee, can we?" Melinda said, as we sat at one of the tables. "Do they still think that's what made you sick?"

I shook my head. "I'm not sure they think anything, if by they you mean the police."

"Really?" Sara asked, taking the seat on the other side of me. "They're not investigating anymore?"

"Not that I know of." I needed to come up with a change of topic before I had to explain that they thought I'd done it myself and why.

Jesse sat down across from me. "As if they investigated much to start with," he harrumphed.

147

"I know," Sara agreed. "They didn't do much besides take the pieces of your coffee cup away."

Jesse leaned forward. "We should investigate."

Melinda laughed. "I think somebody read a few too many Hardy Boys mysteries when he was a kid."

"Seriously," Jesse said, holding up his hand like a traffic cop. "There are security cameras all over the building. We could at least look at some of the video to see who was around the kitchen."

My heart started to beat like a whole flock of birds had suddenly taken up residence in my chest. "Do you think they'd still have the tape?"

"It's been less than week," he said. "I think they don't record over them for like three weeks."

It was all I could do to stay at the table and not leap up and run down the street to Bellefountaine. Someone had put that salicylate in my coffee. If I could give Detective Pagoa a name, maybe he would listen to me. Maybe he'd stop looking at my past and help make sure I actually had a future. "Who would I talk to?"

Jesse wrinkled up his forehead. "I think Pete Collins in HR would be a place to start."

I tried to conjure up a mental image and failed. "I don't think I know him."

"I do," Jesse said. "He played shortstop on the company softball team when I played first base. You should really join the team. It's fun."

"My general reaction to a ball coming toward me is to duck and scream," I said. Plus the whole team sports thing looked like it led to hugging. Plus it blurred those nice walls I had erected between my home life and my work life. Plus…

Well, I guessed there wasn't another *plus*. That's all I had. Work and home.

Sara waved her hand in the air. "No one cares if you can play. They'll put you out in left field. Just make sure to stand your round at the bar afterwards."

The conversation shifted to the hysterical shenanigans gotten up to at the games and afterwards. I let the conversation flow around me, still thinking about the security cameras. I didn't think there was one in the kitchen, but there was definitely one in the hallway. It took forever for everyone to finish their lunches and order for Anna. I was nearly dancing at the door by the time everyone was ready to leave, then Sara froze in the doorway. "I can't walk outside in that. I just can't."

"You can. You have to," Melinda said, pulling up the collar of her coat.

"No. I'm going to stay at the deli until spring. You guys bring me my laptop. I'll telecommute." Sara didn't move.

I considered bodychecking her out of the way to get out the door, but luckily she took a deep breath and went out on her own. After the moist heat of the restaurant, the dry cold air was especially bracing. Sara stamped her feet on the ground. "I'm not sure how much more I can take."

"I suppose throwing a tantrum might warm you up," Melinda said, taking Sara's arm and walking her down the street. "But it won't warm up the weather."

Jesse glanced over at me as we fell into step behind them. "We can go see Pete Collins as soon as we get there."

I smiled at him. "Thanks."

He took my hand and tucked it into his arm like Melinda had done with Sara. I couldn't figure out how to snatch it back, and after a few minutes, I wasn't sure I wanted to.

We piled into the lobby of Bellefountaine with Sara chanting, "Cold, cold, cold, cold, cold."

"Not exactly a newsflash, girl," Yolanda said as we made our way past her. The door to the right of Yolanda's desk led to the administrative offices. The door to the left led to the research and development division. Both doors required the swipe of a security card or being buzzed through by Yolanda. Jesse swiped his security card and let us all through to R&D. Back in the lab, Jesse and I dumped our coats and then went back out to the lobby and had Yolanda buzz us in to the admin section of the facility.

"Should we have called first?" I asked.

Jesse shrugged. "Maybe. Worst -case scenario, he tells us to come back later."

I knew that wasn't true. Worst -case scenario was always much worse than that. Terrorist attacks. Fire. Zombie plague. I could spin worst -case scenarios all day long. I envied Jesse a life where he really thought someone telling him to come back later was the worst that could happen in any given moment.

As it turned out, none of our worst -case scenarios came to pass. Pete Collins was a large African-American man with a bald head and one of those little wrinkles at the back of his neck that made my fingers itch to pinch it. He stood up partway and shook both our hands as we walked into his office.

"Ms. Sinclair," he said. "I'm glad you're back. I've been meaning to stop by and see how you were feeling. Got a little swamped, though." He gestured to the shifting piles of papers on his desk.

"I'm feeling much better. Thank you." I glanced over at Jesse, not sure how to ask for what it was we wanted.

"We were hoping we could look at the security footage of the area outside of the kitchen the morning that Amanda got sick," Jesse said, settling into one of the two chairs across from Collins. I sat in the other.

Collins's eyebrow went up. Then he nodded. "You want to see who went in and out of the kitchen area to see if someone could have done something to her coffee here." It wasn't a question.

"It's a thought," Jesse said.

"I was under the impression that the police had ruled out the coffee as a possible source of the poison." He steepled his fingers together.

"Actually, it was more that they really couldn't find anything to test," I chimed in. "It had all been cleaned up before the police were even notified."

Collins sat very still for a moment or two and I held my breath. Then he dropped his hands and said, "If it's someone here at Bellefountaine, I want to know, too. Whether it was deliberate or a prank gone wrong, well, it's unacceptable."

I let out the breath. "So we can look?"

"I can access all the cameras from my computer." Collins started tapping on his keyboard. Jesse and I exchanged a glance while we waited, his with raised eyebrow and a little smile, mine with a grimace and a shrug. Suddenly I wasn't sure I wanted to know which of my coworkers had poisoned me. Work had always been where I was safe, known for just being me. Now that had changed. As much as I knew it was a done deal, I had the irrational sense that ignorance might really be a little bit of bliss.

"Here," Collins said, turning his computer monitor so all three of us could see it.

I edged my chair closer to Jesse's to get a better view. The monitor displayed the hallway outside the kitchen. The date stamp was Monday, February 20, 8:14 a.m. Collins put the tape on fast -forward and we watched as most of Bellefountaine's R&D staff entered and exited the kitchen, some walking in with lunches and walking out without them, presumably dropping them off in the refrigerator. Some coming out with cups of coffee. Finally we hit me walking toward the kitchen.

"Back up," I said. "Who came and went right before I did?"

Collins hit the bar at the bottom of the image to take us back a few minutes. First through was one of the janitors. He was one I didn't recognize. Tall and a little gaunt, the custodial uniform hung off him. He left his cart and went into the kitchen. He came out a few seconds later with a full bag of garbage that he dumped in the bin on his cart. Then he moved on.

Next Sara came into the frame and entered the kitchen. Then I entered and exited. After I was gone, Sara came out with a mug in her hand. Sara's coffee was from a fresh pot, so she wouldn't have gotten sick. She'd let me take the last of the old one and made the fresh one herself.

I chewed on the edge of my thumbnail. Sara. Sara, who had been in my apartment and would have had time to find the COGG necklaces. Sara, who knew my schedule. Sara. But why? What possible reason could she have to do me harm?

"Go back to that janitor dude," Jesse said. Collins clicked the requisite buttons. "I don't recognize him."

"He wasn't with us long," Collins said, peering at the screen. "Only a few weeks. Didn't give notice when he left, either."

"When was that?" I asked.

"Tuesday. Day after this, as a matter of fact," Collins said, nodding at the computer.

"Weird," Jesse said. "What was his name?"

Collins leaned back in his desk chair. "Palmer. Simon Palmer."

Jesse pulled out his phone and typed in a note. "You have an address or phone number for him?"

Collins drummed his fingers on his desk. "I can't give out that kind of personal information."

Jesse's head shot up. "Come on, man. He might know something about what happened to Amanda. Hell, he might be the person who laced the coffee."

"I can see that, but there are rules and regulations about this kind of thing." He leaned forward. "Now, if the police asked…"

I shook my head. The police weren't going to ask. I was pretty sure that a janitor who emptied garbage from the kitchen and quit soon afterwards wasn't going to be a sufficiently compelling story to get Pagoa to reopen his investigation. My heart started to thump in my chest. I knew what would be compelling enough…

But I couldn't. Amid everything that had happened after Jackson's death, it was the one thing I'd never breathed a word about. Not to my father. Not to any of the therapists I'd been to. Not to anyone. My mother never brought it up, either, not even when she was out of her head with guilt and shame and horror, not even when she was flying high and deluded out of her tree.

What would happen if I told now? I had more perspective on it now than I had as a teenager. I knew I wouldn't be prosecuted. I wouldn't be locked up the way they'd locked my mother away. It would be news, though. Big news. I would be news. Everything I'd built, my whole carefully constructed, anonymous existence would be destroyed, smashed beneath the boot heel of the truth.

"Amanda?" Jesse said.

I realized I'd been staring into space, off in my own world. "I understand," I told Collins. Then something occurred to me. "Can you call him?"

He sighed and pushed back from his desk. "Yes and no. I tried to call him when he didn't show up for work. The number he gave us has been disconnected."

My head shot up. That sounded familiar. Lois Brower's number had also been disconnected. It was too crazy to think the two might be linked, but then again, the whole situation was crazy. It wouldn't hurt to check. Maybe Sam could see if Palmer had been seen around Elgin.

"Thank you for letting us review that. Is there any chance I could get a printout of a still? Just so I have a photo of Palmer in case I see him some place else?" I asked.

"Of course." He hit a few buttons and a printer in the corner whirred to life. Collins gave us the photo, which was surprisingly good, and Jesse and I headed back to the other side of the facility.

"I think that's pretty suspicious," Jesse said. "That this Palmer dude suddenly disappeared."

"I agree, but I'm not sure there's much I can do about it, except watch out for him." Jesse didn't need to know I had any other plans for that photo. We walked into the main lobby and waved to Yolanda as we walked in the other door.

As soon as the door shut behind us, Jesse took my arm. "Amanda, tell me why someone like Palmer might want to hurt you. What is going on? It's hard to help you if I don't know the big picture. I'm like one of those blind guys trying to describe an elephant."

I almost laughed, but he clearly was so sincere. I looked into those big melting -chocolate eyes and thought about what it would be like if I told him who I really was, what I really was. Maybe if it was just him and me, I would be able to do it. Maybe if I could explain, he would understand how it all fell apart. But it wouldn't be just him and me, and I wasn't sure I could explain it even to myself.

"You don't have to help, Jesse. There's nothing to do. It was probably some kind of misunderstanding or prank." I turned to continue walking to the lab.

He grabbed my arm again, more forcefully this time, and pulled me back. "What is it you won't tell me? I see it in your eyes. You have some kind of huge secret and it weighs on you. Let me help."

I felt like my throat was swelling shut, like even if I wanted to push words out, I wouldn't be able to. I extricated my arm from his grasp. Mercifully, he didn't cling. I swallowed hard to remove the lump in my throat. "Even if I told you everything, there wouldn't be anything you could do. It's very sweet what you're offering, but I can't. You can't. I'm sorry." I walked back to the lab.

I slipped the picture of Simon Palmer into my messenger bag. I wasn't sure what good it would do me. He was simply one more loose end out there. I started up my computer and tried to focus on what I'd been doing before lunch, which seemed like it was years ago instead of hours. Ah, yes. The Ames tests. There wasn't much more I could do, since it would take two days for them to run. For once, my timing was good. They'd be ready for me on Monday morning.

CHAPTER
13

Friday, February 24

IF THE GANG FROM THE lab was going out for drinks Friday evening, they didn't mention it to me. I was relieved. I still didn't feel quite myself after my adventures in poisoning earlier in the week, but even more, I didn't want to get my drink on with someone who was falsifying scientific research that I was supposed to put my name on. As I made my way home, my anger grew. Whoever had fudged those numbers would besmirch the reputations of everyone in the lab when the truth came out.

And the truth would come out. If I caught the weird numbers in those charts, surely someone at the FDA would, too. That's part of what I didn't understand. The FDA would rerun these experiments and whatever wasn't right with the faked data would come out. Why bother?

Then another thought occurred to me. What was in the data that needed to be hidden? The idea was to show that Cover Me would be safe for long -term use. Was there something wrong with the product? Could it be harmful under certain circumstances? I lifted my hand to chew on the side of my thumb but remembered in the nick of time that I was wearing gloves.

I got off the train and started the walk back to my apartment, using the heat of my anger to stay warm. I was at the door when it occurred to me that I should have been looking around. Sure enough, Homeless Dude stood at the end of the block. Our eyes met and he gave me a small salute. I nodded and went inside. Did he think he was my guardian angel? I'd seen worse kinds of crazy in my day. Here's the thing about having been in a locked ward for twenty-one days: you learn what crazy is and what crazy isn't. Or at least, what I considered to be crazy and not crazy.

Schizophrenics are crazy. They can't help it. There's some chemical/wiring crap going on that is completely out of their control. They hear things. They think things. They see things. It sucks for them and for their families.

Bipolar folks? Also crazy. It's chemical. They're no happier about it than anybody else is.

Then there's the people that aren't crazy but have something wrong with them. Something inside them is not right. Something got twisted up or damaged or was defective before they ever left their mothers' wombs. They can't help it, either, but it's different than crazy. It's called being evil.

Me? I wasn't crazy. I wished like hell I was.

Upstairs in my apartment, I walked in and froze, listening intently but hearing nothing above the usual comforting silence. I couldn't help myself, though—I went around inspecting the closets and looking under my bed. It helped to have a place without many walls. There weren't many spots a person could hide. Still, someone had been in here before without me noticing. Someone had come in and taken the necklace from my jewelry box without disturbing anything else. I dragged a chair from my dining room table down to the door and propped it under the handle so it couldn't turn. I'd at least know if someone was coming in.

I settled down on my couch with a glass of wine, relieved to have the week behind me. It struck me that it had been nearly exactly a week since I'd received the phone call telling me my mother was dead. By that time, she'd been dead for well over twelve hours, possibly longer. Shouldn't I have felt something when she passed? Some lightening in my universe? Some sense of a burden set down?

I hadn't, though. I'd felt nothing. Of course, by this time in my life, I'd gotten pretty good at shutting down any kind of psychic connection with my mother.

I dragged my computer onto my lap and opened it up. I knew what I wanted to do. I knew what site I wanted to see. I tried like hell to stay away from it, but somehow I couldn't. I was drawn back to it over and over again. Maybe now that my mother was dead, this would be the last time.

I typed in the URL for the Children of the Greater God website. It was nicely done, definitely professional designed and maintained. Photos of smiling people of all races and all ages filled the home page, as always. Sometimes I thought it looked like an ad for a healthyliving housing development. I knew better, but how many other people did?

Tonight there was something different: a breaking news alert.

On Monday, *COGG* founder Patrick Collier will be released from prison. Our community rejoices in Reverend Collier's freedom from the wrongful prosecution that has held him in its bonds for nearly a decade. Come rejoice with us the following Sunday at two p.m. in a special ceremony to welcome *him* back to his rightful place at the head of our fold.

Below was a second message from Andre Schmidt, the man who had been Patrick's second in command back when I'd been part of COGG and had been running it while Patrick was in prison.

It's been my privilege to be the steward of Children of the Greater God for these past ten years, but I am thankful that our true prophet will be back on the pulpit where he belongs.

I wondered if he really meant that. Hard not to feel some ownership of something you've run for a decade. I can't imagine it would be easy to step aside.

161

Not that anyone would be putting their hidden resentments on the home page of their organization's website. Still, disingenuous much?

There was one more message, one that nearly sent me over the edge.

Our hearts go out to our lost sister, Linda Framingham, who took her own life last week. Linda lost sight of her place in God's grand machine years ago, but we still mourn her passing.

I slammed the laptop shut then drummed my fingers on top of it. One thing COGG wasn't trying to do was hide its connection with my mother. If they'd had something to do with her death, wouldn't they want to stay as far away from her as possible, both physically and figuratively?

They certainly weren't distancing themselves from Patrick, either. He was being welcomed back with open arms and hearts. Interesting, since as far as I knew, the money he'd supposedly siphoned out of the Children of the Greater God's coffers had never been found. Patrick had never stopped saying that he was innocent, and it looked like COGG believed him. I'd never really understood how the people running COGG made their decisions, even when I was part of the group, even when I would have done anything to have Patrick's approval. Even when I did do whatever had to be done to get Patrick's approval. That is, until what he asked me to do had gone too far, which all brought me back to the place I didn't want to go. It brought me back to Marcus. Much as I wanted to place all the blame for what happened to

Marcus at Patrick's feet, I knew part of it was on my shoulders.

I'd been the one to first interest Marcus in COGG, after all. Our group was down at the bus station. Celeste and I had sat down a few seats over from a skinny blonde girl hunched over on the seat like she was either cold or sick or both.

We did what we always did. We started talking. Not about anything in particular, at first. Then we'd start to talk about the compound. How good the food was. How much we liked it. Then we'd kind of fold the girl into the conversation. Pretty soon, she'd be asking to come with us. Some of them practically begged. A warm bed? Good food? A shower? A place to stay where you didn't have to pay for it on your knees or on your back? They all wanted to come to the compound.

Only this time, we snared more than the girl. I'd seen Marcus when he'd gotten off the bus from Cleveland, but I didn't figure him a good COGG prospect. He walked too tall, looking around like he was surveying the place, like he wanted to see whether it met his expectation. Not like a scared kid. Not like someone running. Not like someone who wasn't sure where his next meal was coming from or what he would have to do to get it.

I'd watched the girl raise her head a little bit to listen to Celeste and me talk. Out of the corner of my eye, I saw her lean a little toward us. Celeste gave me a nod when she saw the girl taking covert little glances at us. But it wasn't the girl who spoke to us first. It was Marcus.

"Hey," he'd said. "What's this compound place you're talking about and how do you get there?"

I'd turned to appraise him, surprised that he'd been listening. "It's a cool place. Away from the city. Clean, you know?"

"What do they want from you once you're there?" the girl asked, her tone suspicious. I didn't know how long she'd been out on her own, but it was long enough to know what to ask.

"Everybody works, mainly in the gardens," Celeste said. "In the winter there are other chores."

"Like what?" she asked, her eyes narrowed.

"Like cleaning and cooking. Sometimes some office work." I may have been answering her questions, but it was Marcus I was looking at.

"Do you live there?" Marcus asked me. "Because that would be some major incentive."

I felt the heat rush to my face. "I, uh, well, not yet." It had been a deal struck with my Dad that my mother still complained about. We could live with her as long as we stayed in the house and didn't move out to the COGG compound.

"But you come around a lot?" he asked.

"Pretty much every day." My lips felt dry. I licked them.

He smiled and stood up, slinging his backpack over his shoulder. "How do I get there?"

Ten minutes later, we were in the van with Marcus and the girl, Gina. I'd known Marcus wasn't a good prospect. I'd known he didn't fit the profile. I also knew he had beautiful curly dark hair and dark brown eyes with completely ridiculous eyelashes.

I pressed my clenched fists against my eyes. I'd only been sixteen. I hadn't known what I was doing. Not really. Not fully. I hadn't known yet that there was something inside of me that was rotten.

Saturday, February 25

I called Dylan on Saturday morning. I'd waited until ten, but I still had clearly woken him up.

"Hey, sis. How's it going?" He yawned.

"Fine, kiddo," I lied. "How are you? Any more weird things showing up on your dorm room door?"

"Nope. Nothing. It's been mellow."

"Collier's getting out of prison on Monday." I'd thought about not mentioning it to Dylan, but it was the kind of thing that showed up on news feeds and I didn't want it to take him by surprise.

He yawned again. "You think that's why someone put the necklace on my door?"

"It's too big of a coincidence not to be related. I don't know what they thought they would get from it." I swiveled back and forth in my desk chair.

"Me neither. COGG was your thing. Yours and Mom's. I only went if she made me."

That was true. I'd been Mom's mini-me, wanting to do whatever she did, especially after Dad left. I'd been

165

angry at him, furious at his desertion, at the way he acted as if he was the victim in the whole situation. I'd been terrified of Mom sinking into one of her depressions where she refused to get out of bed or shower. When she'd started going to COGG it had felt like it was literally the answer to my prayers. God, in the form of Patrick Collier, has swooped in and given my mother a sense of purpose.

According to Patrick, her job as our mother was given to her by God, so it was important for her to get us to school on time, clean and fed with homework completed and checked. God wanted our house to be clean and for her to treat the neighbors with respect, so things were vacuumed and dusted and whatever imaginary slights the neighbors might have perpetrated were met with a turn of the cheek. I was happy to go with her to a place that was telling her to make our lives so nice, so normal.

Plus there were the other kids. Kids like Celeste and Ryan and Brandon. Some lived at the compound. Some lived at home and came in with their parents, like me. They were nice to me. I had friends. It had been hard to hold onto friends when Mom had been more erratic. Other moms shied away from her, never knowing if she'd be wildly pursuing one of her audacious plans to start new business ventures or run for office or if she'd be barely managing to brush her teeth in the morning. They didn't much want their daughters spending time around her or, by extension, me.

At the COGG compound, however, my mom quickly became a person to watch and so I did, too. Patrick took a special interest in our family, something that had not impressed Dylan in the least while Jackson was too little to notice. I had been a totally different story.

I had loved it. I had loved the way Patrick's eyes seem to light up when our family came into the room. I loved the special interest he took in the questions I would ask at Bible study. I loved how his attention elevated us to a certain status.

Unfortunately, once you're raised to a certain height, you have a longer way to fall.

After our marathon conversation two nights before, Dylan and I didn't have much to discuss. "Tell me if anything else comes up, okay?" I said. "And be careful for the next few days. You know, just in case."

"I'll be careful," he assured me as we said good-bye.

I poured myself another cup of coffee and tried to read. The words blurred and faded on the page in front of me. Why would anyone from COGG threaten Dylan? He didn't know anything. He'd stayed away from the compound unless Mom made him go.

The only reason to threaten Dylan was to send a message to me. It was the same message they'd sent with the decapitated Spiderman toy. Be quiet. Keep your mouth shut. Leave us alone.

The irony was, I would have probably done exactly that if they hadn't threatened my brother. COGG had taken one brother from me. They weren't getting another one. Ever.

CHAPTER
14

Monday, February 27

PATRICK COLLIER WAS RELEASED FROM prison Monday morning. I didn't attend. Based on the news coverage, close to a hundred COGG members did. If it hadn't been a news event already, the crowd ensured that it was.

It reminded me of news footage of some of those early Beatles concerts. Women were crying. Several men dropped to their knees, clasped hands raised to the heavens. Children sported colorful signs welcoming home their spiritual father.

I did my best to ignore it. After a quiet weekend, I went to work. I got in early and made a beeline for the incubator. I pulled the wells out, ready to start counting how many wells had turned from purple to yellow in each one. The color change would indicate that one of the substances was indeed mutagenic and at what concentration it turned that way. The first few looked pretty much as I expected. The negative control remained purple and the positive control had turned nearly completely yellow. That meant that I'd done the test correctly. A substance I knew to be mutagenic had indeed adversely affected the Salmonella bacteria. A substance I knew to be harmless, hadn't. The other four sections remained mainly purple with a smattering of yellow cells at the highest concentrations. Anything can be bad for you if you over do it, after all. I'd count the actual wells later. The third plate I removed, however, made me gasp. Nearly all the higher dosage section was yellow. The lower doses had a higher rate than the other substances, but there was a huge jump in the final dosage increase. I checked my label. Cytothelate acid. The active ingredient in Cover Me. The thing that made it special. The thing that made it so valuable to Bellefountaine. I cursed softly.

"That doesn't sound good," Sara said behind me. "What's up?"

I jumped. I hadn't heard her come in. I quickly shuffled the plates around so the one with too much yellow would be hard to see. "Oh, nothing much. I think I screwed up one of the plates. I'll have to rerun it."

She walked up next to me. "Plates for what?"

"Double-checking some of the Cover Me data for the FDA report." It didn't make sense to say I was working on anything else. Cover Me was pretty much all that was on anybody's mind.

"You're going all the way back to the Ames?" she asked, slipping out of her coat.

I shrugged. "It seemed like the right place to start."

"Well, don't forget how many false positives you can get with Ames. Maybe you didn't screw up. Maybe it went a little haywire on you." She went back over to her bench area to hang up her coat.

I quickly stacked the plates and went back to my desk, feeling like Sara's eyes were drilling into my back. When I glanced over my shoulder, however, she was already back at work on her own data. I was getting paranoid.

Sara was right; Ames did give you a lot of false positives. That was the flaw of the test. Negatives you could count on. Positives, well, not so much. There was still a chance that that's all that had happened here. Maybe I was even more paranoid than I knew, seeing conspiracies around me all the time. One more personal problem I could lay at the feet of Patrick Collier.

The next step would be to run a quantitative reverse transcriptase polymerase chain reaction or, as we call it in the biz, qRT-PCR, to see what the heck was going on with the RNA here. In qRT-PCR, you take RNA and convert it through reverse transcription into a complementary DNA sequence. You then take the DNA and amplify it using electrophoresis. All this happens in a gel agarose mixed with a dye that binds to the DNA, which is why we call it running a gel. We also put two measuring ladders in the gel, one for base pairs and one for molecular weight.

Again, somebody had to have done that the first time around. I pulled up the digital lab notebook where we all input our notes. Each of us had our individual notebooks that we kept as sort of rough drafts, but at the end of each and every test or experiment, we uploaded our findings into the lab's digital notebook. Our own notebooks? Well, they were ours. We could take them home or do whatever with them. The lab notebook, however, belonged to the lab and never went anywhere. Time was that it would have been a physical notebook kept in a locked drawer. Now it was a password-protected set of zeros and ones kept in the Cloud.

It didn't take me long to find the gels that were run based on the substances I'd run the Ames tests on. They were right where they should be and showed exactly what they should show considering the numbers in the original report. Exactly.

I stared at them and sighed. I looked from one to the next. Each progressed exactly as it should according to the numbers in the chart. Maybe too exactly, but could that be an anomaly in and of itself? If a room full of monkeys would eventually type a Shakespeare play, maybe a set of experiments would have numbers that looked too perfect and it would mean nothing.

I chewed on the edge of my thumb. Then I saw it. It would have been so easy to miss it. I had been looking for something wrong. What I saw were things that were too right. Nothing is ever really perfect, and we don't try to make it that way in the lab. When we run a gel, there's always something a little bit off. One lane will be a little distorted. A band will be a little too light. Something might smear. There's always something. In this case, it was one lane that veered a little more to the left than its companion lanes. No big deal, it happens all the time. Somehow, however, it had happened every single time in the gels that accompanied the numbers from the Cover Me data. Always the same lane. Always to the left. Always at the same angle.

I wouldn't have been able to do that if I'd tried. There was only one way for that to have happened. Instead of running individual gels for each level of the test, someone had taken the same gel, copied it, pasted it, altered it slightly, and marked it as its own unique experiment. Someone had falsified the results.

Photo manipulation programs like PhotoShop have made labeling and sharing scientific images a million times easier. They've also made it way easier to cheat. Most scientists use photo manipulation to resize images, heighten the contrast, sharpen the details. Stuff to make the image clearer and easier for people to understand. For some people, however, the temptation to go further than that is too great. It's so easy to take part of one image and paste it over another to get an illustration that will support your hypothesis. A little rubber stamp here or there and suddenly you have something that might get you more recognition and a better publication. Unfortunately it was happening more and more. At least, people getting caught was happening more and more. Who knew what else was going on? If the people whose unethical manipulations had been exposed were the tip of the iceberg, as was usually the case with getting caught, then how many more were doing it? At what levels?

When scientists did get caught, it was usually because someone tried to either reproduce a result or take the research further and got strange results because the basis of the new hypothesis was faulty.

Which was why it made no sense at all for someone here at Bellefountaine to falsify results. This report was going to the FDA, who would almost certainly rerun these self-same experiments. If their results were different, then our proposal would get bounced and all the work and money Bellefountaine had put into Cover Me would be for nothing.

Maybe it had been a mistake. We'd been under a lot of pressure to get this report ready. That pressure had only increased once the bigger cosmetic companies had started sniffing around. Bellefountaine had a lot of good products, but Cover Me was going to be great. And great products made great amounts of money. I was pretty sure that Will Friedrichs had wanted the FDA approval so he could ask for an even higher buyout amount. He had really turned up the heat on our Bunsen burners to finish the report. Perhaps someone had simply pasted something unintentionally over something else while rushing and fatigued and hadn't noticed the error. It actually wouldn't be that hard to do. I got confused all the time when I was working with multiple images at the same time. Everyone did.

Sara knocked on the wall next to my desk. "Coming to the lab meeting?" she asked.

I quickly switched off my computer screen and gathered up my notebook and a pen. "Of course." It was kind of a silly question. Monday -morning lab meeting was mandatory.

Usually Ollie Lopez, head of R&D, ran our lab meetings, but today when we walked in Will Friedrichs was sitting at the head of the table. Sara and I exchanged glances and then slipped into spots near the other end of the table.

There was no set seating arrangement, but there was definitely a bit of a hierarchy. The lower you were on the laboratory food chain, the farther down the table you sat. As lab techs, Sara and I were lucky to even have seats in the room.

Once everybody slid into place, Will started the meeting, then almost immediately turned it over to Ollie, who ran through the usual things. What we had done last week. What we were doing this week. Upcoming items. The big difference was that he then turned the meeting back over to Will.

Will stood. There was an intense energy to the man, like a coiled spring. He paced the front of the room. "As you know," he said, his voice too loud for a second. Next to me, Sara jumped.

He started again in a softer tone. "As you know, some big cosmetics companies have become interested in Bellefountaine."

We all nodded. Well aware of the rumors.

"The basis of their interest is Cover Me."

Again, not a news flash. I glanced around the table. Everyone was either nodding or casting looks around like I was.

"If anything, interest is mounting. We currently have two companies vying for us."

I sat back in my chair. That was news. Two companies meant a bidding war. A bidding war meant the price was going to go up.

"So what I need to know is what is holding up the FDA report." Will planted his fists on the table and leaned against them.

Every head in the room swiveled to me. I felt heat rush to my face. "I'm double-checking some numbers that didn't seem quite right to me."

Will grimaced. "What kind of not right, Amanda?"

I hadn't been ready to go public with the information and wasn't about to lay out everything, but I might as well let people know I wasn't crazy. "The too - perfect kind of not right."

Ollie snorted. "You're saying our results are too good?"

I shook my head. "Maybe not too good, just too perfect. I'm rerunning some tests to see if I can reproduce the results."

"And how long will that take?" Will asked.

"A week, maybe two?"

"Which is it, Amanda? One week or two?" His voice was cold. He'd never spoken to me quite like that.

"Two to be safe," I said, trying to sound more definitive.

He pressed his lips together. "Look, Amanda. We're all aware of your recent…problems. Would it be better if someone else took this off your hands? It's really imperative that it be done soon."

"No!" I said too loudly. Would someone else see what I was seeing? They hadn't before. I was as anxious as everyone else for everything to go well for Cover Me, but that meant making sure the data we submitted to the FDA was rock solid. "No. I've got it."

"If you're sure," Will said, sounding anything but sure himself.

"I am. It's my number -one priority. It will be done as soon as possible," I assured him.

He sighed. "All right then. I know it's a lot on your shoulders right now. Make sure to let me or Ollie know if it's too much and you need some help."

From whom? I almost asked. From someone in my lab who might well be the very one who had dry-labbed the data in the first place? I didn't think so. "I will."

"Fine. Meeting adjourned."

We all filed out. Jesse maneuvered his way through the group to walk next to me. "You okay?" he asked, his voice soft.

I shrugged. "As okay as I can be after that. I didn't feel like our illustrious leader was exactly happy with me."

"Yeah. I caught that vibe." He patted my shoulder. "Let me know if you need help, okay?"

I nodded. "It takes the time it takes, you know? I can't exactly get DNA to replicate any faster than it does."

Jesse laughed. "Truth."

I turned into the restroom on the way back. When I got back into the lab, Sara was over by my desk. "Is there something you need?" I asked her.

She blushed, her dusky skin going rosy. "Uh, no. Just looking for a pen I thought I might have left on your desk."

I looked at the top of my desk. There were about seven pens scattered around on its surface. "Take whatever one you want."

"That's okay," she said, backing away.

I watched her as she returned to her own desk alcove, wondering again exactly how that necklace had gone missing from my jewelry box and if she had something to do with it.

I turned my computer screen back on to look at the gels that had clearly been manipulated. They had to have been created by someone in this lab. My gaze flitted between them. Melinda. Anna. Sara. Jesse. It had to be one of the four of them. If I figured out who had done it, I would have to report it to Will. Falsifying results was an ethical violation that demanded immediate termination. That could seriously put a crimp in someone's plans. He would also have to understand why we couldn't possibly send manipulated data to the FDA. It wasn't a conversation I relished having.

The next step to figuring out who had falsified the gels would be to figure out who had run them in the first place. The place to do that would be the physical lab notebook.

While the digital lab notebook was the official record of what happened in the lab, we still had a physical one where originals were kept after being scanned and uploaded to the Cloud. Ours was permanently bound and we were directed to write in it in pen, no pencil. If there was any question about when an experiment was run, how it was run, who ran it, or any other details, it would be answered in the lab notebook. It never left the lab.

I strolled over as nonchalantly as I could and retrieved the notebook from the shelf where it was kept.

"What are you up to, Miss Amanda?" Sara asked.

Apparently my nonchalant was pretty chalant. Figured. "Double-checking some gels."

"The gels are bothering you, too? Not just the numbers?" Anna asked, stopping what she was doing to stand up and stretch.

"Less so. I figured out my problem, I think." I opened the notebook and started paging through it to avoid looking either of them in the eye.

Dylan had on occasion told me that I was living a lie. By going as far out of the way as I did to keep anyone from associating me with Mom, I'd created a fake Amanda out there in the world. While he didn't advertise what our mother had done, he didn't go as far as I did to hide it. He had friends he hung out with. He went to parties. He was...normal, for lack of a better word.

I didn't think of it as lying, though. In fact, it was what kept me from having to lie. If no one knew much about me, they couldn't ask the kind of pointed questions that would lead back to Mom and Jackson and COGG and I wouldn't have to figure how to deflect those questions. I was actually a pretty crummy liar. Hence using the notebook as a distraction.

"I'm glad you figured it out," Anna said, returning to the microscope she'd been leaning over. "Sounds like Will be pleased as well."

I went through the notebook once quickly and didn't see any mention of the particular gels I was looking for. I went through again more slowly. Again, nothing.

I went back to the report to try to get a sense of the date they would have been run. It would have been sometime in November. I went back again to the notebook, going over it even more slowly. That's when I noticed it. There was a gap in the dates. There was a lab notebook entry on November 10 and then another on November 14. There should have been at least one or maybe two entries between those two dates.

I spread the notebook open and that's when I saw it. Pages had been cut out of the notebook. Whoever had done it had done a masterful job. If I hadn't been looking for precisely those dates, I would never have noticed the missing pages.

There was no way this was a simple mistake. This was deliberate, careful, painstaking. I peered out in the lab. Anna was still bent over her microscope. Sara was at her computer, and Jesse was at his. Melinda appeared to be on break. One of them did this. One of my coworkers committed one of the most egregious and fraudulent actions a scientist can commit.

But which one?

And why?

CHAPTER
15

WHEN I GOT HOME, I flicked on the news. I wanted to see the coverage of Patrick's release, if only to see how the media was couching it. Was he a hero returning to his flock? A despicable man who'd gotten away with something? A fallen man who had paid his dues?

I didn't have to wait long until the blonde woman on the television set said, "Earlier today, controversial religious leader Patrick Collier was released after spending ten years in prison for mishandling of funds for the church he founded. We take you to his press conference."

Seriously? A press conference? Someone was doing a much better job with COGG's public relations than they had back in the day.

The scene switched to an anonymous -looking room. Patrick sat behind a long table with a small forest of microphones in front of him. Andre Schmidt sat to his right. A woman I didn't recognize sat to his left. Patrick began to speak and I leaned toward him. Even through a television screen, I could still feel his pull. With conscious effort, I sat back in my chair.

"I am so grateful to be back in the arms of my brothers and sisters today." He paused to turn and smile at the people next to him. "It has been a long hard journey, but today I breathe free again and I can do no more than give thanks for that."

"Reverend Collier," one of the reporters shouted from off screen. It was a man.

Patrick nodded. "Yes?"

"Do you still claim you're innocent of the charges that you were convicted of?" the reporter asked.

Patrick dropped his head then looked up again. "I do. I always have. Nothing has changed."

Another voice called out, this time a woman. "Where's the money, Patrick?"

Patrick's eyes narrowed. "I don't know. I've never known." He looked directly into the television camera. I shrank back. It felt like he could see me here in my apartment. "Someone does know, however. Someone out there knows exactly where the money went. The Lord will balance the scales of justice. It may not happen right away, but it will happen."

"Are you looking for revenge, then?" someone else asked.

Patrick shook his head. "You misunderstand me. While I am the Lord's instrument, revenge is not the charge he has given me. I've spent quite a bit of the last ten years praying. Praying and reading the Bible. My duty is clear. I am here to make sure COGG continues to spread the word of brotherhood and sisterhood and how we are all part of God's grand machine." He pushed back from the table and said, "That's all for now."

The camera followed him as he stood and turned to walk out of the room. Now I could see the faces of the people who stood behind him, COGG members all, judging by the necklaces that sparkled at each person's throat.

At first I couldn't believe what I was seeing. I scrambled for the remote, hit a few buttons, and rewound the television to replay it again and again. Then I picked up the phone and called Sam. As soon as he answered, I said, "I found Lois Brower."

I stared at her face on the television. She was beaming. It was like there was a glow coming from within her. At her shoulder was Simon Palmer, the janitor who had disappeared from Bellefountaine right after I'd been poisoned. I had it. Proof that there was a connection between what happened to my mother and what happened to me and COGG. Seeing it in pixelated flesh left me gobsmacked.

The arrogance of the leadership at COGG thinking they could get away with this stunned me. Yes.

Patrick had always preached that we were all cogs in God's grand machine and as such we were replaceable, interchangeable, but he'd also preached that each part of the machine was necessary. He'd said we might not be able to see exactly what purpose we served, but that God knew and like a huge machine that can be brought down by the malfunctioning of one small component, it was imperative that we all play our part. Had they forgotten that part of Patrick's teachings while he was away? Had he forgotten how important he made each one of us feel? Had they only remembered that each one of us could swapped out for another and were therefore expendable?

"Where did you find her?" Sam asked.

"I'd rather show you," I answered.

Sam said, "I'll be right over."

I let Sam in my apartment and rather than say hello, I said, "Do you want a drink?" I needed one and didn't want to drink alone on a weeknight.

"Uh, sure."

"Your choices are limited. I have wine and wine."

"Wine's fine."

"Good choice." I walked down the hall to the kitchen and pulled a bottle of red out of the cabinet.

"So tell me about Lois," he said as he accepted a glass from me.

"I'll show you instead." I'd found the press conference on the Internet. A website called Chicago Cult Watch had the whole thing ready and available for viewing. Very handy. I tried to ignore the sidebar that they'd dedicated to my mother on the COGG page. Less handy. We sat down on the couch and I hit the play button, then froze it when Patrick stood up and walked past Lois.

Sam made a sound somewhere between a gasp and a grunt. He set his wineglass down slowly and deliberately, then leaned forward to rewind the video and play it back again. He leaned back on my couch, head resting on the back, and pinched the bridge of his nose. "That is not good."

"No. It isn't. Want to know what else isn't good?"

He raised his head and opened his eyes. "Might as well."

"That guy next to Lois? He worked at Bellefountaine until the day after I was poisoned. He was one of the last people to go in and out of the kitchen area before I went in to get my cup of coffee." I watched his face, not sure how he was going to react.

"We have to call Detective Pagoa." There was no hesitation.

"And tell him what?" I wasn't surprised at Sam's reaction. It really was a perfectly normal response. At least, it was a normal response for anyone who had never been let down by the system.

The system hadn't exactly been helpful when my mother had stopped functioning. It hadn't helped the kids I used to help recruit out to the COGG compound. No one was even looking for most of them. They were runaways, kids who'd already been in trouble from families who didn't know how or didn't want to take care of them. When people said that someone slipped through the cracks of a system, it made it sound like the cracks were small, little spaces between good solid slabs. They weren't. The cracks were huge. The poorer your family was, the bigger the crack. The crazier your family was, the bigger the crack. If you were unlucky enough to be from a poor crazy family, the whole system was nothing but a giant crack.

"We tell him that there is now a demonstrable link between what happened to your mother and what happened to you and Children of the Greater God," Sam said. He paused for a moment, then he said, "And we tell him why it is the cult would still be interested in hurting you."

I picked my glass back up and took a long sip, not looking at him. "Why would that be?"

"I don't know. I'm hoping that you trust me enough to tell me. Before you do, though. I have something more to tell you." He looked down at his hands.

"Oh?" I asked, relieved to have a slight reprieve.

"Your mother's autopsy report came." He still didn't look up at me.

My head shot up. "I thought we knew the results. They said it was a suicide."

Now he did look up and I got the full force of those too-blue eyes. "I don't see how it could be. I can see why the original finding came in that way. Whoever did this knew how to make it look convincing." He turned his wineglass in circles.

I moved my glass out of the way entirely and leaned forward on my elbows. "So why don't you think it's a suicide?"

"The tox screen. Your mother had a large amount of Lorazepam in her system."

"Lorazepam? The sedative?" I asked.

"Yep. That's the one. It's pretty commonly used in residential situations, especially with patients who are easily agitated. The thing is, your mother wasn't usually one of those patients." He rubbed his face. "I mean, it was on her med list. It was there if it was needed. She'd been given it occasionally before, but never enough of it to show up in her bloodstream like that."

My mind raced through the possibilities. "So how did she get it?"

"That's the question, isn't it? I can't say for certain, but I have some suspicions. Remember I told you that the night before your mother's death, another patient became very agitated?" he asked.

I nodded. "You said the staff was distracted and the floor was all in a jumble."

"Exactly. Well, that patient, the one who became so agitated, he gets regular doses of Lorazepam. He's a big man. He requires a big dose." Sam went back to turning his wineglass in circles.

"Are you saying someone somehow gave my mother the Lorazepam meant for that patient?" That would have been a whopping mistake.

He nodded. "It's my guess."

"Is there any way that could have been an accident? Some kind of mistake?" Or had someone purposefully drugged my mother into submission?

"Of course. No matter how many double-checks and safeguards we put into place, mistakes can be made. I don't see how, but it's always possible. Here's the thing, though. Even if it was a mistake, it doesn't matter. With that much Lorazepam in her system, your mother would have barely been able to sit up much less manage to harm herself the way she did. The cuts she made...they were nearly surgical in their precision."

I winced at the idea of my mother's wounds. My fingers went to the scars on the inside of my own arm. I knew precisely how hard it was to make those kinds of cuts.

"Someone killed your mother, Amanda, and I think that whoever did it is somehow connected to Children of the Greater God." He reached out and took my hands in his. "Please tell me what it is you know that made you and your mother into targets for them. I know there's more than you said. Please trust me."

I looked into his eyes. I'd seen that look before, that pleading, that desperation. The eyes had been brown, not blue, with lashes so ridiculously thick it looked he was wearing eyeliner and mascara. Marcus.

Tears welled in my eyes. I had never told anyone, never breathed a word. Through all the questioning by the police, by therapists, by my father, I'd never said anything.

"Amanda," Sam said. "Here's the thing about secrets. They only have power over us while they're secret. Once they're out in the open, they lose their power over us."

I wasn't so sure about that. Back when it had happened, I'd been certain that if anyone knew, I'd be arrested and locked up like my mom. Then later, as I'd come to understand that I wasn't responsible for what had happened, I worried that I would be arrested for my role in covering it all up. An accessory after the fact. Even more than that, though, was my very deep shame.

My secret was, in the end, the key to everything. It explained what happened to me, what happened to my mother, and what happened to Jackson. It was the missing piece of the puzzle that the police and my mother's doctors and my own therapists had tried to get to for years and year. It was the one thing I wouldn't give any of them. Ever.

No one ever understood what pushed my mother over the edge. No one could figure out what had made her take the dark turn that led her to suffocate my little brother in his bed and to wake me to help her do the same to Dylan. After all, COGG had seemed to make my mother better. After getting involved with Children of the Greater God, my mother had been doing a better job of meeting her responsibilities, of taking care of her children and her house, of taking care of herself. It had been part of why I'd been so supportive of her involvement with COGG and why I went with her willingly when Dylan refused and Jackson whined.

Of course I'd gotten something out of it, too. I'd gotten the warmth of Patrick's attention and the approval of other COGG members. I'd gotten friends for the first time in a very long time. There was an element of enlightened self-interest in the way I encouraged Mom to take part in everything COGG had to offer. Bible study classes. Working on the land. Community dinners.

So what had happened to make my mother feel that it was better for her children to die than it was to force them to live as sinners in this world?

"Part of what I did for COGG when I was a teenager was outreach," I said slowly. "A group of us kids would go to places like the bus station downtown and talk to the kids we saw there about COGG."

Sam nodded. "You recruited. It's pretty standard cult behavior."

"Patrick trained us what to look for, who to target." I swallowed. "We were to look for kids who looked hungry, kids who looked scared, kids with bruises."

"Runaways," Sam said.

"I felt like I was doing those kids a favor." I covered my face with my hands and took a deep breath. "COGG had places for them to sleep, food for them to eat."

"And what was expected in return?" Sam asked.

I look over at him, sharply. "Not what you're thinking. Not sex. Never sex." My cheeks got hot anyway. It hadn't been much of a secret that I'd had a major crush on Patrick. I'd unraveled most of the knot that had tied me to him over the years. A strong older man when I had an absentee father. A steady, calm presence to counteract my mother's wild cycling between mania and depression. Attention when I'd gotten so very little of that from either of my parents. I'd been sixteen and my hormones had been raging. He could have had me if he'd wanted me, but the same was true of at least half the women and girls that came to the compound or lived there. He could have made it his harem. Enough of the men were in thrall to him that I doubt they would have raised a peep at the seduction of their wives and daughters and sisters and mothers.

But that wasn't what Patrick was after. He was after something more, something purer, something harder to give. He was after commitment to COGG and to God. He was after loyalty and admiration. If anything, it had made me love him more.

"Then what?" Sam prompted.

"Our obedience, mostly. For the kids from the bus station, it was mainly work." I scooted back into the corner of the couch and crossed my legs tailor-style. "Collier was into organic farming. It was a lot of how COGG supported itself. Raising vegetables to be sold at the farmers' markets and to restaurants that catered to people who wanted locallysourced organic food. It wasn't bad work, but it was work, you know?"

Sam nodded.

I swallowed. "There was one boy, a boy I recruited. His name was Marcus." I couldn't believe I'd said his name out loud. It had been more than ten years since I'd let those two syllables pass my lips. "He was cute. I liked him and he liked me."

"And Collier disapproved?" Sam's eyebrows went up.

"Not exactly. I mean, there were some pretty strict rules about how boys and girls were supposed to behave with each other, but he didn't get in the way of all the little romances. No, the problem he had was with Marcus." I wanted to chant his name. Now that I'd finally said it, I wanted to say it again and again and again.

"Why?"

I sighed. "He was lazy. I mean, I don't suppose he was much more lazy than a lot of other teenage boys, but lazy enough for people to notice." And he had a mouth on him and he was confident—at least, more confident than most of the broken, beaten boys who ended up living at COGG.

"And what happened when it was noticed?" Sam asked.

"Patrick thought the best cure for laziness was more work. So Marcus got extra chores. Instead of being able to relax in the evening after a day in the fields, he'd have to wash dishes after dinner or mop the floors or chop wood." It had almost been a game, finding more chores for Marcus to do while the other kids read or played cards.

"Harsh."

I shrugged. "Actually, that wasn't the harsh part. There was an element of social conditioning."

"How so?" Sam asked.

"Nobody wanted to be associated with the kid who wasn't being a good cog in God's machinery. In part because no one wanted to be seen as guilty by association, but also because after a few weeks at COGG, you really wanted to be part of it. You really wanted to feel that you were part of something so much bigger than you, so much bigger than your family or your school or even your country. Somehow Patrick made us all want that." I remembered the first time I'd felt it. It hadn't been during a church service. I'd seen other people, even some kids, literally fall to their knees while Patrick preached. Celeste was standing right next to me when she did it, garbled words coming out of her mouth, arms waving in the air, tears streaming down her face. It frightened me. When I asked her about it later, she told me none of it had been of her own volition. She said she'd felt the spirit move through her and take over her being. She spoke about feeling like she was bathed in a warm soft light and was surprised I hadn't been able to see it glowing from within her. I'd been jealous. The joy on her face as she'd sunk to her knees had been unmistakable. I wanted some of it, but it didn't come.

At least, not right away. No, when it had hit me, we'd been in the dining hall at one of the big communal dinners. Mom and I would come to them at least twice a week, more if Dylan was going to a friend's house and we could sneak away. There'd been this huge hustle and bustle of people getting food to the tables. Everyone was laughing and smiling, working together. It was all so different than the dinners we had at home, which were silent and sullen and full of tension. Then Patrick stood and everyone found their places and he said a prayer over the food thanking God not just for the food, but for bringing us all together. I looked around and saw so many shining eyes, clasping hands, and the warmth flowed over me and through me and if I hadn't been sitting down, I too would have fallen to my knees as Celeste had done.

"Patrick was—is—very charismatic," Sam observed.

I snorted. "That's an understatement."

Sam leaned back in his chair. "So people shunned this Marcus kid? Did you shun him?"

I shook my head. "No. He was my recruit. I felt responsible for him. I wanted him to see how great COGG was. I really did. It wasn't bullshit. I really believed that we were all going to go some place special, that we were something special because we were part of COGG. I wanted that for him, too. I wanted him to feel it."

"But he didn't." It wasn't a question.

"No. He didn't. He kept asking questions, ones I couldn't answer, about how the money worked and who had made Patrick the boss of all of us. Things I'd never questioned." I picked at the seam of my jeans. "And he kept shirking. He kept saying his stomach hurt."

"And he kept getting punished?"

I nodded again.

"And ostracized?"

"And bullied. The other kids who lived at the compound would pick on him. Nothing horrible, but a lot of pushing and tripping, so even when he did try to do the work, it would be difficult." He'd told me about it, told me how Brandon had waited until he was walking down a row with a full bushel of strawberries and had tripped him, sending everything flying into the dirt. How Tony had ripped apart his bunk after he'd gone to take a shower so he'd get in trouble for not keeping his space tidy and clean the way God and Patrick wanted it. He asked me for help, for protection.

Sometimes I told myself that I hadn't had any protection to give. I was as vulnerable as he was, but I knew it wasn't true. Besides, it really was the least of it.

"Why didn't he leave? He could have gotten away, couldn't he?" Sam asked.

"Yes and no." It was another one of the stories I told myself. No one had locked Marcus in or chained him to his bed. He could have walked down the long driveway to the road and hitched a ride into Chicago to continue on as he had been before our paths crossed in the bus station that night. It wouldn't necessarily have been easy. People might have tried to talk him out of it. It was a long walk and he wasn't feeling well. It was still do-able.

Yet, part of the reason he was at COGG in first place was that he really had no other place to go. No one was looking for him, not really. No one cared. He was one of those kids who seemed to slip everyone's mind. A runaway dropout with an absentee father and a strung -out mom. It wasn't even that unique of a story. Celeste's was pretty similar. So was Brandon's. Even mine wasn't all that different except my mom wasn't doing drugs. Her brain was the drug. I shrugged. "I'm not sure he knew how to leave."

"Okay. So he couldn't leave. What happened next?"

"He got sicker. He started throwing up. His skin looked clammy." My voice had begun to sound robotic.

"So he was visibly sick now, clearly not faking," Sam said.

"Yeah, but everyone was so convinced he had been faking they still didn't believe him." I chewed my lip. "They kept giving him more and more work."

"What did you do?"

I shut my eyes and felt the tears spill over. I swiped them away. "I took over some of his chores, so he might be able to rest a little, but we got caught. Or I guess I got caught."

"Were you punished as well?" Sam's forehead creased.

I shook my head. "Sent home. That's all." Here was the part that was truly hard to say. "He begged me to take him with me." Literally begged me. On his knees. Doubled over with pain. And I had walked away. "He died that night."

Sam winced. "Do they know why?"

"Best guess was a burst appendix. He'd been going slowly septic. They had made him chop wood and haul water while his own body was poisoning itself." All I could think about was how much pain he'd been in, how terrifying it must have been to have your body shutting

197

down and have no one be willing to help you. "The people who supervised the teenagers found him dead in his bed the next morning. They were able to pull the body out before any of the other kids knew. They told them they'd taken him to the hospital."

"So how do you know what really happened?"

"I kept asking questions. I wanted to know which hospital so I could visit him. I wanted to know when they'd taken him, who had taken him, how. Finally Patrick dragged me back to where they were hiding him to shut me up. He was afraid if I kept asking questions, the other kids would, too."

"Oh, Amanda. I'm so sorry."

"I'm not done." I had to get the last little bit out. I felt like I was removing an infected splinter from my side. It all had to go. If even a tiny bit stayed inside, it would continue to poison me for the rest of my life. "I helped bury him. There was a spot toward the back of the property, an area that we weren't farming yet. No one went back there. There was no reason to. We hauled his body back there and dug a grave."

People talk about digging graves as if it's no big deal. It's backbreaking. It takes hours. "A while ago you asked me what I knew that the cult wanted me to keep quiet about."

"A dead teenager would be a big secret to keep," Sam said.

"That's not all, though. There were other mounds back there. I think that means there were other bodies. And I know where they're all buried."

CHAPTER

16

WE SAT IN SILENCE FOR a moment or two as Sam let my words sink in. "Who do you think the others were?"

"I'm not sure." It wasn't as if I hadn't thought about it over the years. Who else had Patrick needed to bury under the elm trees? Kids had disappeared before, but I always thought they'd left. A few adults had gone as well, vanishing into the night.

"Amanda, why didn't you tell anyone about this?" Sam sounded anguished.

I hid my face in my hands. "Patrick told me that the police would think I was as guilty as they were, that Marcus's death was as much my fault as everyone else's at the compound. I...I thought I would be arrested for murder."

"Oh, Amanda..." He sounded so very tired.

"I was only sixteen. I didn't know. These were people I trusted." I swallowed. "Then Patrick took me aside and explained how much it would hurt COGG if I told. The whole operation could be shut down. Everything good he'd tried to do would be ruined."

"And you didn't want to betray him."

I shook my head, sending the tears finally spilling down my cheeks. "No. Never. I...I loved him."

Sam shot me a look. "Amanda, did you... Did he—"

"No. Not that I wouldn't have if he'd tried. I had about as big a crush as a girl can have on a grown man." Saying it like that trivialized it, but I didn't have words big enough. I had burned for Patrick. My skin had tingled for hours anywhere he touched it. When he was in the room, it was hard for me to breathe, to move, to talk, to walk. My feelings for him were a potent stew of love and worship.

"Even after what happened with Marcus?" He looked like he was trying really hard to understand, but simply couldn't. I didn't blame him. I didn't totally understand and it was myself I was trying to explain.

"For a little while. Until..." Could I? Could I finally let all of it out into the open? Suddenly I wanted to. I wanted to have it out in the open, on the table, exposed to the light. Maybe if I did I would finally stop feeling like I had to always cling to the darkness.

"Until what?" Sam prompted.

"I had a hard time after Marcus died. I'd liked him. I hadn't been as crazy in love with him as I'd been with Patrick, but he was a boy I liked. He was dead and I felt—I'd been told—it was my fault. I had bad dreams. I had trouble eating, sleeping. I found myself bursting into tears at odd moments."

"You were grieving."

"Yet I couldn't. I'd been told not to. If anyone found out Marcus was dead, we'd all be in trouble. All of COGG was counting on my silence and COGG was the very thing that kept my family from disintegrating as well. Everything I had that was good and true counted on COGG being okay and me keeping that secret." I tried to explain the convoluted logic that had twisted me up so.

"That's an awful lot to ask of a sixteen-year-old," Sam said.

"Like I said, I was having a hard time. I went to talk to Patrick about it, to get his advice. I wanted him to know that I was doing this really hard thing for him. I wanted him to appreciate me." I'd had a whole picture in my head of how it would go down. I'd tell him how difficult it had been. He would put his arms around me. Once my body was against his, he would realize I wasn't a little girl anymore. He'd know I was a woman. He'd lift my chin. Our lips would meet. The clouds would open up and angels would sing.

"But he didn't?"

"I didn't get a chance to tell him." His office door had been locked, which was unusual. It was hardly ever even closed. I thought I heard movement inside, but when I knocked no one answered. I waited around for a minute or two then decided to look for him on the grounds. I left the building that held his office and took a short cut to get back to the community room, a shortcut that took me under the windows to his office. I looked in. It never occurred to me not to. It never crossed my mind that I'd see something I shouldn't see, that I wouldn't be able to unsee. "I wasn't supposed to see. He was…with my mother."

Sam's eyebrows shot up. "With her? You mean, like sexually with her?"

"Yep." It had taken me a moment to figure out what they were doing. I was that naïve, that innocent. They were on the couch, my mother in his lap, his hands on her hips, urging her up and down. I couldn't hear them, but I could see how my mother's head was thrown back. I could see Patrick's face contorted in an expression that could have been pleasure and could have been pain.

I ran.

I did what Marcus didn't do. I ran down the driveway and stuck out my thumb and caught a ride back into Chicago. I was drunk by the time Mom got home.

"So you saw your mother with the man that you both worshipped as a father figure and wanted for yourself shortly after helping to hide the death of a friend," Sam said, shaking his head. "It's amazing you even walk upright."

I snorted. "I'm not sure I did for a while. I sort of went off the rails after that."

"What does that mean?" He asked.

"I stopped going to school. I started drinking. I, uh, started acting out sexually." My whole face grew hot. He might as well know, though. There was worse to come anyway.

"You became promiscuous." The way he said it somehow took the sting from it, removed the judgment.

"I went from being a virgin to getting caught having a three-way in the boys' cabin at the compound." I blurted it out.

"Wow."

"That's one way to describe it." It hadn't exactly been wow for me. It had been more like oblivion.

My head had swum and my skin had tingled. Everywhere I turned there had been more skin. Skin and hands and mouths. I'd had no idea whether I was up or down, in or out. My whole world had been reduced to sensation, touch, taste. The only sounds were moans and groans. All the other stuff was gone. School. My mother. My brothers. My dad. Marcus. Gone.

I didn't know when the second boy had come in. I didn't know his name. I wasn't sure I knew my own name.

I didn't care.

And then the screeching started.

My name. Apparently I did know it. "Amanda Framingham, what are you doing?"

Then there were other hands. Not hands that caressed or explored. Hands that yanked and pulled. "Get off her! Get off her!" the voice screamed.

I was being pulled from the bunk. I tried to grab onto its rails, but my hands weren't strong enough. I wasn't fast enough. The boys scattered, clothes clutched to their groins. They ran from the cabin.

It was just me and my mother, face -to -face. I braced myself for the inevitable slap across the cheek or twist of my arm. It didn't come. Instead my mother looked at me and said, "You dirty little whore. We'll see what Reverend Collier has to say about this."

"I'm not talking to him." I started pulling my clothes back on as Mom threw them at me.

"Yes. You are." She grabbed my arm and twisted it up behind me—I'd known something like that would come eventually— and frog marched me from the cabin.

"Stop it!" I screamed. "You're hurting me."

Mom spoke directly in my ear. "What are you going to do? Call your father again?"

My face burned. I couldn't believe he'd told her. If there had been one thing I'd thought I could count on, it was my parents not being a united front. The one time I really needed them not to talk, they were suddenly communicating. "What are you going to do? Fuck Reverend Collier again?"

She dropped my arm. "What did you say?"

"You heard what I said. I saw you, you know. I saw what you two do with each other." I spit the words at her.

Her face turned white. "When?"

"Last month. The day I left."

She buried her face in her hands. "You were never supposed to see. You were never supposed to know."

"Well, I did see. I do know. So you can stop pretending you're so virtuous and good. I might be a dirty little whore, but I learned it from somewhere." Now I did actually spit.

She grabbed my arm again, but changed direction.

"Where are we going?" I struggled against her pincer grip.

"Home," she said. "We're going home."

And we had. We'd gone home and everything had come apart in ways that I'd never dreamed possible.

Sam said, "So you tried to go live with your Dad and when that didn't work, you started acting out."

"And somehow something inside Mom broke. That's when…It's when…" I couldn't say it out loud.

"It's when she killed your brother." Again, he didn't ask it. He stated it.

"She and I were both damaged, impure. Dylan and Jackson weren't. They still had an opportunity to be part of Greater God's children. That's why she killed Jackson. It's why she wanted to kill Dylan. It's why she didn't want to kill me. I was too damaged for even God to take me back."

"Amanda." It's all he said, just my name.

The kindness in his voice nearly undid me. I wouldn't let it, though. "Because there was something so deeply wrong inside of me that even my mother knew it."

"But you didn't do it. You didn't help her kill your brother. You saved him. You're the hero of the story." He reached for my hands.

"Don't you see? The story wouldn't have needed a hero if it wasn't for me. I broke her. Not Dad. Not Patrick. Not Marcus. Me. I'm the reason my brother is dead. I'm probably the reason my mother is dead. I'm definitely the reason Marcus is dead. In my own way, I killed them all."

After long minutes of silence, Sam insisted I talk to Detective Pagoa again. He insisted that this time I tell Pagoa everything, not some redacted version of events.

I insisted that I still had to go to work the next day. I wanted to get a look in my coworkers' personal lab notebooks. Someone knew something about those missing pages and those manipulated photos. Someone had been deliberately hiding something.

"I'll pick you up at lunch time," he said.

"Don't you have to work?" I asked. Elgin was a long trek from Bellefountaine, then add in the time it would take to go to the police station and back.

"This is my work, Amanda. Your mother was my patient. It was my duty to protect her," he said.

"This White Knight thing you've got going is going to get you in trouble." I wished I could keep my mouth shut. I wanted him to come with me. I didn't want to say it out loud, but I was scared, nearly as frightened of facing Pagoa again as I was of whatever it was COGG was up to.

He shrugged. "Let it come then. I'm ready for it."

Tuesday, February 28

On my way to work the next morning, I stayed far back from the train tracks and intersections. The gray skies had returned and the wind whipped up and down the concrete canyons of the Loop. My eyes stung with the combination of cold and grit picked up from the streets as the wind buffeted me around.

One good thing about the damp cold was that my homeless stalker didn't seem to be anywhere around. It was too cold even for him to be hanging around Printer's Row. I'd have to remember the creepy feeling I got when he saluted me and shooed me to my door the next time I was tempted to do more than shove a dollar in someone's hand. Apparently no good deed goes unpunished. If anyone should know that, it should be me. How many times would I have to learn the same lesson?

It took me a little longer to get to work than usual. I hadn't realized how important an assertive attitude was to being a pedestrian in Chicago. If you didn't push to the intersection, you were going to have to wait through a few signal changes before you got to cross. If you didn't shove into the train, you weren't going to get on it. By the time I walked into the lab, everyone was there and already working.

"You okay?" Jesse asked as I walked in.

"Sure. Why?"

He shrugged. "You're not usually late and well, with everything that seems to be happening in your life right now…"

I winced. He was so sweet. Every time I shut him down he responded with care and concern. "Sorry. It didn't occur to me that anyone would worry. I'm fine. Just taking my time getting to work today."

He nodded and returned to his bench. I dumped my stuff off and hesitated. Normally I'd go get a cup of coffee. I decided to wait until lunch and got to work. There wouldn't be any way for me to check anyone else's notebooks with everyone in the lab. Besides, there were plenty of other tables and gels to check in the FDA report. If one set was suspect, well, who knew how many other pieces of data had been faked? I needed to go through the whole report again with a fine-tooth comb.

At eleventhirty, my cell phone pinged. Sam was waiting in his car downstairs. I put on my coat.

"Where are you going?" Sara asked.

I hesitated. When had everyone gotten so interested in my comings and goings? "Out."

"Want company?" she asked, a smile on her face.

"Uh, I already have some company. Thanks." I felt the burn on my cheeks.

"Oh!" she said, her own cheeks turning a little pink. "A lunch date. You're going out. Not just out."

I decided not to explain that going to the police station to confess that I knew the location of dead bodies didn't really feel like first -date material. "Yep. I'm going out."

Sara looked behind me. I glanced to where she was glancing and saw Jesse, who looked crestfallen. I felt like a jerk. I'd have to fix it later, though.

I waved good-bye and walked out of the lab, out of the building, and into Sam's car.

CHAPTER
17

DETECTIVE PAGOA SAT VERY STILL behind his desk. "Start at the beginning again, please."

Sam had made an appointment and Pagoa had been waiting for us when we walked in. He had accompanied us through the metal detectors and other hoops we had to jump through to get inside and then brought us to an interview room. I looked around for the big plate glass window that seemed to be a fixture in every cop show I had ever watched, but I didn't find one. There was, however, a camera up in the corner.

I wasn't sure where the beginning was. Was Marcus the beginning? Or was the beginning what appeared to be my mother's murder? I'd blurted out so much information to him the second we sat down, I wasn't even sure I'd told him everything I'd left out before or all of the new information Sam and I had discovered since the last time I spoke to him.

"Which beginning?" I asked. "Start with the boy. Marcus. Was that the name?" He glanced at his notebook.

"Marcus. Okay." I took a deep breath. "He was one of the kids who came to work at the COGG compound."

"When did he come?"

"It must have been September. It was still warm. The harvest wasn't finished. It was busy."

"What was his last name?"

I shook my head. "If I ever knew, I don't remember it. He was always just Marcus." A lot of the kids who came to COGG safeguarded their personal information, at least at first. Whether they were runaways or had other reasons, they often didn't want anyone knowing exactly who they were or where they were from. "He might not have even really been Marcus. That was the name he gave, though."

"Where was he from?" Pagoa made a note. I couldn't imagine what it would have been.

"From a city or a town, for sure." I wasn't sure I'd ever seen anyone so surprised at how much work it was to raise a crop. "I don't what city or town, though."

"Accent?" Pago asked.

I shook my head. "No. At least, not that I ever noticed."

"So probably not the south or back east." Pagoa made a note. "Race?"

"Not sure." It was another question that we didn't ask. COGG didn't care whether you were white or black or brown or some combination of all those.

"Skin tone?"

"Darker than me, not as dark as you." I blushed.

Pagoa stared at me for a second and then laughed. "That leaves a lot of room on the spectrum. Anything else? Scars? Tattoos?"

I shook my head. "Not that I ever saw."

"Now tell me about where he's buried." He leaned forward onto his desk.

My throat constricted. For a second, I wasn't sure I would be able to get words out. "It was at the edge of the compound, as far from the road as you could get." I paused. "Not exactly at the property line. I don't think they wanted someone from an adjacent piece of land noticing it."

Pagoa nodded. "Any distinguishing features?"

"Trees. Elm trees." I shut my eyes. "The ground sloped downward there. You could walk right past them if you didn't know they were there."

"And there was more than one."

I nodded. "Four. Four mounds."

"Do you remember anyone else ever going missing from the compound? Any of the kids?" He asked.

"Sure. COGG wasn't for everyone. Some kids would come for a few days, get a few hot meals, and then disappear." It had never seemed sinister before.

Pagoa tilted his head to one side. "Do you think those kids are the ones under those other mounds?"

"I don't know. I really don't." It was the truth. The other part of the truth was that I hadn't wanted to know. I'd wanted to forget that those mounds ever existed.

"Who else could they be?" he pressed.

I shook my head. I had no more words. Sam reached over and took my hand.

"Did anyone give any indication of who they might be?" Pagoa made a note in his notebook.

"I asked," I finally blurted. "I asked Patrick that night."

Pagoa sat up a little straighter. "And what did he say?"

I remembered Patrick's face, how sad it had seemed. He'd looked older than I'd ever seen him look. The vital energy that coursed through him had somehow faded, leaving him deflated. "He said sometimes God's will was harsh."

"Do you think you could lead us to those mounds, Amanda?" Pagoa asked.

I nodded. "I think so."

He stood. "I'm going to see about getting a search warrant and putting out an APB on Lois Brower and Simon Palmer."

The COGG compound was located out on Interstate 290 toward Elmhurst. Patrick had inherited the roughly twenty-five acres from his grandfather when he passed away. He could have made a fortune. Developers drooled over the rolling hills and copses of trees. It would have been an amazing high-end housing development, simply amazing.

It had been one of the things that had made me admire Patrick back when I still thought he could walk on water with Jesus. He could have made millions, literally millions. He would never have had to work a day in his life. Instead he'd started his ministry. He'd built his church. He'd started working the land.

When he first started preaching, he had a congregation of ten. Within two years, his worshippers had increased tenfold. It had grown from there. With each year, he had added new buildings, ploughed new fields, expanded his services. By the time my mother and I joined COGG, it was a busy farm plus a church plus dorms plus a community hall plus administrative offices. It had been huge.

By the time Pagoa and Sam and I started down the interstate toward the compound, it was already getting dark. I'd called into Bellefountaine and explained I needed the afternoon for personal business. I felt bad about not being in the lab when there was so much work to be done, but I knew this had to take precedence, if only for today. I'd work late tomorrow. I'd probably have more luck figuring out who was responsible for the faked gels when no one else was there anyway.

Somehow the press had figured out that something was happening. The caravan of police cars and vans was followed by a parade of media vans, satellite antennas casting distorted shadows along the medians in the waning light. Sam and I rode with Pagoa in an unmarked car. I'd told Sam he didn't have to come with us and he had given me a look and changed the topic.

"How did they know something was up?" Sam asked, gesturing at the news vans.

Pagoa shrugged. "Sometimes I think they've all got someone on the payroll in the judges' offices. They always seem to know. This was particularly fast, though. It felt like they were mobilizing even before I walked the search warrant through Judge Steiner's office."

I shivered, pulling my coat tighter around me.

"Cold?" Pagoa asked. "I could turn the heat up."

I shook my head. The chill in the car kept my head clear. I needed to stay focused and not let the swamp of memories cover me completely and suck me under.

We arrived at the compound and Pagoa walked to the front door of the administrative offices, where a light was on, and I'm guessing served the warrant. Sam and I waited in the car. Then we drove onto the property and down as far as the roads would take us. Then we got out and walked.

That night was burned into my brain like a brand, but nothing stays the same for ten years, even the Illinois countryside. I turned a few times before I reached where I thought the mounds should be.

"Amanda?" Pagoa said.

I held up my hand. "Give me a minute." I remembered a tree. I probably couldn't have named it then, but I knew now that its distinctive jagged and pointed ends made it an elm. There was nothing like it anywhere near.

I walked several yards north, then east. It was near here. I knew it was near here. My skin prickled with the knowledge. Then I spotted it. Not a tree. A stump. I picked up my pace, nearly jogging toward it. The ground rose slightly as I made my way toward it, snow crunching beneath my feet in the cold, and then dropped away on the other side. It was only a hillock, but it had been enough to block what was on the other side from my view and from the view of anyone casually walking along the COGG property line.

Four mounds in a row, set out with a nearly mathematical precision. It had been ten years. They could still have been missed if you didn't know what you were looking for, if you hadn't been there the night a seventeen-year-old boy's body had been put in the cold dark earth without so much as a sheet around it.

I pointed. "There."

Lights ringed the area. It was entirely dark. The city created a glow in the sky in the distance like a fuzzy dome, but I could still see the stars, hard white pinpricks in the velvet night sky. It felt as if the temperature had dropped ten degrees with the sun, numbing my face and toes. A couple of the crime scene unit officers had tried shovels, but the ground was too hard, frozen solid. I'd thought they would give up, come back tomorrow, but that's when Pagoa called in the backhoes.

Now amid the hissing lights and diesel fumes, the top was taken off the first mound. I huddled close to Sam, for warmth and for comfort. "You did the right thing," he said to me, his voice soft.

"I know." I did know, too. I should have done it years before, as soon as it happened. I should have done it as soon as I knew the nature of my mother's relationship with Patrick Collier. I should have done it before my mother decided my brother would be better off with the angels than with her on this sin-ridden joke of a planet. The fact that I hadn't had been my secret shame for over a decade. Based on the number of news vans parked along the road verge just yards away, it would not be a secret much longer.

The backhoe broke through the frozen crust and the crime scene workers moved in with their shovels and picks again. I couldn't hear what they said to each other. The backhoe still idled nearby, belching its noxious fumes. The lights still hissed. My eyes watered in the cold.

Finally Pagoa came over to where Sam and I stood. "You two might as well go home. I'll have one of the uniforms take you back to town."

I couldn't stop myself from asking. I both wanted and didn't want to know. "Did you find him?"

Pagoa shook his head. "Not yet, but it could be hours. They have to take it slow. Everything in there could be evidence."

"What things are in there?" I didn't remember the hole being filled with anything but dirt.

"Now's not the time to discuss this, Amanda. Go home. Get some rest. I'd recommend taking your phone off the hook." He nodded toward the news vans. "Those vultures have ways of figuring out who people are and how to contact them. You, too, doc."

Sam nodded and led me away. The officer assigned to take us back to the city looked as exhausted as I felt. Luckily, he stayed awake longer than I did. The heat in the car and the swaying motion coupled with the relief of finally showing someone where Marcus was buried lulled me to sleep almost before we hit the highway. I didn't wake up until we were in front of my apartment building.

"Do you want me to come up with you?" Sam asked.

I shook my head. "It's late. I'll be fine. I just want to fall into my bed and sleep." The thought of being both warm and horizontal overwhelmed me and I was afraid I'd fall back asleep right there and then.

"I'll call you tomorrow then." He got back in the cop car and was gone.

I went upstairs, curled up in my bed, and cried myself to sleep.

Wednesday, March 1

The first phone call asking me to comment on the police excavation at the COGG compound came in at five thirty the next morning. Within an hour, my phone was blowing up. I turned the ringer off and let them all go to voicemail, watching the caller ID as they went. Detective Pagoa didn't call until seven thirty. He sounded exhausted. I wondered if he'd slept at all the night before.

"Can you come to the station, Amanda?" he asked.

"Sure. When?"

"The sooner the better. I want to discuss what was found at the COGG site you pointed us to."

"How many?" I asked. "How many bodies were there?"

He paused. "I think it would be best if we spoke in person."

I called Bellefountaine and left a message saying I would be late. I was going to have to let them know why I needed all this personal time sooner or later. I sincerely wanted it to be later.

I texted Sam and then dressed quickly and hailed a cab a couple of blocks from my apartment and rode to the police station. I faltered when I got out of the cab. Too much glass. Too much brick. I wasn't sure where to go. Then suddenly Sam was there. By my side. Taking my arm. Guiding me. I slumped against him in relief.

This time Pagoa sent a uniformed officer to walk us through security and back to the same interview room we'd sat in before.

"Let me tell you what we found." Pagoa sat down on the edge of the table. "Garbage."

"Excuse me?"

"Garbage. All four of those mounds had nothing but rotting garbage in them." He crossed his massive arms over his chest.

I couldn't be hearing right. It had to be some kind of joke, but Pagoa didn't seem the joking type. "But…"

He held up his hand to stop me. "The lab will continue going over what we found to make sure there are absolutely no human remains, but I thought I'd give you a chance to save us all a lot of time and you a lot of heartache, Ms. Sinclair."

I noted I was no longer Amanda. "It's where I saw Patrick bury Marcus. I swear it is." My voice broke. I had finally unburdened myself of this terrible knowledge and now he was telling me it was all for nothing?

"What about Lois Brower and Simon Palmer?" Sam asked. "There's no doubt that they're part of Patrick Collier's supporters and were at Elgin and Bellefountaine and left immediately after Amanda's mother died and after Amanda was poisoned."

Pagoa held up a shovel-like hand. "I know. We're still looking into that, but don't you think it's possible that Brower and Palmer realized that when their affiliation with Children of a Great God came to light they'd both be blamed and left ahead of that?"

I sat back in my chair, stunned. "Are you serious?"

Pagoa swiveled toward me. "I am. Very serious. You should be taking this very seriously as well, Ms. Sinclair. Do you have any idea of the cost of last night's search? Of how many other cases were set aside to focus on information you gave us? Information that proved to be unreliable?"

"Someone must have moved the bodies," I said. "It's been ten years. They had plenty of time. Maybe they were worried I'd tell eventually and moved the evidence?"

"And maybe some kids too lazy to take garbage to the dump buried it on the back of the property," Pagoa said.

"That's not what happened." This was part of something bigger. I could feel it.

"So you say. Right now, however, we only have your word for it. We can't find a record of a missing teenager matching your description of this Marcus from that time period. We can't find any evidence of a child ever dying at the COGG compound. The only things we have evidence of are your mother's crime and some of your subsequent behavior."

My cheeks flamed. I wanted to protest. I wanted to scream. Finally, after all these years, I'd told my terrible secret and no one believed me. I should have kept my mouth shut. I stood, my legs shaky beneath me, and walked toward the door.

"Not so fast, Ms. Sinclair," Pagoa said. "I warned you once about this. If you continue to make false accusations to stir up trouble, eventually the department will press charges. This is your second strike. You don't want to find out what strike three will get you. Are we clear?"

"Crystal," I said and continued out the door. I hadn't even realized that Sam had followed me until I was in the lobby.

"Amanda, wait," he said as I headed to the doors.

I turned, not sure what he could possibly say.

"Can we talk?" he asked.

The one thing I was pretty certain I couldn't do was talk. I was afraid that if I opened my mouth, nothing but a wail would come out. Some sort of primeval keening noise that would rip my throat in two as it clawed its way out of my lungs. "About what?"

There were a lot of things that weren't clear back then. My whole world had shattered in a matter of days. I'd felt fragmented, not sure of who I was. COGG had been at the center of my being and once it was gone, there was nothing in its place. I'd tried booze, pills, sex. They'd all left me feeling more empty.

After the worst happened, after my mother killed my brother, I'd stopped searching. I knew for sure then that there was no point. I hit the lowest point, the point that led me to take a razor blade to the tender flesh on the insides of my arms, and I had survived.

I seemed to always survive. Somehow, there seemed to be a message in that. Enough of one that I was willing to keep putting one foot in front of the other, taking one breath after another, living through one day after another. Then I found science. Numbers and data and statistics became my religion and my refuge.

Whatever was happening with COGG was out of my hands. I couldn't do any more than I'd already done. I'd given the police everything I knew and nothing was going to come of it. Nothing. No one was going to investigate my mother's death. No one was going to investigate who might have poisoned me. No one was going to investigate COGG. Nothing was different than it had been a week before. I might as well go back to living as if nothing had changed either. I'd done exactly what COGG had warned me not to do. I'd talked. They were still fine. The only logical course of action would be for them to leave me alone.

So I would go back to work. I might as well practice my own religion since the one I'd had before had been trying to kill me.

CHAPTER
18

I KNEW SOMETHING WAS WRONG the second I walked in the door. Yolanda half stood behind her desk and then sat back down. "Hey, Amanda," she said. "You okay, honey?"

"Fine. Thanks." She didn't say anything more, but I felt her swivel and watch me as I made my way to the lab side of the building and let myself in.

Jesse, Sara, and Melinda clustered around one of the computers in the lab. They all stopped talking when I walked in.

"What?" I asked.

Looks were exchanged. Meaningful ones. I still didn't understand until Sara turned the monitor so I could see it. It was an article about the search warrant served at COGG. It had a good-sized color photo of Sam and me standing on top of the hillock looking down at the backhoe.

I sank down into a chair, letting my messenger bag bang onto the floor. I winced when I thought of my laptop, but couldn't be bothered to check it.

"What does it say?" My voice came out in a croak.

Sara turned to monitor back toward herself and read. "A former member of COGG told authorities that bodies had been buried on this site on COGG property. She further claimed that COGG members had threatened her life. Patrick Collier, charismatic founder of Children of the Greater God was released on Monday after serving ten years for violation of fiduciary responsibilities, charges he has always claimed to be innocent of."

Jesse looked at me. "Is it true?"

"It's true. All of it." I figured I might as well connect all the dots for them. It was all going to come out now anyway. "My mother was Linda Framingham."

"Who?" Melinda asked.

Sara clicked some more buttons and brought up a story about my mother's death and turned the monitor to Melinda.

Jesse looked at the monitor and then up at me. "That's the call you got when we were out that Friday night. You got the call about your mother."

I nodded.

He rubbed his face. "Oh, man. No wonder you had to get out of there like that. I'm so sorry. I thought maybe it was, you know, a guy and you were blowing us off. I thought…" He stopped and leaned against the bench. "It doesn't matter what I thought."

The computer made a funny blipping noise. "There's breaking news," Sara said.

We gathered around the computer and watched a live streaming video. The anchorwoman said, "We're getting word that Andre Schmidt of COGG is about to make a statement."

The picture cut to the front of the COGG compound. Andre stood with COGG members flanking him on either side in front of the gates to the property. He held a piece of paper in his hand.

"Last night, our peaceful home was disrupted by law enforcement officials digging up parts of our property with backhoes." Each word came out with a little puff of steam into the cold. "We bear no ill will to the police officers, who were only doing their job. In fact, we bear no ill will toward anyone. We are deeply saddened by the circumstances that led to this situation.

"A young woman who was for a time a treasured member of this community has chosen to bear false witness against our leader, Patrick Collier, and against our community as a whole. There is no doubt this young woman suffered greatly and is looking to place the blame somewhere."

He looked into the camera. I felt like he was looking directly at me. "We pray for you, Amanda. Please know that if you want to return to us, we will welcome you with open arms. We know you're in pain. Let us help you bear it. We are all parts of God's grand machine. Let us be a part of your life again. We mourn for you and your mother and your brother, Amanda. Come back to us, let us bring you the joy we once brought. I remember your face, shining with tears as you became part of our community."

Without thinking, my hand went up to my throat as if to finger the COGG necklace that no longer hung there. It felt like Andre's eyes were boring directly into mine.

"Come home, Amanda."

I swayed toward the computer. "Whoa there!" Jesse cried as he stepped forward to steady me. "Are you all right?"

The press conference ended. Sara shut the window. "How can we help?" she asked.

They all three sat there, faces turned toward me like expectant flowers, pure and unsullied. Like Jackson had been. I shook my head. "There's nothing. Nothing I can think of."

"What were the police digging for?" Sara asked.

"I...I can't talk about it," I said.

"Got it." She nodded. "Ongoing investigation, right?"

The only investigation that might be ongoing would be one into me and my actions, but I couldn't bear to say it. Not out loud. Not to these people. I nodded one more time and headed to my desk.

Ten minutes later, my cell phone lit up like a freaking Christmas tree. Paula Spencer from Channel 10.

Ray Blair from Channel 32. Minnie Colon from the Tribune. Did I have a comment? What had they been looking for? How was I connected? I turned it off and stuck it in my purse.

I had come back to work to bury myself in something that made sense, but of course what I was dealing with was the thing that made no sense: the manipulated gels.

Before I even finished working my way through the morning deluge of emails, my office phone buzzed. It was Will Friedrichs. "Hi, Amanda. Do you have a minute to come to my office and talk?"

I couldn't imagine an employee saying no to that. I picked up a notebook and a pen as if we were going to be discussing some new experiment I would need to take notes about and left the lab. Yolanda buzzed me into the administrative side of the building, giving me a nod as I went past.

Will's office was on the second floor of our building in the corner, as befitted his rank. It was the closest thing to a view that any of the offices at Bellefountaine had, but it wasn't magnificent. The desk and chairs weren't crazy luxurious either. I mean, it was nicer than my little alcove in the lab, but Will clearly was more interested in running the company than in the trappings of running a company. I knocked on the open door of the office. "Hi, Will."

He looked up from the papers he was reading and motioned me in. "Shut the door, Amanda."

I sighed. This wasn't going to be good. I did as he asked and shut the door and sat down in one of the chairs opposite his desk.

"I think we need to talk about your present situation, Amanda." He leaned back in his chair. The expression on his face was as regretful as his overtight skin would allow.

I willed myself to keep my breathing even and deep. It's not like I hadn't known this was coming.

"I think it might be wise for you to take some time off," he said. He laced his long fingers and set his hands on the desk in front of him, the actions of a man who had made up his mind.

"Please," I said, hating the wobble in my voice. "Please don't."

His eyes narrowed. "I would think you would welcome the time to deal with everything that's happened. Even if it had just been the death of your mother, I would recommend taking some time."

I shook my head. "You don't understand. That...that's not what I want my real life to be. I want my real life to be here. At the lab. At Bellefountaine. I love this job."

Will leaned forward on his desk. "I know you love this job. I know you have a passion for your work, Amanda. It's why we recruited you right out of school. Every one of your professors and references said the same things about you. Dedicated. Professional. Smart. Sharp. But we all have things in our lives that make us miss a few steps. Take some time. Sort things through.

Your job will be here waiting for you when you're ready."

But the FDA report wouldn't be. That would be assigned to someone else. Someone else in my lab. Someone else who might have been the very person to falsify data in the first place. I didn't have enough proof yet to tell Will, but I would soon. "Just give me until the end of the week. If things haven't settled down by then I'll follow your advice and take some time off." I couldn't help it, a tear escaped my right eye and slid down my face. I wiped it away with the back of my hand. "Please, Will. Don't make me go home."

He dropped his head. "Amanda, you're killing me here." He took a deep breath and held it for a moment. "Okay. Until the end of the week. If you change your mind at any moment, let me know. You don't have to come in to talk to me. Shoot me an email. The last thing I want is for the pressure on you to become unbearable. Okay?"

I nodded, not trusting myself to speak without more tears. I stood up to leave. He stopped me as I got to the door.

"Amanda?"

"Yes," I managed to say.

"Let me know if there's anything else I can do for you, okay?"

I nodded again and made my escape.

Was there anything more embarrassing than crying in your boss's office?

Well, yes. There was. There was being the subject of everyone's interest everywhere you went. I stopped in the kitchen to get a bottle of water from the refrigerator. Kristy Wilkins and Clark Mendez had been standing by the coffee machine talking. I'd heard the murmur of their voices as I walked down the hall. It stopped the second they saw me.

"Hey," I said as I pulled the bottle from the refrigerator, like I did all the time, nearly every day.

"Uh, hi, Amanda," Clark said. "How are you?"

I stood up and gave him a blazing smile. "Fine. Thanks. You? How are the kids?"

"Great. Great. Thanks. Donny made it onto the varsity soccer team." He smiled, but it looked like his lips were sticking to his teeth.

"Super. See you later." I walked out, keeping my head high. It wasn't a new skill. I'd had tons of experience. I spent two years of high school having conversation stop when I walked into a room. It didn't make my heart sink any less, but at least I was practiced at handling it.

It was the same everywhere I went that day. The kitchen. The bathroom. My own lab. Who could blame them? I was news. Juicy news, too. What could there possibly be more interesting to discuss? The Bulls hadn't even played the night before.

Understanding why it was happening didn't make it any easier to deal with, though. I kept telling myself it didn't matter, but lying to myself was getting more difficult by the second. Plus I had no one to blame but myself. I was the one who'd wanted to stay. Will had given me a perfectly acceptable way to gracefully bow out while the full heat of my infamy was revealed, and I'd turned it down. I turned it down because I wanted to lose myself in my work. I decided that that was exactly what I was going to do.

I checked again for the dates of the missing pages from the physical lab notebook. I couldn't exactly go nosing around in other people's notebooks while they were here, so I started where every good investigator should start: with herself.

The set of questionable gels would have been run fairly late in our tests. They had to do with long - term use of Cover Me. I pulled out my personal lab notebook that covered the period of time when we first realized what Cover Me could do. In addition to the official lab notebook, each of us lab techs had our own individual notebooks. It's where we make our rough notes, jot down impressions, ask questions that we might want to follow up on later. Then later we take turns writing down outcomes in the official lab notebook—the one with the missing pages, in this case.

I smiled as I flipped through my notes. Anyone would have been able to tell how excited I was by the way my handwriting started getting bigger and loopier. Don't get me started on the exclamation points. I'm not generally an exclamation point kind of gal and my notes on Cover Me were peppered with them.

I opened the report to try to decide where in our testing the faked gels would have come in. It wasn't long before I discovered the original source for the faked gel, the gel that had been copied and reproduced in the report.

It was mine. It was one of the first ones we'd run when we realized what Cover Me might be able to do. I'd run this particular one to try to find how much of the active ingredient in Cover Me might be the right amount to produce the effect we wanted without harming the skin.

Fine. The original came from my work? Then I should be able to duplicate it and figure out what was going on. I started preparing my agarose, measuring, microwaving, cooling, pouring it all into the gel tray.

"What are you doing?" Jesse asked.

"Getting ready to run some gels." It seemed pretty obvious to me, but it never hurts to answer an obvious question.

"Which ones?" he asked. "Do you need help?"

"I'm fine." I turned to him. "Seriously. I'm okay. I can handle this. I want to double-check something in the FDA report, make sure it's replicable. The other stuff?" I waved my hand toward the computer monitor where we'd all watched Andre Schmidt publicly shame me in the name of trying to welcome me back to COGG. "I can't do anything about that. I tried. It's over." I gestured to my lab bench. "This I can do. This makes sense."

"I hear you." He smiled. "When in doubt, run the numbers."

"Exactly." I smiled back. It was nice to talk to someone who understood. I returned to my gels. I added buffer and then started the very careful process of loading in a molecular weight ladder into the first lane of the gel.

A gel is basically a medium we use in the lab to suspend particles of things that we wouldn't be able to see with a regular microscope. I loaded the tAE buffer and went to work. By five o'clock I was more than ready to go home, but I had one more thing to check and I didn't want to do it with my lab mates watching. Luckily, they all seemed to be putting on their coats and gathering their belongings to leave.

Jesse walked over to me. "Want to go out for a drink?"

I stared at him, not quite sure I could believe what I was hearing. They knew now. They knew who I was, what I was. They should be running as fast as they could in the opposite direction. "I think I should just go home. Besides, it's only Wednesday. Kind of early in the week, isn't it?"

Suddenly Sara was by Jesse's shoulder. "I think going home alone is exactly what you shouldn't do. You shouldn't be alone. You should be with friends. Plus Pedro's will be so much less crowded on a Wednesday."

"You guys don't have to do this," I said.

"You're right," Sara said. "We absolutely don't. We want to. Please, Amanda, let us show you some support. Let us be your friends."

I couldn't speak. If I opened my mouth to let out a word, the tears would come pouring out and I wasn't going to do that. I nodded instead. Then I took a deep breath and cleared my throat. "I'll catch up with you. I just need to finish up one more little thing here." I quickly wished it didn't have anything to do with proving that one of them should be fired.

Sara and Jesse exchanged glances but eventually agreed and left, telling me not to dillydally because there'd be a margarita with my name on it waiting at Pedro's.

Once they were gone, I made my way over to the minus eighty freezer. The minus eighty was where we stored actual tissue samples. The name referred to the temperature at which it was kept. It was where the tissues and gels from the experiments we'd run would be.

Our particular minus eighty was an upright model. It looked like one of those fancy stainless steel refrigerators you see in ads for ultra-modern kitchens, except it got much much colder. Much. Average refrigerators generally run from thirty-five to forty degrees. Plus they didn't have alarm systems on them that went off if the temperature started to rise. Our minus eighty did. If it got too warm, hundreds of experiments representing hundreds of thousands of research dollars would be destroyed.

I opened the minus eighty and began sorting through the shelf I thought the samples I was looking for would be on. There was plenty there. Stacks and stacks of plates and petri dishes. The search took a long time because I had to keep closing the door of the freezer periodically to keep the temperature from rising and setting off the alarm. After a half an hour, I still hadn't located the samples. I had a very bad feeling that they simply weren't there. I decided to take one more look and then call it a night.

"What are you looking for?"

I slammed the freezer door shut and whirled around, surprised to see Jesse standing there. "I thought you'd gone to Pedro's.

"I did, but we were worried when you didn't show up. Sara and Anna sent me back here to see if you were okay." He leaned against the doorframe and gestured with his chin at the minus eighty. "What were you looking for?"

I shrugged one shoulder, not quite ready to come clean with him or anyone else from the lab yet. "Some tissue samples to match the gels I was trying to replicate."

He nodded as if he understood. "Find them?"

I shook my head.

He held out his hand. "Come on. Let's get you a margarita. I'll help you look tomorrow."

CHAPTER

19

THERE'S NOTHING LIKE TWO -FOR -ONE margaritas on a Wednesday night to make you forget that you tried to lead police to evidence of murder, or at least manslaughter, and had instead ended up looking like a lunatic fool. Or to forget that you actually might be a lunatic fool, because maybe your memory was not so sound. Maybe everything you remembered didn't happen. Maybe you were more your mother's daughter than you ever wanted to admit.

I poured myself another drink from the pitcher and saw Melinda and Sara exchanged glances. "Maybe you should slow down a little," Melinda said. "These are pretty strong."

They weren't. They were typical happy hour fare: lots of ice, lots of mixer, not so much tequila. I didn't want to argue with my friends, though. Friends! I had friends like a normal person. They even knew who I was and they still wanted to be my friends. I picked up my water glass and took a long swallow of that instead after raising it toward Sara and Melinda as if I was making a toast.

"Good choice," Melinda said. She shoved a plate of nachos toward me. "Maybe a little food, too."

I eyed the nachos. That might be more than I could handle. Besides, food in my stomach would interfere with the wonderful woozy lightheaded feeling that was so much better than the rock I'd felt I was carrying around for most of the week. I took a chip from the edge that wasn't too loaded down with cheese and meat and sour cream and nibbled it.

Melinda patted my hand and went back to discussing tropical vacation destinations. I let the noise from the bar turn into a background buzz that I found soothing. There was something about the ebb and flow of it, rising and falling, swirling around me. Jesse caught me beneath the elbow. "You okay there?"

I realized I'd nearly fallen off the high stool on which I perched. I must have started to sway with the vibrations around me. "Fine," I assured him. "Perfectly and totally fine."

He laughed. "I'm not sure I've ever seen you smile this much."

I smiled wider.

"Maybe it's time someone made sure you got home in one piece," Sara said, giving Jesse a meaningful look.

He nodded and stood up, shrugging into his heavy coat. He helped me get my arms in my coat, too. Then Melinda wrapped my scarf around my neck and pulled my hat on for me. It was a little too much touching for me, but when I tried to lift my arms to protest I nearly fell over.

We made it outside into the night. I was pretty certain it was cold. The insides of my nostrils got that instant frozen feeling. Somehow, it didn't seem to bother my face or my ears or my hands, though.

Jesse stepped into the street to hail a cab.

"Let's walk," I said.

"You sure?" he asked.

"Totes. It'll help me sober up a bit." I didn't relish the idea of getting home this drunk and having the room spin around me once I managed to fall into my bed. I slid my arm through his and started to skip Wizard of Oz –style toward the intersection.

He pulled back. "Let's maybe just walk. It's kind of icy in places."

He was right. The sidewalk glinted black beneath the fizzing street lights. I slowed down. We walked along in silence. I couldn't imagine what I could possibly say and apparently Jesse couldn't either. At least, not until we were only two blocks from my apartment. He'd taken a couple of breaths in that I'd thought were preludes to conversation, but he was apparently having trouble getting whatever it was to come out.

When we were stopped at the intersection of Wells and Harrison, waiting for the green light, he loosened his grip on my arm and turned toward me. "I don't care what happened when you were a teenager. I thought you should know that."

I started up into those melting chocolate eyes. His face was dead serious. No trace of his adorable dimple. No flash of white teeth. I reached up and put a gloved hand on each side of his face and pulled his lips down toward mine. We kissed through an entire cycle of the lights. We kissed until the stars circled above me. We kissed until I wasn't sure where his lips ended and mine began.

"Wow," he said, breathless, staring down at me. "That was even better than I'd imagined it would be, and I've spent some time imagining that being really great."

I'd imagined it a time or two myself. I laughed and stepped into the crosswalk as the light turned green again. He hurried to catch up. We stopped on the other side to kiss again. Then halfway down the block. Then at the next intersection. Then we were nearly at my building. I turned to kiss Jesse once more. Out of the corner of my eye, I saw a heap of blankets in the recessed doorway.

It was cold out, fiercely cold. I knew that even if I had too much tequila in my bloodstream to feel it. My homeless knight in stinky armor would not survive a night spent out here. I touched my finger to Jesse's lips and said, "Hold that thought."

I dug in my purse and found a couple of twenties. Maybe that would be enough to get him a spot in a hostel or a shelter. I walked to the doorway and crouched down next to him. "Hey," I said. "Hey, buddy. It's cold out. Why don't you find somewhere warmer to sleep."

He didn't budge. I didn't particularly want to touch the blankets. They were so dirt -encrusted I wasn't sure there was any blanket underneath, and I had looked at way too many things under microscopes to want to get any of it on even my gloved hands. I stood and nudged him with my toe. "Buddy, wake up. Come on. I'll help you. You can't sleep here, though."

"What are you doing, Amanda?" Jesse called to me.

"Trying to help this guy. I think he's been sort of guarding me lately." I nudged him again with my toe, but still nothing. He must be seriously burrowed in. There was nothing for it, I was going to have to touch the blankets. Whatever. I'd burn the gloves once I got inside. I tugged the blanket back and breathed in to rouse him again. Then I saw why he hadn't responded to my voice or the nudges with my toe. Suddenly I was stone cold sober.

Someone had slit his throat from ear to ear.

Jesse and I sat on the steps inside my building's foyer and watched out the door as the red and blue lights swirled outside. He pulled his glove off and took my hand. "This wasn't exactly how I saw this night going."

I snorted. "Me neither. Although I'm fairly accustomed to things not going the way I expect them to at this point."

A slender policewoman with black hair pulled into a sleek bun at the nape of her neck knocked on the apartment building door. Jesse stood up and pulled it open for her. She nodded her thanks at him and then turned to me. "You're Amanda Sinclair?" she asked, checking her notebook. "You found the body?"

"Yes." I stood and brushed off the back of my coat.

"We're going to need to ask you some questions." She sounded almost bored. Probably finding the dead bodies of homeless people was an everyday occurrence to her. I would have thought the whole slit - throat thing would have at least added some urgency, though.

"Of course. Do you want to do it here? We could go up to my apartment if you wanted. It'll be warmer there at least," I offered.

A slight tinge of pink colored her dusky skin. "It'd be better if you came down to the station."

I turned to Jesse, who looked as confused as I felt. "Is that really necessary?"

"We think it would be best." She didn't meet my eyes.

I looked at my watch. It was already nine o'clock and with the buzz shocked out of my system, I was tired. "How about tomorrow? It's been a long day. I'd like to go to bed."

She shook her head. "Now would be best."

Jesse shrugged. "Fine. Let's get it over with."

"Oh, not you, Mr. Garcia. We only need Ms. Sinclair." She smiled at him.

That's when the alarm bells started going off in my head. "But we both found him."

"Primarily you, though" the officer said. "And you're the one with a prior relationship with him as well."

"And if I refuse to go with you?" I asked. I was pretty certain I didn't have to go if I wasn't under arrest.

Her lips tightened. "I'm not sure why you would want to start this out on an adversarial foot."

"She's not the one—" Jesse started.

I held up my hand to stop him. There wasn't any point. "I'll go. You're right, Jesse, I should get it over with." I stood and followed the police officer out the door with a backward glance at Jesse, who stood in the foyer with a frown on his face.

It didn't surprise me when Detective Pagoa walked into the interview room. I'd been in there for quite a while. Forty-five minutes at least. A guy in a uniform had brought me coffee, or at least something masquerading as coffee. The liquid in the Styrofoam cup wasn't drinkable, but it did help warm my hands for a little while.

The door slammed open. If Pagoa thought he was going to make me jump, he probably shouldn't have let me sit for so long. I'd been hard -pressed not to fall asleep. There wasn't any jump left in me.

He sat down across from me, dwarfing the metal chair he sat in. "I didn't expect to see you again so soon, Ms. Sinclair."

"It wasn't exactly my idea." He knew that, though. I was fairly certain he was the only reason I was there at the police station.

He put on a pair of reading glasses, opened a file he'd brought in with him, and leafed through some of the pages. "Seems like you have a nose for finding dead bodies."

"Actually, not so much, as you'll recall." If he *had* found dead bodies in the place I'd told him to look, he'd probably be happier with me.

"Point taken." His lips twitched as if he was fighting back a smile. "So what can you tell me about Rex Weber?"

"Who?" The name didn't ring any bells.

He glanced at me over the top of the reading glasses. "The gentleman whose body you found tonight."

His name had been Rex. Rex for king. Someone long ago had named him that and expected great and wondrous things for him. No matter what they'd named him, I'm sure they hadn't expected him to end his life alone and halffrozen in a doorway on Wells Street. "There's not much to tell."

He looked at me expectantly, pen poised over pad of paper.

When had it all started? "A week or so ago, I gave him a pair of gloves."

"When exactly was that?"

I thought for a second and then it hit me. It had been the night I'd heard that my mother died. I flinched. Pagoa's eyebrows went up. I wasn't going to be able to fudge this one. He'd know I was lying now that he'd seen that recoil. Too bad he was so observant. "A week ago Friday."

He paused with his pen still over the pad. He'd recognized the significance of the date. "Why'd you give him the gloves?"

"It was cold. I was nearly home. He had rags wrapped around his hands. I didn't want him to freeze his fingers off." It wasn't just a turn of phrase. It had been cold enough to do precisely that.

"Why not give him a dollar or two instead?" he asked.

I threw my hands up in the air. "I don't know. I'd had some bad news. Maybe I wasn't thinking clearly. He looked cold. I gave him my gloves. I went inside and went to bed."

Pagoa nodded and made a note. "You see him after that?"

I nodded. "He hung around that area. He liked to sleep in that doorway where…where I found him tonight."

He made some notes on his pad. "Any more interactions with him?"

I tilted my head back and thought. "He held the door open for me one time when I was carrying groceries. And he was doing something the other day where it was almost like he was following me."

"Why would he do that?" Pagoa asked, his tone sharp.

I hesitated. "I really don't know."

"Anything else?" He looked up from his notepad, head cocked to one side.

I thought for a moment. "No. That was it."

"What about tonight?" He asked.

"What about it?" I was pretty certain I'd covered that as thoroughly as I could.

"Why did you stop? You say he slept in that doorway a lot. What made you look closer?" He leaned in toward me.

I was surprised it wasn't obvious. "Do you know how cold it is out tonight? It's got to be hovering around zero."

"Minus three, actually."

I held out my hands as if that explained everything, which it sort of did. I decided to elaborate anyway. "It's way too cold to be sleeping outside. I thought…I thought I could give him some money and maybe he could find someplace indoors to sleep so I wouldn't end up finding him dead in the doorway in the morning." The irony of the statement didn't hit me until it was already out in the air.

"And instead you found he was already dead," Pagoa said.

I'd been doing my best to block out the mental picture of his staring eyes, the blood-soaked blanket, the gash across his throat. Pagoa's words brought it rushing back. "Yes," I whispered. Suddenly shivering with cold, I pulled my coat tighter around me.

"You ever see him in any altercations with anyone else? Was he ever aggressive?"

I shook my head. "Not really. I mean, he'd maybe follow you a little bit, but he didn't frighten me. It was more like…"

"Like what?" Pagoa pressed.

"Like he was looking out for me. Watching my back, you know?" It sounded stupid now. Why on earth would a homeless man whose name I didn't even know be watching my back? Was a pair of gloves and the occasional loose change that important?

Pagoa blew out a breath. "Well, okay then. I guess you can go."

I tilted my head to the side. "Really?"

He tilted his chair back. "Really what?"

"You dragged me down here for that? Why couldn't the officer on the scene have asked those questions back at my apartment?" A little spark of anger lit in my chest. I welcomed its warmth.

The front of the chair came down with a thump. "Think about it, Ms. Sinclair. If you were a police officer and you had spent an evening digging up part of the frozen Illinois countryside looking for corpses on someone's say -so and coming up dry, and then got a report that the same someone found an actual body less than twenty-four hours later, wouldn't you have wanted to look that someone in the eye and ask some questions?"

He had a fair point. I didn't care. "I didn't make up that story about COGG. Those bodies are out there somewhere."

"So you say. I'd be careful about continuing to say it, though." Pagoa's lips tightened.

"Why?" What difference did it make if I said it to him again?

"Defamation of character? Libel? Slander? I can't keep 'em all straight, but I'm pretty sure they could make a case for one or the other." He stood up. "Would you like to go home now?"

More than I could possibly say. So I didn't. I just stood up and walked out.

CHAPTER
20

Thursday, March 2

I WOKE FROM A DEAD sleep to the sound of the dead bolt on my door clicking open. I sat straight up and immediately wished I hadn't. My head swam. I should have downed a gallon of water before I went to bed, but I hadn't. I'd fallen onto the pillows wearing panties and the camisole I'd had on under my blouse the day before. I looked around to see if there was anything I might use as a weapon. Nothing.

"Amanda?" a voice called from the entryway.

I pulled my knees up and leaned my forehead against them. There were no weapons that would be effective against this particular onslaught. "In here, Dad."

He peeked around the corner. "Are you decent?"

"Sort of." I could only imagine what he was seeing from the doorway to my room. Or what passed for a doorway to my room in the loft. Hair standing up. Yesterday's make-up halfway down my face. My clothes strewn on the floor.

"I'll make coffee," he said and ducked back out.

"Thanks, Dad," I called after him.

"I tried to call," he yelled from the kitchen. "It kept going to voicemail."

Then I remembered shutting my phone off. "Sorry. I turned it off. Too many reporters were calling." I pulled on yoga pants and a t-shirt and headed for the bathroom.

"I can imagine."

The coffee grinder went on, saving me from replying. I washed my face, brushed my hair and teeth, and tried to mask some of the last night's damage with a little concealer and blush. It wasn't going to fool Dad, but I knew the fact that I was making an effort would give him some solace. I wasn't completely down in the pits of hell if I still cared about dark circles under my eyes. I hoped my deodorant would cover the smell of tequila seeping from my pores. I took a deep breath, blew it out, settled my shoulders, and walked out of the bathroom.

"There you are." He wrapped his arms around me in a bear hug. My dad was fifty-seven years old and still pretty dreamy as far as dads go. He and Jessica worked out at least four times a week. Even though his jaw was a little soft these days, his arms and abs were not. His hug was strong and warm and made me feel like things might be okay for a second or two.

Then he stopped hugging me and the cold world rushed back in. Sometimes I wondered if that was how it had been for my mom. If the only way she could feel that safe warmth again after my dad left her was through her involvement with COGG. I knew how it felt to have that hug withdrawn. It wasn't pretty.

"Now," he said, sitting down at the table. "What the hell happened?"

I filled him in on all that had happened, including seeing janitor Simon Palmer and nurse Lois Brower at Peter Collier's press conference. "COGG is involved in this somehow, Dad. I know it. They had something to do with Mom's death, too."

He checked his watch and went to pour the coffee from my French press. "COGG was not to blame for any of the things that happened with your mother, pumpkin. It maybe fed her illness, but there was something broken inside her. I wish I'd realized how broken it was. Maybe I could have kept you kids safer, but I didn't. I have to live with that. COGG wasn't to blame."

"But Dad, don't you think that's an awfully big set of coincidences? To have all this happening at once?" I took my mug of coffee and wrapped my hands around it. Just the smell of it made me start to feel better.

He added cream and sugar to his mug. "Yes. I do. I can see why you feel everything's connected, but you know that saying about the hammer? How to a hammer everything looks like a nail?"

I nodded.

"Maybe all you're seeing is COGG because you want to hammer them for what happened to our family." He took a long sip.

I shook my head. "No, Dad. That's not it. I would have never suspected anything was strange about Mom's suicide if it hadn't been for that picture of Jackson in her stuff, and I would never have probably even noticed Lois Brower if I hadn't been looking for her to get an explanation about it."

He put his hand over mine. "That aside, what were you telling them to dig for?"

I'd been dreading that question. I knew it would come. It would be pretty much the first thing I would have asked. There didn't seem to be any room for wiggling out of answering it at this point. He might as well know. "A body."

His chest heaved with a sigh. "Whose body, Amanda?"

"A boy's. A boy who died on the compound. He said he was sick, but no one believed him. They made him keep working, and then..."

"He died," Dad finished the sentence for me. "Why didn't you ever say anything about this before?"

I turned my coffee mug in circles in front of me. "When it happened, I was too scared. Patrick—" I had to stop and clear my throat. Saying his name seemed to clog it up. "Patrick said that since I helped bury him, I'd be an accessory. Then Mom was arrested."

"And you thought you'd be arrested, too?" Dad's eyebrows went up.

I nodded.

"Surely you eventually figured out that wouldn't be true," he said.

"I did. But by then, so much time had passed. I wanted to never think about COGG again, never have anything to do with any of them. I wanted to bury them in my past the way they'd buried Marcus." I looked down at my coffee mug, not willing to look him in the eyes.

"But all that changed with your mother's death." Dad leaned back in his chair. He sighed again. "Honey, nothing's changed. Leave this all alone."

"I was planning to. Did you hear the part where someone poisoned my coffee?" I asked.

"I did. Trust me, it worries me, but maybe it was some kind of accident. I know what it's like in a lab. No one obeys all those safety instructions. Stuff happens." He reached across the table for my hands again. "How sure are you about this boy you say died?"

I blinked. "Pretty darn sure. I saw his body. I watched them put it in the ground."

"Honey, you were so messed up then. Your mom was losing it. I wasn't around. That Collier character was poisoning your mind with all kinds of claptrap. Could it have been something you imagined?

Something you dreamed?" The kindness in his eyes made his words cut that much more deeply.

It was one thing to have Detective Pagoa not believe me, but my own father? I felt like my heart had turned to ice. "It's not the kind of thing you dream up, Dad."

"Not under normal circumstances, no. But those weren't normal circumstances. I remember what you were like after...after Jackson." Even he had a hard time saying his name.

"This happened before Jackson, but I think any teenager would be distressed after turning her mother in for murder." My tone had gone sarcastic. It wasn't the best way to reach Dad. I knew that, but I couldn't seem to stop myself.

"Amanda." It's amazing how much parental information can be conveyed in saying just your name. A lifetime of patience being pushed almost to the breaking point. Frustration. Worry.

I held up my hands. "It doesn't matter, Dad. The police won't be pursuing it any further. With any luck, whoever at COGG thought I might be a threat to them now knows I'm not and will leave me alone."

Dad gave me a wan smile. "Take a few weeks off. I'm sure your boss wouldn't mind. Rest a little. Come home. Let Jessica and me coddle you a bit."

Home. The house Dad shared with Jessica and his new family had never really been home. I'd known from the second I walked through the door when they first moved into it that I was a temporary squatter.

After all, when I'd actually asked to come home, I'd been put off. I called my father, begged to be allowed to come live with him. I knew I was out of control, that Mom was whirling closer and closer to the edge, too. I called him, a last -ditch effort to save myself.

That day I listened to the phone ringing. One. Two. Three. Four. I'd already gotten my father's voicemail three times. I hadn't left messages, didn't want him calling back when Mom was nearby. If he didn't answer now, I probably wouldn't get another chance to call him until the next day. I twisted a lock of her hair around my finger while I listened to the phone ring.

"Hello," his voice said.

I let out a whoosh of a sigh. "Daddy," I said. "It's Amanda."

"Well, hello, sweetheart. It's good to hear your voice."

That was a good start. He was happy to hear from me. That wasn't always the case. "How are you, Daddy?"

"Fine. Busy at work, like always, but fine."

"And Jessica? Is she okay?" I'd made a note to ask about my new stepmother. It wouldn't do to seem hostile.

"Amanda, what do you want?"

Damn. I'd overplayed my hand. He knew something was up. I probably shouldn't have mentioned Jessica at all. "Mainly to say hello. I haven't seen you in awhile."

"Your mother keeps telling me that you're busy at church. Some kind of youth outreach program?"

That was one way to put it. "Yeah. Sort of."

"Well, I can't say I'm crazy about that Reverend Collier, but doing volunteer work will look good on your college applications." That was Dad. Always worrying about things like grades and college. It used to drive me crazy. Lately I missed the normalcy of it all .

"That's the thing, Dad. I'd kind of like a break from COGG. Just for a little while." I twisted my hair harder, hard enough for it to hurt a little.

There was a pause. "I'm not really in charge of that, Amanda. You need to talk to your mother."

Dad wasn't really in charge of anything that had to do with me, Dylan, or Jackson. "Yeah, Mom is kind of hard to talk to about COGG. She's so into it, you know?"

Dad laughed. "All too well."

"That was why I was hoping that maybe I could come to live with you and Jessica for a little bit. Not forever. Maybe a week or two, to take a break." I closed my eyes as I spoke, as if I was making a wish on my birthday candles.

There was a long pause. "You know, kiddo, usually there's nothing I'd like more than having you come for a visit. It's just that both Jessica and I are crazy busy with this new project at work."

I let his words hang out there for a minute, hoping he'd go in a different direction if I didn't acknowledge them.

"You still there, honey?" he asked.

"Yeah, Dad. I'm still here." Stuck here, apparently.

"How about this. Let's make a plan. Maybe next month, you and the boys can come for a long weekend. How does that sound?"

A long weekend? That wasn't going to help. I needed to get away, and I needed to do it now. "Sure, Dad. Sounds awesome. See you then."

I'd hung up the phone and then sat and knocked my head against my desk over and over and over and over.

I knew Dad felt bad about it now. Just like he felt bad about leaving us with Mom. Just like he felt bad about not stepping in to get us out of COGG. Just like he felt bad about Jackson's death. Feeling bad didn't seem to change anything, though.

I knew Will Friedrichs would be more than happy to give me the time off if I asked, but what would I do out there in the suburbs? Lie around on Jessica's cushy sectional couch and watch afterschool TV with my little sisters? Eat nutritious balanced meals sitting at the dining room table, asking Jessica to pass the salt? I felt my throat closing up thinking about it.

"I'd rather stay here, keep busy," I said.

"Okay, then. Is there anything I can do to help?" he asked.

Besides believe me? "No, Dad. I'm fine. I've got everything I need."

"Okay, then. I've got to get to work." He got up to leave. "Take care of yourself. Check in once in a while. Oh, and call your brother. He's worried, too."

I'd forgotten about Dylan. What must he have thought when he saw the news coverage? "I will."

Dad left and I turned on my cell phone. I thought it was going to short out with all the notifications it tried to push through at once. When it finally stopped, I dialed Dylan's number.

"Way to keep a low profile, sis," he said when he answered.

"I've always been an overachiever," I said breezily.

He snorted. "Seriously, what possessed you? Those people are nut jobs of the first order. Stay away from them."

"I plan to. From now on. I swear." Why not? What else could I possibly do?

"On a stack of Gino's pizzas?"

"On a stack of Gino's pizzas with Frango mints on top."

"Serious stuff there, Amanda." He paused. "Speaking of serious, though. Are you okay?"

"Sure. I'm always okay, aren't I? How about you? Anybody put two and two together and figure out you were my brother?" I asked.

"Nah. Sinclair's a common name. No one batted an eye."

"That's good." I'd screwed up my own life pretty successfully. I didn't want to screw up his. He, after all, wasn't the one who was broken inside.

We said good-bye and hung up. I hauled out my laptop to check my email, relatively certain my inbox would be filled with requests from reporters and media outlets. I wasn't wrong.

One message did catch my eye, though. The subject heading was *Need to talk to you*, and it was from Kelly@IllinoisCultWatch.Com. I clicked on it.

Dear Ms. Sinclair,

I saw the recent news coverage of the excavation at the Children of the Greater God compound. I understand that nothing incriminating was found, but I believe that only means authorities haven't looked in the right place yet. I run a cult watch website. I was hoping I could interview you regarding your time in COGG and the tragic end to that time.

Please contact me when and if you're interested.

Sincerely,

Kelly Harris

I was disappointed. When I'd seen the Cult Watch domain name I'd hoped it was someone with information for me. Instead it was one more person trying to use me to gain a little notoriety. I was good copy, I supposed. Well, she'd have to make that copy without me, particular with that "tragic end" crap.

No one, me included, ever knew what to call what happened to Jackson. The district attorney hadn't had much trouble. He'd called it like he'd seen it. First

Degree Murder. Filicide. Killing one's own son. Everyone else? Well, we kind of danced around it. Jackson's death. The tragic event. Our family's troubles. Nothing ever felt right. Either it was too much of a euphemism or not enough of one. Too distant and cool or too full of emotion. There never seemed to be a happy medium.

I deleted the email.

My cell phone rang and I cursed myself for not remembering to turn it back off. I was about to when I saw that it was Sam calling. A flash of kissing Jesse streaked across my mind like a lightning bolt. I couldn't pretend I didn't know why I felt guilty about it, but I knew it was stupid at the same time.

I answered. "Hey."

"Hey, yourself. Are you okay? I've been trying to call you."

"Yeah. Sorry. I turned the phone off. Too many reporters."

"Oh. That sucks."

I laughed. "Pretty much."

"Do you want to talk?"

"I'm not sure there's anything more to talk about."

"Amanda…"

Again, someone who seemed to be able to pack a huge amount of emotion into saying my name. "Really. What's more to be said? That's where they buried Marcus and now he's not there. They must have moved the body and whatever other bodies were buried there. At any rate, I'm not a threat to them anymore. Detective

Pagoa wouldn't believe me if I told him the sky was blue at this point." I cringed thinking about facing him across the table in the interrogation room the night before.

I was so busy thinking about that, that I didn't notice Sam's hesitation at first. "How totally sure were you about Marcus being buried there, Amanda?"

"What do you mean?"

"I mean, you were young, your world was in turmoil, your mother was poised to spiral completely out of control. Could you have misremembered about Marcus?"

My father had said nearly the same thing moments ago. "I suppose maybe. But that spot seemed so right. The tree. The fence. The way the ground sloped down. The mounds."

He cleared his throat. "I didn't mean that you had misremembered where Marcus had been buried. Could you have possibly misremembered about his death?"

I couldn't have answered if I'd wanted to. My face felt too frozen to move. Somehow Sam's doubt was even worse than my father's.

"It's not uncommon for things that people have imagined to seem very real to them, especially when those dark dreams or delusions come at times when we're very vulnerable."

"You think I made this all up?"

"Not deliberately. Could things have become exaggerated in your memory?"

"What about my car being broken into? What about me being poisoned? Pushed into traffic?"

Now he didn't say anything.

"You think I made that up, too?" Except the poisoning. I couldn't have made that up. Which meant only one thing—he thought I'd poisoned myself. "How crazy do you think I am?"

Had he been humoring me this whole time? Trying to keep his crazy patient's crazy daughter under control?

"I don't think you're crazy, Amanda. I think that your mother's death and the questions surrounding it had to have brought up a lot of unresolved issues—"

"Unresolved issues? That's what you call this? Tell me, Dr. Ashmore, how exactly am I supposed to resolve the fact that my mother may have been murdered while serving a life sentence for murdering my brother?"

"No one said this is easy. I think that's part of the issue. The situation is inherently fraught."

"Oh, for fuck's sake, fraught? Do they have a special class in euphemisms in shrink school?"

"Amanda, I know you're angry..."

"Damn right, I'm angry. I thought you were on my side. I thought you had my back on this." I had thought that. Now I wondered what had possessed me.

"I do. I absolutely one hundred percent do."

"Funny way to show it, doc." Throw a little more gas on the self-doubt fire, why don't you?

"I'm showing it in the only way I know how. I'm asking you to stop and examine the situation."

"Tell you what. And you can tell Lois Brower this, too, if you ever find her. I am done examining the situation. I'm out. I gave it everything I had and ended up nearly burying myself. Don't worry, I won't be bothering you again." I hung up and shut the phone off before he could call back.

I dragged myself into the shower. I had one last bit of solace left to myself—I could go to work. I could go to the land of data and science and numbers. I stood under the hot water until it started to run cold. Wrapped up in a towel, I stared at my face in the mirror and marveled at how normal I looked. Oh, I still looked like I'd been run hard and put away wet, but normal all the same. I didn't look like a woman who would make up dead bodies in one spot and find them unexpectedly in another.

I stared harder. Was I?

I looked like her. I knew that. There'd been a time that had made me proud. People would say I was the spitting image of my mother and I'd feel my spine lengthen like I was actually getting taller, like it meant something, like it said something about who I was.

Then it had been a source of horror, and not just for me. I'd seen it on Dad's face on occasion. Those moments when I must have made a gesture or a facial expression that was a little too much like her. There'd be a softening, but that was just a reflex, a throwback to his youth when he and Mom had been young and in love.

On its heels would come realization and revulsion. The last thing he wanted was for me to be like her.

Dylan had been the same. He'd been eleven when we went to live with Dad. All kids had nightmares, but Dylan's were a million times worse. One of the first times he'd had a nightmare after moving in with Dad and Jessica, I ran to his room when I heard his scream, ready to comfort him, to hold him, to rub his back like our mother had done when she was well. In the dim light of his room, he'd taken one look at me and begun screaming in earnest. I looked too much like her. Instead of calming him, I'd terrified him more.

I cut my hair short, dyed it blonde. I could still catch glimpses of her in the mirror, though. The shape of my cheekbone. The curve of my eyebrow. The arch of my lip. I'd never be free of her.

And that was just what was on the surface.

What lurked beneath? Everyone wondered. I saw the question in Dad's eyes, in Jessica's, in the eyes of my counselor at school. I didn't know myself. What I did know was that there was something in me that made my own mother think I would get up in the middle of the night and help her kill my brother. Maybe she thought I would because I'd already watched one boy I cared about die and be slipped into the earth and hadn't done a damn thing to stop it.

Or had I? I leaned closer to the mirror, staring into my bloodshot morning -after -tequila eyes. Had they seen what I thought they'd seen? Had I dreamed the whole thing? Had there ever been a Marcus? My mother had never fabricated an entire person, at least not that I remembered. There'd been plenty of other delusions, though. Plenty of other things she'd seen that no one else had.

How crazy had I become? Or had it always been there and only started surfacing now?

CHAPTER
21

POLICE TAPE STILL CRISSCROSSED THE alcove where my homeless friend had died. I couldn't understand why anyone would bother to kill a homeless man like that. What could possibly have been the motive? Money? Territory? That slash across his throat had been nearly surgical in its precision. Whoever did it knew just where to cut and had a good sharp knife to cut with as well.

The temperature dropped another ten degrees as I neared the track at my L station and the moist moldy smell with its overtones of disinfectant and urine stung my frozen nostrils. I shoved my hands in my pockets and watched the puffs of steam my breath made in the air.

When I walked into the lab, Sara was sifting through the papers on my desk. I leaned against the alcove wall. "Looking for something?"

She whirled. Clutching her chest, she said, "You scared the bejeesus out of me, Amanda!"

"Sorry. I didn't really think I needed to make an announcement to walk to my own desk."

Her face flushed bright red. "I was looking for…" She seemed to run out of words.

"For?" I prompted.

"The FDA report. I wanted to see how your review was going."

I kept my face blank. "It's going."

"I knew you were running some gels and I was curious about which ones."

I shouldered past her and didn't answer. I restacked the papers on my desk and turned my back toward her. The huggy invasions of my personal space were bad enough, but mushing in my work papers? It set my teeth on edge.

"Well?" she asked.

"Well, what?"

"Which gels are you running?"

"Why do you need to know?"

She held up her hands in front of herself and backed away. "I don't. I was curious. You know, friendly coworker kind of stuff?"

I let my head drop for a second. What the hell was I doing? No. I wasn't overjoyed about finding Sara going through things on my desk, but we were a team. We all needed to know what the other people in the lab were up to if we wanted to work effectively. That could be all this was. Or she could be the one who falsified the data or the one who took a COGG necklace from my jewelry box. Either way, it wasn't smart to snap at her. I needed to maintain my cool. "I'm sorry. It's been a shitty couple of weeks and I'm jumpy as hell."

She dropped her hands. "Sorry. I know."

I unwound the scarf from around my neck and started sorting through what I had on my desk. Sara got a phone call and left the lab. I fired up the electron microscope. The strands of DNA we examined on our gels were way too small for an optical microscope.

I leaned my forehead up against the brace to look in and focused. I leaned back and looked at the images in the report again. They were nothing alike. Nothing. They couldn't have been more different if I'd been looking at tests of two entirely different substances.

I'd expected a little variation, but not this. Not what looked like completely unrelated results. Wherever the original results came from, they didn't come from any experiment run with Cover Me. This wasn't just fudging; this was a major breach of scientific ethics and what's worse, according to these results, we would also be endangering every person who used the product.

I sat back. We were going to have pull Cover Me from FDA review. There would be no choice. I was going to have to tell Will Friedrichs about it. He needed to know about this right away. I couldn't imagine how devastating it would be. Without Cover Me, none of the big cosmetic companies that had been making offers to buy Bellefountaine would be interested. Oh, we had some good products, some great ones even, but nothing like Cover Me. Cover Me was revolutionary. The only problem was that after it helped you reduce the scars on your face, it would apparently give you skin cancer.

I printed out copies of the results to show Will and my own phone buzzed. It was Ollie Lopez, head of R&D. "Amanda, could you come see me right now."

I looked down at my printout. I'd take it with me and go straight to Will after I spoke to Ollie. "Sure. See you in a minute."

Sara, Anna, and Jesse were all in Ollie's office when I walked in. It suddenly occurred to me that the lab had been terribly quiet. I'd been so intent on what I was looking for that I hadn't noticed. "What's going on?"

Ollie gestured to the one empty chair in the room. I sat.

"Last night the alarm on the minus eighty went off," he said.

My heart sank. If the alarm went off, it meant the minus eighty had been getting too warm, endangering all our samples. I scanned my memory. I knew I'd locked it when I finally left for Pedro's, was sure of it. One hundred percent sure.

"Your lab mates here tell me that you were searching in it before you left last night," Ollie continued.

I nodded. "I was, but I'm positive I shut it completely and locked it down when I was through."

"Then why was it only half latched when I came in at two o'clock this morning to see why the alarm was going off, Amanda?" Ollie asked.

I looked around at my lab mates, at the people who had convinced me they were my friends. None of them met my gaze. "I don't know. Someone must have come through after I left."

Ollie made a noise in his throat, something between a cough and a grunt. "Look, Amanda, we're all aware of how much pressure you've been under with what's going on in your personal life."

Here we go again. My messed up personal life.

"The FDA report is an added pressure. I know you want to do it, but it's simply too important to let you continue with it when you're making these kinds of mistakes." He put his hands flat on his desk. "I'm going to insist that you take a personal leave."

"But I didn't make a mistake," I protested. "I locked the minus eighty. I know I did."

"Amanda, please don't make this more difficult than it already is." He looked sincerely distressed.

"Ollie, look. I found something, something that needs to be addressed with Cover Me before we send it to the FDA." I inched forward in my chair. "It's important. There's something wrong with our results. I think someone might have been falsifying data."

"Someone here? At Bellefountaine?" he asked.

"One of us?" Sara asked, her eyes narrowed slightly.

I looked at her briefly before refocusing on Ollie. "Yes. One of us. I don't know who or why or how, but some of the data in that report isn't right. I've been trying to tell you that for weeks. I have proof now."

"Proof that you obtained while you've been in this very stressful situation?" he asked.

"That has nothing to do with it," I protested. I squared my shoulders. "I want to speak to Will."

"He's not in today," Ollie said. "He's working from home."

"Then I'll speak to him about it tomorrow. I'll show him. I have the proof. He'll believe me." I knew how much he cared about this company. No way was he going to let falsified data go to the FDA.

All Ollie said was, "Amanda, please don't make me have security escort you out."

In the end, security escorted me out anyway. At least I managed to shove the printout under my sweater before they arrived at my desk. They took my key cards and my Bellefountaine ID, and I felt like a cop handing in his gun and badge. My lab mates stood around awkwardly trying not to look as I was marched down the hall and out into the lobby. Even Yolanda couldn't meet my eye as I walked by.

Out on the sidewalk, I blinked at the sun, nearly blinding as it glinted off the packed snow on the edge of the sidewalks. I felt lost, unsure where to go or what to do. The paper crinkled underneath my sweater. I had to get that information to Will.

But first I had to go home. Ridiculous, I knew, but I needed my car. It was easy enough to get to Winnetka by train, but once you were there, you'd better have a car waiting. I walked to my usual L station and waited, bouncing on my toes to keep warm.

When the train finally arrived I leapt in, grateful for even its paltry warmth. I tried to recall the sensation of riding the train in July, when the heat and humidity inside its cars would be enough to make me nearly swoon. My imagination wasn't quite good enough, though.

I got off and walked to the garage, grateful that I had my car keys on my key ring and hadn't left them at the apartment. Then it was onto the Edens Expressway and out to Winnetka. Well, it would have been except for the evening traffic that had already piled up.

By the time I pulled onto Will's block in Winnetka, the sun had lowered in the sky and streetlights were coming on. Warm light shone out of windows. In a few I could make out figures—people making dinner, preparing for a night out or a night in, watching television, reading. It all looked so calm and normal. Of course, it was nearly impossible to tell from the outside. Our house had looked exactly like these ones once. The yard was mowed in the summer, the driveway cleared of snow in the winter. The paint was fresh and unpeeled, the windows clean. Dad made sure of all that. Those were things you could throw money at. It was what was inside that had been so terribly broken.

I pulled to the curb a few blocks from Will's house. I needed to marshal my thoughts. I knew dropping in on the CEO of my company unannounced was unprecedented, but I couldn't take the chance of waiting for an email to reach him or a voicemail message to be listened to. Of course, I could ring the bell and find out he wasn't home at all. I was willing to take that chance.

I pulled out my papers and went over them, jotting notes in the margins of things I wanted to make sure to point out. As I sat, another car drove past me and pulled into the driveway. This car looked more out of place on the block than my crappy Escort. Older. More dented. Spots of rust near the wheel wells. I sank down in my seat to see who might get out of it.

I sank even farther when I realized it was none other than Lois Brower, the CNA from Elgin who had packed my mother's belongings and then virtually disappeared. She locked her car door, walked to the front steps of the house, and rang the bell.

What the hell was she doing here? What possible connection could there be between Lois and Will? Was this some kind of crazy coincidence?

Will answered the door. I picked up my phone and started snapping pictures. He smiled, grabbed Lois by the waist, and pulled her tight against him.

Then he kissed her.

I'm not sure how long I sat in my car after Lois Brower entered Will Friedrichs's house. Well, entered

273

didn't quite describe it. It was more like she was swept off her feet into his house. It had been a romance-worthy moment, at least from out here in my cold car. I'm not sure how much longer I would have sat there, either, if my phone hadn't rung. I was still holding it in my hand from taking photos of Lois Brower and Will Friedrichs in a lip-lock. It buzzed in my hand and I dropped it as if it had suddenly come to life and bit me.

I scrambled to find it on the floor beneath my feet, finally fishing it out from under my seat. Then I nearly didn't answer. It was Jesse. The various humiliations of the night before came rushing back to me. Kissing him. Finding a dead guy. Being dragged to the police station for questioning. He was probably calling me to tell me that he was taking out a restraining order to keep my away from him.

Wait. Why *was* he calling?

I hit the button and said hello.

"Are you okay?" he asked.

"I'm…" I'd been about to say that I was fine, even though I was anything but. Screw that. I needed someone to talk to. Someone to sort this all out with. "I'm really hoping you'll meet me for a drink," I said instead.

There was a pause on the other end, and for a second I thought maybe I'd gone too far. Maybe all the drama and craziness were enough to finally push Jesse away. Then he said, "I can be at Pedro's in half an hour."

Pedro's. Noisy, bustling Pedro's. "How about Heaney's Ale House instead?" Heaney's was significantly divier than Pedro's, one of the few holdouts to the gentrification that had swept through Printer's Row turning warehouses into loft apartments and high -end locavore restaurants run by graduates of the Culinary Institute of America. "It's near Clark and Division."

"Got it," he said, sounding like he was about to embark on a mission to Mars.

I hung up the phone and looked down at what I'd put on that morning. Jeans, a long loose shirt, boots. It would have to do. There wouldn't be time to go back to my apartment and change. I rummaged through my purse and found a lipstick. What the hell. Heaney's was dark .

I made a U-turn so I wouldn't even drive past Will's house and headed back to the Loop.

Jesse already sat at the bar when I walked in. He turned and I felt a little warmth in the pit of my stomach at the way his face lit up. "Hey," I said, rushing up to him.

He gave me a hug and for once I didn't stiffen up as if I thought he was about to try to steal my wallet. I hugged him back, relieved to have someone who seemed always to believe me, no matter what. "What'll you have?" he asked. "Margarita?"

"Good lord, no. Not here. Just a beer." I settled onto the barstool next to his. Ordering a margarita at Heaney's would be like ordering a hamburger at a Chinese restaurant. "I need to show you this."

"Okay," he said, signaling the bartender.

I pulled the sheaf of papers out of my bag. "Someone really is falsifying test results on Cover Me."

Jesse's movements slowed, then he heaved a sigh. "I was afraid you were going to bring that up again. Amanda, are you sure?"

I rubbed my forehead. Everyone knew I was supposed to be doing quality control on the Cover Me report. I supposed it wouldn't take a genius to figure out that I'd found something I didn't like. I'd even said as much in a meeting a while back, when Will was pressuring me on how long the report was taking. Although I hadn't known how bad it was at that point. "It's bad, Jesse."

"How bad?"

I shoved the papers across to him. "It's causing mutagenic cells at a fairly low concentration."

He took a second to read through the pages, then pushed them away on the bar is if he could push the truth away. "Amanda, this is a disaster."

"I know." Having your product that would provide relief to thousands if not millions of people with scars end up giving them cancer? Disaster didn't really sum it up. There was a cruelty to it, a twist of fate that felt like a sucker punch.

"Do you know who's responsible for the switched results?" He flipped the pages facedown on the bar as if not seeing them would make them go away.

"Not yet. I've been more focused on whether or not they were wrong. I think I'll be able to track them back, given time." I looked over at him, nervous to say what I was thinking out loud, but desperate to have someone else to talk to about it. "How well do you know Sara?"

Jesse sat up straight as if I'd poked him. "Sara? She's great. She's accurate, careful, reliable."

Exactly the kind of words you'd want to have applied to you as a lab tech, but it didn't really address what I was wondering about. "But do you know her? Like what's going on in her personal life?"

"Just what we talk about at work or over drinks on Friday. You know pretty much everything I do. You can't really think…"

"I don't know what to think. If you'd asked me two weeks ago about this, I would have told you that there wasn't a single person in our lab who would pull something like this. Clearly I was wrong." Once again proving myself to be a crappy judge of character. Story of my life.

Jesse stared at the papers. "You have to tell Will. I think that has to be your first step."

I wasn't surprised that he'd said that. After all, it had been my first inclination as well. "Well, about that…" I did my best to give Jesse an abbreviated version of what had happened.

"Wait," he said, holding his hand up like a traffic cop. "Wait one minute. You're telling me that you saw the nurse who disappeared right after your mother's death kissing Will Friedrichs in his doorway? You can't possibly think he was part of that cult your mom was in. That's crazy."

I'd been afraid of that response. Honestly, it sounded crazy to me, too. "I know, but I also know that I saw what I saw. My mother's dead. Someone either killed her or pushed her to kill herself, and I was poisoned. In both cases, someone from COGG was there. Now I find out that one of those people is involved with my boss? My head is spinning. I was so glad you called. I desperately needed someone to talk to."

"And you didn't want to call that guy who was at the hospital? Sam?" Jesse asked, his eyes hooded.

I let my head drop. "No. I didn't want to call Sam. After the whole debacle out at the COGG compound, I don't think he believes me much anymore."

"What about that cop? That detective?" Jesse asked.

"You mean Pagoa? Pagoa believes me even less than Sam." Someone had to believe me, though. It was too important.

"So what are you going to do?"

What I really needed to know is if there was more of a connection between Will and COGG than a booty call. I chewed my lip. "I think I'm going to contact this woman at a cult news website. She emailed me after the coverage of the COGG compound excavation. I blew her off, but if anyone would know whether or not Will is really involved with COGG, it would be her."

"What website?"

I told him then stood. "I should go. Thanks for meeting me. I really needed someone to talk to." I shrugged into my coat.

Jesse grabbed my hand. "I'm always here if you need someone to talk to." Then he pulled me toward him for a kiss. It wasn't the dizzying affair that the other night's kisses had been, but it was still pretty darn good. "If you want someone for more than talk, you know where to find me."

I swallowed hard. "Got it. Things are so crazy right now. I don't know—"

He stopped me with a finger to my lips. "I know. I understand. I just want you to know and understand that I'm here and I'll wait."

I backed away and nearly ran from the bar before I changed my mind and dragged him home with me.

The cold outside smacked into me, cooled my flaming cheeks, and slowed my raging libido down a bit. It had been a long time since I'd been with someone, longer still since I'd been with someone that I actually might want to be around with for more than a quick roll in the hay. Maybe I'd held myself in solitary long enough. Maybe it was time to let someone in, someone who believed in me, someone who heard the craziest things from my mouth and didn't ask if I was sure I'd seen what I'd seen.

Back at my apartment, I sifted through the trash folder in my email until I found the message from

Sabrina Hall of Cult Watch. I took my chances and dialed the phone number she'd sent.

"Sabrina Hall," she said upon answering.

"Ms. Hall, my name is Amanda Sinclair. I'm—"

"I know exactly who you are." She sounded as excited as if I'd said I was Santa Claus. "I'm so glad you're calling me. Did you decide to do the interview?"

I hesitated. "Maybe. Actually, I was hoping you could help me with something."

"Anything," she said, almost too quickly.

"I've had some strange things happening to me lately…" I trailed off, not quite sure where to begin.

"I've heard."

It was going to take forever to get through this if she kept interrupting me. I took a deep breath and counted to ten. "I think some of it is related to COGG, but I…well, I'm not sure about all of it."

"How can I help?"

"I went to my boss's house tonight and saw him with a woman that I recognized from one of Patrick Collier's recent press conferences. I'm trying to figure out if there's a connection between my boss and COGG." I could hardly believe what I was saying. How could Will Friedrichs have been part of COGG? Surely I would have recognized him? Even if he hadn't been part of Collier's inner circle, I would have seen him around the compound.

Then I thought about Collier's tight and shiny forehead, the nearly invisible scars by his ears that pointed to a face lift, the dyed hair. Maybe he didn't look the same back when I was at COGG.

"Do you have a photo?" she asked.

"I have one of him on my phone, with the woman I mentioned. I could text it to you right now."

"Do it," she said.

I did and waited until I heard the ping.

"I can work with this," she said a minute later. "Give me a day or so and I'll see what I can come up with, okay?"

"Okay." I felt an immense relief wash over me. Maybe, just maybe, I'd be able to prove I wasn't as crazy as everyone thought. I wanted something that would convince Pagoa and to Sam, but the person I most wanted to convince?

Myself.

CHAPTER

22

Friday, March 3

I FELT CAGED IN MY apartment, like a tiger pacing its enclosure over and over. The hope I felt talking to Sabrina the night before had evaporated shortly after my paltry breakfast. Every time I made a round in the loft, I walked past the box of my mother's belongings and felt a tingle go up my spine. I didn't want to look through it again. I didn't want to see it all again. Yet somehow I couldn't throw it out. I couldn't bring myself to do much of anything except wait.

My phone rang. The caller ID indicated it was Sabrina. "Hello?"

"I actually don't have much to tell you. It's more something to show you. Could you come by this evening?"

My schedule wasn't exactly packed today. "Sure. What time?"

"Around seven would work."

She gave me her address and I made a note of it in my phone. "Great. See you then," she said.

It was just after two in the afternoon. That left quite a few hours for me to kill between now and then. I felt antsy and anxious. Not sure what else to do, I texted Jesse about Sabrina's phone call.

The woman I told you about, the one who runs the cult watch website. She says she has something to show me.

He texted back right away: *Did she give you any idea of what it was?*

No, but it's got to be something about WILL, *doesn't it? Some connections she's found.*

Not necessarily. Maybe it's about that NURSE *person*

I blew out a breath. He was right.

I'll have to wait and see. I'm meeting her tonight so I won't have to wait long.

Tonight? That's soon.

No time like the present, right?

Have you decided what you're going to do with the Cover Me information?

Not until I understand what's going on with WILL *and* LOIS. *He might not even know that she has anything to do with COGG. She wormed her way into Elgin,* MAYBE *she wormED her way into his life,* TOO.

I wish we knew what her agenda was, what she wanted.

Me, too. Maybe whatever Sabrina Hall has to say will help me figure that out.

I hope she's not trying to get a look at you so she can plaster you all over her website.

That hadn't occurred to me. What if she didn't have anything? What if was just a ruse to get me there and get information from me?

I answered*: There's only one way to find out.*

It was dark by the time I got to Sabrina Hall's home. Dark and cold. There weren't a lot of places to park on the street and I ended up several houses down from the address she'd given me. Unlike Will Friedrichs's neighborhood, it looked like a lot of people parked curbside here, probably because they didn't have five- or six -bedroom houses to store all their crap, which ended up in their garages.

I pulled to the curb and sat for a moment, marshaling my nerves. I felt beyond exposed, but what I'd told Jesse earlier was still true. The only way to find out if Hall any useful information would be to meet her and hear her out. My nerves were raw. I'd spent the day hiding in my apartment, ignoring phone calls from the press and from Sam.

I got out of the car and walked toward her house. A porch light shone on the front door and I could see lights on inside. She was home, as promised. I knocked on the door.

Nothing. No footsteps. No one calling out that they'd be there in a minute. I looked for a bell but didn't see one. I knocked again harder and still got no answer.

I stepped down off the porch and tried to peer in the living room window. I could make out a television and a framed print of the famous Seurat that lives at the Art Institute of Chicago, but nothing else. No movement. No people.

I took out my cell phone and called her. Maybe she'd stepped out for a moment or hadn't heard me knock. I waited as the phone connected and then very clearly—way too clearly—heard the sound of a cell phone ringing around the corner of the house.

I walked toward the sound of the phone. There was a side porch and entrance into the house. That door stood open. My breath caught. This was not the kind of night for a person to leave a door open. This wasn't a humid summer evening where people might leave a side door ajar in the hope of a breeze that would blow the fug out of the house. It was no more than ten degrees. Doors got slammed as fast as possible.

I crept toward the door. The phone stopped ringing and went to voicemail. There was no other noise except for the crunch of my boots on the snow. Three more steps and I was at the porch.

"Sabrina," I called. "Sabrina, are you all right? It's Amanda. Amanda Sinclair. We had an appointment?" I hated the rising, questioning tone of my last statement.

No one answered. A gust of wind picked up and the screen door slammed shut and back open again, the noise as sharp and hard as the crack of a gun. I flinched, then forced myself forward and up the side porch steps.

I smelled the blood before I saw it. Warm, coppery, sweet, and cloying. I gagged. I lifted my head to let the cold air cleanse my nostrils and then looked back into the house. The door led directly into the kitchen. Everything looked so normal—teapot on the stove, two pans on the draining board, dishtowels hanging from drawer handles...

A hand extending into the kitchen on the floor. "Hello?" I called. "Are you okay?"

No response. Not even a twitch from the hand.

I walked in, careful to keep my hands at my sides. "Hello?" I called again.

Nothing.

Three more steps and I could see the rest of the body the hand was attached to. An African-American woman probably only a few years older than me. Her eyes stared up at the ceiling, unblinking, unseeing. Blood crusted her long ringleted hair, leaking from the huge slash in her throat. A slash that looked altogether too much like the one I'd seen on poor Rex Weber's throat.

A sob escaped me. I backed away. For a moment, I had a nearly overpowering urge to run, to get in my car and drive away, to pretend I'd never come to this house, never seen this woman, never smelled her blood. I couldn't, though. Wouldn't. I would do what was right. I would call for help as soon as I could catch my breath, which had started coming in gasps as if I'd run three miles.

Behind the woman, I could see her desk. Three flat -screen monitors, all dark, ranged across it as if she was some kind of one-woman command center. For all I knew, she was. I stepped around her, breathing through my mouth, careful not to step into any of the blood. With my gloved hand, I nudged the mouse. The screens blinked to life. On the middle screen was the cell phone photo of Will Friedrichs and Lois Brower that I'd sent Sabrina the night before. The screen on the left had a series of photos. I squinted. Patrick was in all of them. My mother was in two. I was in one, my arm slung around Marcus on one side and Celeste on the other. They looked like photos you'd use in a brochure, happy smiling people, eating together, working in a garden together, praying together. For all I knew that was exactly what they were. I'd never seen the photos before, although I recognized most of the people in them. Most, but not all. I hit the print command on the keyboard and heard the printer whir to life.

The screen on the right had a different set of photos. These were all of Will, but not all of them were recent. Most of them looked like head shots, the kind of thing that would be put in a company brochure. Each one was a little different. I hit the print commands for those, too.

Once the printer was finished, I gathered all the papers, folded them, and slipped them into my purse. Then I walked back out the door I'd walked in, vomited into the snow, pulled out my phone, and dialed 911.

I sat on the curb in front of the house until the police arrived, shivering. A uniformed officer, an Hispanic male this time, ordered me to stay there while he went into the house. As if I might have had other plans.

He was back outside talking on his radio in about two minutes.

"Sorry about the barf," I said when it seemed like he was in between conversations.

He waved the comment away. "I've seen worse. At least you made it outside."

Ooh. I'd done something right. Good to know. I'd tuck that in my pocket and come back to it to warm myself.

He crouched down next to me. "You touch anything in there?"

I shook my head. No one needed to know about those pictures in my purse. At least, not yet.

"So what brought you here?"

That was a trickier question. How much of that should I divulge? "Ms. Hall ran the Cult Watch website. She wanted to interview me."

His eyes narrowed. "Why? You in a cult?"

"Not now, but back when I was a kid." I tried to say it the way someone else might say that they'd been in marching band.

His eyes narrowed a bit more. "What did you say your name was?"

"Amanda Sinclair."

He rose and walked a few feet away and started talking into his radio again. I had a feeling I was going to be paying another visit to Detective Pagoa. I also had a feeling he wasn't going to be super pleased to see me again.

I was right.

This time, Detective Pagoa came to me. Officer Mendoza didn't leave me on the curb too long, which was good. By the time he shepherded me into the back of the police car, I was shaking with the cold. Even half numb with shock, I was freezing.

The police car wasn't exactly toasty, but it was out of the wind, which helped. Of course, it also smelled like what I now suspected all police cars smelled like in back: fear, sweat, and piss. I almost wished I was on the curb. I tried to breathe through my mouth.

I watched as five police cars, red and blue lights swirling but no sirens, descended onto the block. An ambulance was next. Then several unmarked cars arrived. Around the time Pagoa arrived, the news vans started to show up, too.

"Ms. Sinclair," Pagoa said as he eased himself into the front seat.

"Detective Pagoa," I replied.

He twisted in his seat to look at me. "This doesn't look good."

"I know." What else was there to say?

"Can you explain how you keep stumbling on people whose throats have been slit?" The question wasn't funny, yet somehow a bubble of inappropriate laughter swelled in my throat. I choked it back. Pagoa looked worried.

"I can't," I said. I decided not to explain that two people didn't really constitute a pattern, at least not the kind he was indicating. Two could just be coincidence. A third person? That would constitute a definite pattern. I shuddered at the idea.

"You okay?" he asked.

"Not particularly." Why pretend? I was not okay. I wasn't sure when I would be again. Pagoa might have a professional concern over me finding dead bodies, but I might never be able to close my eyes again without seeing all that blood.

He flipped open his notebook. "Officer Mendoza said you were here because Ms. Hall wanted to interview you? Because of your involvement with COGG as a child?"

It wasn't a complete lie, only a slight smudging of the truth. "She figured out how to get in touch with me after…after our evening out at the COGG compound." After I'd led the police to a spot where bodies weren't buried and damaged my credibility to the point that no one could take me seriously.

"Can you think of any reason someone would want to hurt Ms. Hall?" Pagoa asked.

"I'd never met her before. I talked to her on the phone once, but I don't really know her. I'm not sure what her favorite color is much less who her enemies are." I wondered how long it would take before they found the photo I'd texted her, the one of my boss kissing my dead mom's nurse. Surely they would be checking her phone calls and emails and texts. I wondered if they'd care once they did. "It does seem more than coincidental that she would be killed the same way as the homeless guy who had appointed himself my personal bodyguard and that it would happen as Patrick Collier was getting out of jail, what with her running a cult news website."

"As coincidental as you being the person to find both bodies?" He cocked his head and waited for me to answer.

"I'm not so sure that's coincidental." It wasn't something I'd thought through all the way, but a few ideas had begun chasing around in my skull while I'd sat on the curb freezing my fanny off and waiting for the cops.

Pagoa went very still. "Is there something you'd like to tell me? Something about your involvement in these deaths?"

I snorted. "Seriously, dude, you think I'm going to confess something? Get real."

He shrugged. "A man can hope."

"Listen to me. Someone doesn't want me talking about COGG. Someone wants me to know I'm not safe. Timing these murders so I'm the one who finds the bodies is getting that message through loud and clear." I wrapped my arms tighter around myself to stop the shaking that had begun again.

"And yet, here you are, still talking," he said.

291

I leaned forward. "I'm a little stubborn."

He stared at me for a second and then he laughed. It was a rich booming sound that filled the car. "That you are." His face became suddenly serious. "Who knew you were coming here tonight?"

That stopped me short. "Nobody knew. Or at least, not anybody connected to COGG."

"Makes it kind of difficult for them to murder her right before you got here then, doesn't it?" Pagoa cocked his head to one side. At least he was listening.

The only person who knew I was going to Sabrina Hall's tonight was Jesse. Jesse, who also worked for Will Friedrichs. Will Friedrichs, who I'd seen kissing Lois Brower. Lois Brower, who I'd seen in the background at Patrick Collier's press conference and who had also been a nurse at the locked mental ward where I was now fairly certain my mother had been murdered.

What if Jesse had taken it upon himself to tell Will about the falsified test results? And what if Lois Brower had been there to overhear?

Jesse was there when I found Rex Weber dead in the doorway. Jesse knew I was going to talk to Sabrina Hall. Jesse could have easily poisoned my coffee.

My head spun.

All that interest in me. The flirting, the checking in. Had it all been about keeping an eye on me?

"What if I told you there might be a connection between COGG and the place I work?" I asked. Pagoa already thought I was crazy, it wouldn't hurt to bounce my crazy idea off him.

His brow creased. "The cosmetics place? Why would they have a connection there?"

"Exactly." I nodded.

"Ms. Sinclair, you're confusing me." He shook his head. "I should say, confusing me more."

"I'm not sure what's going on, either, but I know there's some kind of connection. There has to be."

CHAPTER
23

A VAN IDLED AT THE sidewalk in front of my apartment. I slowed my walk. It wasn't a black SUV, shiny and menacing, like the one that had nearly run me down coming out of my parking garage or the ones I'd seen cruising the neighborhood. It was brown and dented and the lower panels were crusted with dirty snow.

The back door slid open and suddenly he was standing before me on the sidewalk. Patrick Collier in the flesh.

"Amanda," he said, opening his arms.

I didn't walk into them, although somewhere in my treacherous soul I wanted to. I remembered what it felt like to be in Patrick's embrace both physically and emotionally. I remembered what it was like to be so sure of everything. I remembered the peace and tranquility that had lived in my very core when I had sat at his feet at COGG, listening to him talk about connection to the land and to each other and to God.

Unfortunately, I also remembered it was all a lie.

"What do you want?" I asked him.

"To talk," he said. "It's been a long time."

It had. The last time I'd seen Patrick was the glimpse I'd had of him with his head thrown back in ecstasy as my mother had moved and swayed over him. He'd aged since then. Apparently even white -collar prisons weren't good for your health. His hair was streaked with gray. The coat he wore hung from his shoulders, and his legs were sticks inside his jeans. He held a cane in one hand, and his face was too thin. When I'd known Patrick, he'd been a man of vigor. His arms had been swollen with muscles from working in the fields, his shoulders broad. His skin had been tan even in the winter from the hours he spent outside.

This was a pale ghost of the Patrick I'd known. He couldn't offer me a tenth of what the old Patrick had given me.

"I can't imagine that we have anything to say to each other at this point, Patrick." I started to skirt around him, but he moved into my path.

"Amanda, please..."

I didn't like the pleading tone in his voice. I didn't like his uncertainty. The only Patrick I wanted was the one full of confidence, the one that had made me feel safe. "Please what, Patrick? Please don't tell where you buried Marcus? Too late for that now, isn't it? I already told, but you can rest easy. Someone moved him."

He dropped his head. "Amanda, I've spent the past ten years in prison. Isn't that enough?"

"Oh, poor Patrick. He had to go white -collar prison for financial misconduct. Guess what, Patrick? My mother was locked up for murder. She never got out and now she never will." I walked toward him now, so he'd have to see my eyes. "You should have been in prison for murder, too, Patrick. For Marcus."

His lips tightened. "Marcus was a tragedy, but not a murder, Amanda. You know that. It was…an accident."

"An accident? The good members of COGG let him die as his own body poisoned itself. They did nothing. Actually, that's not true—they punished him. They punished him for being ill and they did it on your orders, Patrick. But maybe you wouldn't have been sent to prison for it. Maybe you would have found a way to weasel out of it. I guess I'm glad they got you for mishandling the money. At least you were punished for something."

"For something I didn't do." He clenched his jaw.

"Oh, blah blah. You're innocent, huh? Like all those other people in prison? Sure you are." I waved him away.

"Amanda, listen to me. I am innocent of those charges." He leaned on the cane more heavily, as if he was suddenly exhausted. Maybe prison had done more

296

than age him. "Someone moved money around without my knowledge."

"Moved it where?" I stopped, faced him, and planted my fists on my hips.

He shook his head. "I don't know. I never figured it out. It wasn't me, though."

I stared into his eyes. Could he be telling the truth? If he was, did it matter? "Why should I care, Patrick?"

His eyes narrowed as if he was getting frustrated. "Because whoever did it is still out there and might be worried that I could figure out who they are now that I'm out."

I took a step back. That hadn't occurred to me. The idea that Patrick could really be innocent of financial misconduct hadn't really been part of my calculations. "So?"

"So they might be trying to make sure all of us at COGG are distracted. What better distraction than trying to defend ourselves against murder charges?" He took a limping step toward me.

I shook my head. "There can't be murder charges without Marcus's body, Patrick. Even if they found his body after all this time, they might not be able to make a case against you or anybody at COGG."

"But they might. At the very least, it would make sure we were focused elsewhere for a while," he said.

"What good would that do? It wouldn't distract you forever." I didn't like how what he was saying was feeding into my paranoia.

"Maybe they don't need forever. Maybe they just need a little while. The financial world moves fast these days, Amanda." He took another step toward me.

I retreated a step. "I don't believe you. I think you're trying to distract me."

He reached out his hand. "I'm not, Amanda. I'm trying to keep you focused. I think it's possible that your mother was murdered."

The delicious irony of the one person who believed me about my mother's death also being the person I held most responsible for her mental breakdown was not lost on me. Nor was the horror of having to do what I was going to do next. I couldn't help myself. I started to laugh. Softly at first, but the hysteria took over and soon I was shaking with deep down belly laughs.

"Amanda, are you all right?" Patrick asked.

I gasped in some air and said, "Patrick, I think you ought to come upstairs with me. There are some photos I need you to look at."

Patrick Collier was in my apartment. The devil was in my sanctuary. I gestured to my dining room table for him to sit. "Don't get too comfortable, though."

He shot me a look but sat. I got the printouts I'd made from Sabrina Hall's computers and laid them out in front of him. "Do you recognize any of these people?"

He looked over them. "Of course I do. That's Noel Cummings, Armando Tucker, and Monique

Rodriguez." He pulled one piece of paper from the group and pointed to another figure. "That's Adrian Horton."

I shoved the photo of Will and Lois embracing across to him. "How about them?"

His brow furrowed. "Her. I've seen her before."

"Is she a COGG member?"

He shrugged. "She's new."

"What about the guy?" I pressed.

He looked and shook his head. "I don't think so."

"Look again."

"Amanda..."

"I'm serious. Look harder." I placed the photos from COGG next to the photo of Will Friedrichs. "Could anyone in these pictures be this guy? I mean, with plastic surgery and hair dye."

Patrick opened his mouth, appearing to get ready to protest, but then abruptly snapped his mouth shut. He leaned forward, pulling one of the COGG photos out of the pile. He set it next to the photo of Will. "Look at the ears," he said.

I leaned over him. "I'm not sure what I'm supposed to notice about the ears."

"The left one. In both pictures. His left." He looked up at me with a smirk and said, "Look closely."

I rolled my eyes, but I did. It took me a few seconds, but I finally saw it. There was a notch in the left ear of both men. I sat down hard. "Hard to fake an ear, I guess."

"Or he didn't think anyone would notice."

"Who is he? I don't recognize him in the COGG photos."

Patrick leaned back. "His name was Walt Freeman. He didn't interact much with the kids. Not really a kid person. Not really a people person, to be honest, but man was he good with the books."

"Are you sure it's him in this other photo, too?"

Patrick shook his head. "No. There could be thousands of men in the world with a notch in their ear from being bitten by a dog as a child. I just don't think there would be thousands of them who would be kissing a woman who started visiting me in prison a month ago."

"So you do recognize Lois?"

He squinted. "That wasn't the name she used, but that woman there, yes." He put his finger on Lois's face.

"Why didn't you say something when I first showed it to you?" I sat down. Could I trust this man? I had once and it had destroyed my family.

"Allow me a moment or two of wishful thinking, Amanda. Or maybe it's hubris. I thought it was me she was interested in." He pushed her photo away.

I took a moment to allow that to sink in. I had it. I had a connection between COGG and Bellefountaine. I still didn't know what it all meant, but it was there. The cops could figure out from here. The only problem was how to get the cops to listen. They weren't exactly going to call out the cavalry on my say -so. Would they listen to Patrick? Possibly. Patrick and me together might make more of a convincing presentation. The more people I had on my side and the more information I had, the more convinced the Pagoa would be.

I picked up my phone and dialed. Sam answered on the second ring. "Amanda, thank God. I've been so worried."

"Can you come over? There's someone I think you should meet."

Sam stood in the hallway that led into the rest of the apartment and looked from Patrick Collier to me and back again. I hadn't had to introduce them. Sam knew the man sitting at my dining room table instantly. "I don't understand," he said.

I didn't fully, either. "Look at these." I handed him the stack of photos that we'd spread out on the table.

"That's Lois Brower. The CNA from Elgin." He tapped the photo with his finger. "Who is she with?"

"My boss. Will Friedrichs." I watched for his reaction. Would he question my sanity again? Ask if I was really sure I had seen what I thought I'd seen? Surely not with a photograph in front of him.

Sam raised his head slowly. "She's dating your boss?"

I blew out a breath. "I'm not entirely sure I'd call it dating, but clearly there's a relationship there."

Sam turned toward Patrick now. "And one with you as well?"

Patrick nodded. "A new recruit to COGG. Very eager." He pressed his lips together into a tight line. I wondered exactly how eager Lois Brower had been. As eager as my mother? My hands curled into fists at my side, but I tried to focus on the reason I'd let this man into my apartment.

"Tell him about Will Friedrichs," I said to Patrick, nodding at Sam.

"I think," Patrick said, "I think this man is Walt Freeman."

Sam's eyes narrowed. "And if he is?"

Patrick shrugged. "If he is, he's the man most likely to have taken the money I was accused of mishandling."

"So what do we do about all this?" Sam asked.

We all stared at each other for a moment and then I said, "We set a trap."

I texted Jesse.

Found more information on WILL'S *involvement with COGG. A little more and I think I will be able to get* THE *police to listen to me again.*

It didn't take long to get a response.

Great! What did you find?

I texted back: *Too complicated. Will explain later.*

"Now what?" Sam asked.

"Now we wait."

We ordered pizza. As long as I focused on simply eating and drinking, the total surreal nature of the

302

situation couldn't get to me. It was hard, though. I was sitting around my living room with the man who destroyed my family and my dead mother's shrink, waiting for my boss to call and threaten me.

It took nearly two hours. Not long to most people, I supposed. It felt like an eternity to me.

When my phone rang, all three of us jumped. I looked at the caller ID. "It's him," I said. The first piece of my theory was confirmed. Jesse was the snake in the grass, the worm in my apple, the traitor. He'd been the only one who knew I was going to meet Sabrina Hall. He'd been the only one outside my apartment who knew I had linked our boss with COGG. He'd probably been the one to falsify the data in the first place. He certainly had access to everything he needed to do it.

The phone rang again.

"You're sure you want to do this?" Sam asked.

I nodded and slid my finger to pick up the call. "Hello."

"Hello, Amanda. Will Friedrichs. I was hoping we could talk. Ollie tells me that you think you found something disturbing about the Cover Me data." His voice was steady and deep. If anything about this situation was making him tense, it wasn't showing in his voice.

"I did. It's bad, Will. Really bad. Ollie didn't believe me, though. No one in the lab did. They all think..." I let my words drift off.

"I know what they think, Amanda. You must admit, it's a possibility," he said. "You're sure about what you found? You don't think you're maybe seeing shadows where there aren't any?"

His voice was so concerned, so reasonable. Part of me still wanted to believe that he was the man I'd thought he'd been. A good boss who cared about his employees and his company. "I don't think so, Will. I think this is real."

There was a pause, a breath. "Ollie mentioned some papers you wanted to show me. Do you still have them?"

"I do."

"Let's meet. You can show me what you found and I'll be the judge of whether or not we need to look deeper. Cover Me is simply too important not to explore possible problems."

My heart sped up. This was exactly what I'd wanted. A face -to -face confrontation. "Where? When?"

"Can you come back to the lab tonight?"

I looked at the clock. It was already ten o'clock. "Tonight?"

"Yes. I'll make sure the security guard knows to let you in. Can you be there in an hour?"

"Absolutely," I said. "Thank you, Will."

"The pleasure is mine, Amanda."

We hung up.

"He's not wasting any time, is he?" Patrick said.

"And you really think it was Jesse who lit the fire beneath him?" Sam asked.

"Yes and yes," I said, feeling slightly sick when I remembered the kisses I'd shared with Jesse on the street. Did he know we'd never make it to my apartment? Or had Rex's dead body been a surprise to him, too? Would he have actually taken his duties as a corporate spy so far that he would have slept with me?

I didn't want to know the answers to any of those questions. I'd trusted him. I'd pitied him a little. Now I wondered how much he had laughed at me behind my back.

CHAPTER

24

FIFTY MINUTES LATER, I KNOCKED at the door to Bellefountaine. I no longer had a key to let myself in and had to wait while the security guard, a man named Gary who looked like he might have been too skinny to qualify as a candidate for the police academy, let me in. As I walked through the door, I let my hand linger over the latch, placing a piece of tape that I hoped would keep the door from locking behind me.

Sam and Patrick waited a block and a half away and would need a way in, too, after all.

"Mr. Friedrichs is waiting for you in the rooftop garden," Gary informed me.

"Seriously? It's like ten degrees outside!" I hadn't anticipated that. I'd expected us to meet in his office or possibly the conference room.

Gary shrugged. "He said he needed the fresh air and that you might, too." He gave me a little side-eye.

I bet Gary knew that I'd been escorted out of here by one of his compatriots not twelve hours ago. I nodded and got into the elevator. As I rode, I quickly texted Sam: *Rooftop garden. Tricky to get to.*

He texted back: *We'll figure it out.*

I shoved the phone back in my pocket as the doors opened. Garden was probably a glorification of what was happening on Bellefountaine's roof. I knew Will had plans for it, but at the moment it was mostly open space with some benches and a few planters. In the summer, it was actually a nice place to have lunch. Tonight, however, it was desolate and bone-achingly cold. Will stood over by one of the portable heaters that had been set up to try to extend the usefulness of the area. I couldn't imagine that its heat was anywhere near enough to combat the cold and the wind.

"Amanda, thank you for meeting me." He turned to face me.

"No, thank you. I wasn't sure what I should do with this information. It's too important to ignore." I crossed the deck area to join him.

"May I see it?" he asked.

I nodded and pulled the papers out of my jacket and handed them to him. He switched on the flashlight app of his cell phone and began reading. After he got to the last page, he said. "Very thorough, Amanda. I imagine you were quite upset by these findings."

"I was." I'd hoped he would be, too. I wasn't so sure anymore.

"Do you have any idea who might be responsible for the falsification?" he asked, as if he was inquiring if I knew when the next Bulls game was.

"I'm pretty sure it's Jesse. He's the one who's been reporting to you about me, isn't he?" I asked, trying to keep my voice calm and matter-of-fact.

Will's eyes widened fractionally for a moment, then his expression returned to its usual calm demeanor. "You figured that out, did you?"

"I wasn't one hundred percent sure, but it was the only reasonable answer." A heartbreaking answer, but the only reasonable one. Had his interest in me always been feigned? Or had Will read the situation and decided to use it to his advantage? I'd probably never know.

Will folded the papers and put them in his own pocket. "So what are we going to do with you, Miss Amanda?"

"Give me a raise for keeping a harmful product off the market?" I suggested.

He laughed. "I don't think so. Cover Me will never make it to market anyway. The FDA will rerun some of those tests and find exactly what you've found."

"That's the part I don't get. We all know they'd find out. Why bother with falsifying the data?" I asked.

"I don't need Cover Me to get to market. I need it to look like it will get to market until we're bought out. I'll have all that lovely money and it won't be my fault that an unscrupulous employee was responsible for the scientific misconduct." He smiled. "No harm, no foul."

"Which employee are you going to hang it on?" I asked. Poor Jesse. He probably never realized that he was going to be double-crossed.

"Why, you, of course. You're the perfect patsy, Amanda," Will said. "At least, you've made yourself into one."

I took a step backward. That was not the answer I'd anticipated. "Me? How?"

"Simple. You were upset. Possibly even deranged. You've done an excellent job of making yourself seem like a dangerous loose cannon these past weeks. I barely needed to do anything at all. But the plan has shifted thanks to your behavior. Originally we were simply going to kill you and make it look like COGG was responsible. You know your connection with COGG was how you got this job in the first place, don't you?" He cocked his head to one side.

My throat tightened. "What?"

"Oh, I kept my eye on you over the years. You and your brother. Then when you went into the sciences in college, I was overjoyed. It was a simple matter to recruit you when you graduated. Did you really think lab techs made the kind of salary you make?" He laughed again, like he'd made a witty joke.

I was speechless.

"I had a feeling you'd come in handy, and I was right," he continued. "When you started talking about the numbers not looking right in the Cover Me product tests, I knew it was time to use your connection to COGG in my favor. And really it let me kill two birds with one stone. I could hide the Cover Me results and discredit COGG at the same time. They'll be too busy denying that they had anything to do with your death to look for the money I embezzled all those years ago."

My head spun. "My what?"

"Your death," he said it slowly as if I might be a bit dim. "You won't be leaving the roof the same way you came up tonight."

I backed away. "You can't. You won't."

"It's okay. I'll help," a woman's voice said behind me.

I turned. Lois Brower. "You? You would kill for him?"

She shrugged. "I already have." She tilted her head to one side and her silky blonde hair fell to one side.

My heart clenched. "My mother."

She nodded. "It wasn't difficult. Once I slipped her all that Lorazepam, she was practically comatose. Two quick slices. I don't think she felt anything, if that makes you feel any better."

I turned back to Will. "Rex? The homeless guy by my apartment?"

"That wasn't Lois specifically—that was someone else—but yes. He'd been getting a little too good at watching out for you. It seemed prudent to get him out of the way," Will confirmed.

"Sabrina Hall?"

Lois rolled her eyes. "Oh, that one. So holier - than -thou with that awful website. That was actually a pleasure."

I started backing my way toward the door. "I won't let you do this. I'm not alone."

Will laughed. "You mean Patrick?" He hit a few buttons on his phone and Gary came through the door pushing Patrick ahead of him. "It really was nice of you to bring him. Now it can be the two of you going off the roof as you struggled with each other. Really, Amanda, it's like you're on my side."

Oh, God. He had Patrick, but what about Sam? Where was Sam?

Gary pushed Patrick closer to the edge of the roof. I wasn't going to stand there and be pushed over the edge, though. I couldn't fight Gary and Lois and Patrick, but I could get away. I could get help. I turned and ran. Lois was on me in a second. She grabbed me by the hair and yanked me backwards.

For a second, I was paralyzed. The last time someone had done that to me had been the night my mother killed Jackson. I'd been fleeing down the stairs to let in the police who were banging on the door. This time, there was no one there to help. No police officers waited on the other side of a door, ready to save me and the brother I still had left. The only person who could save me was me.

Lois was taller than me and had a longer reach, but I had desperation on my side. I went down but tangled my legs in hers and brought her down with me.

I heard a shout from where Patrick had been and hoped it meant he was fighting back, too. I pulled back my arm and punched Lois as hard as I could in the solar plexus. I heard the air leave her lungs in a whoosh. I didn't wait to see if she could still move. I leapt up and ran toward the door to the rooftop.

I tried to shove the heavy door shut behind me, but it wouldn't close any faster than its spring would allow. Instead I ran, racing down the steps in the half - light. I came around the corner and on the landing below me saw former janitor Simon Palmer putting his phone back in his pocket. Will must have called him to warn him I was coming. He was bigger than me and undoubtedly stronger. When he spotted me, a smile spread across his face, but it wasn't a pleasant one. I had to get past him. I had to get out of here and get help. But how? He started toward me, left foot up on the first step. I crouched low and leapt down the short flight of stairs, landing on Palmer and knocking him back against the wall. His head hit the concrete blocks with a crack. We slid down the wall, his body breaking my fall. Well, not entirely. My knee hit the ground and pain traveled up my leg like a strike of lightning. Beneath me, Palmer's eyes didn't open. He was still breathing, but I had no idea how badly I might have hurt him.

A whimper escaped me and bile rose in my throat. I couldn't stop to see if he would wake up, though. Out. Out. Out. It was all I could think. Above me I heard the door from the roof creak open and light steps start down the stairs. Lois. I limped down the next set of stairs and through the door into building. No way could I run. My knee was barely supporting my weight. Each step was another jab of pain from my knee to my hip. I needed a place to hide.

I was on the third floor of the lab side of the Bellefountaine building. Not my floor, but it was laid out the same, which was good because it was difficult to make out much in the dim light and I didn't dare turn on the lights. I tried the door to the first lab, but it was locked. So was the second. I tried to move faster, dragging my injured leg behind me. I slipped into the alcove that held the staff kitchen as I heard the heavy door opening again at the end of the hall.

"Amanda," Lois Brower's voice echoed down the hall. "Don't make this harder than it has to be. Come out now."

I pressed myself back against the wall, hoping she'd go past me. I could hear her trying the knobs of each of the lab doors. I felt around me on the counters for anything I might use as a weapon. Coffee cups. Paper plates. Napkins. Finally, a knife. A big serrated knife with a forked tip they probably used to slice bagels. I gripped it tight in my hand, praying I wouldn't need to use it.

"Amanda, really," Lois said from way too close to where I cowered in the kitchen. "Don't be silly. Let's talk."

I tried to still my ragged breathing, tried not to sob out loud. My knee continued to throb, pressing now against the fabric of my jeans, swelling fast. Tentatively, I put my weight on it only to have pain burst in my brain like a white hot light as it nearly give way beneath me. I wouldn't be running. It had to be here that I stood my ground.

Lights began to snap on in the hallway. The darkness had been my friend. I could cower in the shadows hoping she wouldn't see me as she passed by. The light would make that impossible. I put my hands, knife still clutched in one, behind my back.

Then she was there, snapping on the light to the kitchen. "There you are," she said. She smiled and then pointed a gun at me.

For a moment, my entire life narrowed down to that one black hole at the end of the gun. Nothing else existed.

"Let's go back upstairs, shall we?" She motioned with the gun toward the entrance into the kitchen.

"I hurt my knee," I said. "I'm not sure I can walk."

"Let's give it a try." Her sickly sweet tone turned my stomach.

I inched along the wall using it for balance, still keeping my hands behind my back.

"A little faster, please," she said.

"I need help." I kept my pace slow. Then I was at the kitchen entrance and she was only a few feet away from me.

Her stance relaxed. She thought I wasn't a threat.

Maybe I wasn't, but I had to try to be one. It was now or never. If I went back up to that roof, it would be over. I lunged forward, swinging the knife in front of me and stuck it into her thigh.

She fell backward, shrieking. The gun went off, bullet whizzing by my head so close I felt the heat of it.

"You bitch," she screamed. "You stupid little bitch!"

"That," I said, "was for my mother."

I lurched to my feet and beganto stagger back to the stairs, snapping lights off as I went. If I could get downstairs. If I could get out of the building.

The gun went off again. I heard it hit the steel door.

I made it to the stairs.

I flung open the door and ran directly into the broad chest of Detective Pagoa.

"So tell me again how you got there?" I asked Detective Pagoa. I pulled the blanket someone had wrapped around my shoulders closer, not that it helped. I was shaking, but it wasn't with cold.

"Dr. Ashmore called me," he said, sounding like he might be running low on patience.

Sam put his arm around me. "I called when I saw the security guard catch Patrick. I knew we were in over our heads."

"And you were right there, why?" I asked Pagoa.

"Well, let me put it to you this way. Dead bodies were popping up wherever you were. I thought it was prudent to keep track of your comings and goings." He scratched his chin. "Turned out I was right. Not for the reasons I thought, but that's okay."

"You thought I was killing those people." It seemed completely unreal to me.

"It did seem like a reasonable conclusion. You did appear to be more than a little…unhinged." He didn't look apologetic at all as he said it.

I wasn't terribly happy for the reason he'd been there, but he was right. The end result had been a good one. I might have gotten away from Lois, but there was no guarantee I would have made it out of Bellefountaine alive.

I curled my body into Sam's and felt the shaking in my limbs start to slow.

EPILOGUE

BELLEFOUNTAINE ENDED UP CLOSING ITS doors. Overnight, the company became the pariah of the cosmetics industry. We all lost our jobs. Melinda and Anna don't speak to me. I hear from Sara now and again. Andre Schmidt admitted that the bodies of COGG members who had died under questionable circumstances had been moved from the location I'd known about to another spot. He'd always suspected that I might eventually tell the world about Marcus. That was pure dumb luck for Will Friedrichs (or Walt Freeman, whatever you want to call him). Andre hadn't known about Will or his plans and had no idea how well he was playing into his hand. Of course, none of us did. Will actually said in an interview that he'd been thrilled that I looked so erratic and crazy and had pissed off the police so thoroughly. Until that last night, I could hardly have been more helpful to him if he'd given me a To Do list.

Marcus got a decent burial, as will Rex Weber, the poor homeless man who took a shine to me after I gave him a measly pair of gloves. I couldn't bear to have either of them out at Mount Olive buried with dozens of others by the state. They were able to identify Marcus eventually. That was actually his name. Marcus Moore. His mother died of an overdose not too long before I met him at the bus station in downtown Chicago. His father was in prison at that time. He's out now, but couldn't afford to claim Marcus's body. And Rex Weber had done a pretty good job of alienating his family. Mental illness and drug addiction are an unpleasant combination. They didn't want to claim him. I get it, but I guess it's a little bit like Mom—I can't quite walk away. The burials are expensive, but I don't think I could lay all that had happened to rest without laying them to rest as well.

Will is in jail awaiting prosecution on multiple homicide charges as well as fraud. Lois Brower is also in jail. Irritatingly, she actually looks really good in orange; the newspapers like to run her photo whenever she has a hearing. Simon Palmer somehow made it out of the lab that night and disappeared into the night. I still look over my shoulder for him. That nasty smile he gave me as I came down the stairs occasionally plays a role in my nightmares.

Patrick is back in jail as well. He says knew it was a possibility when he approached me. Marcus's death was most certainly due to negligence. His negligence. He says he didn't think he could live with letting me be cast in the same kind of crazy light as my mother. I think he might actually have loved her. He gets a funny look in his eyes whenever he talks about her. I visit him every other week, but then, a lot of people visit Patrick. He has a way of drawing people to him, even from behind bars.

No charges were filed against Jesse. He really hadn't done anything illegal. It's not against the law to tell your boss what your crazy coworker is doing. It's not even against the law to cozy up to her for more information. I'm fairly certain he's the one who unlatched the minus eighty freezer that night, but even if I could prove it, it still wouldn't rise to something prosecutable. It might get him fired, but we were all out of jobs anyway.

Me? Well, things seem to be working out. Losing my job at Bellefountaine wasn't great, but I've had a few interviews and nobody thinks I'm crazy anymore. Nobody.

Not my father or my brother.

Not Detective Pagoa.

Not Sam.

Especially not Sam.

Especially not me.

THE END

ABOUT THE AUTHOR

Eileen Rendahl is the national-bestselling and award-winning author of the Messenger series and four Chick Lit novels. Her alter ego, Eileen Carr, writes romantic suspense.

Both Eileens were born in Dayton, Ohio. She moved when she was four and only remembers that she was born across the street from Baskin-Robbins. Eileen remembers anything that has to do with ice cream. Or chocolate. Or champagne.

She has had many jobs and lived in many cities and feels unbelievably lucky to be where she is now and to be doing what she's doing.

www.eileenrendahl.com

Read a Preview
of
Veiled Intentions

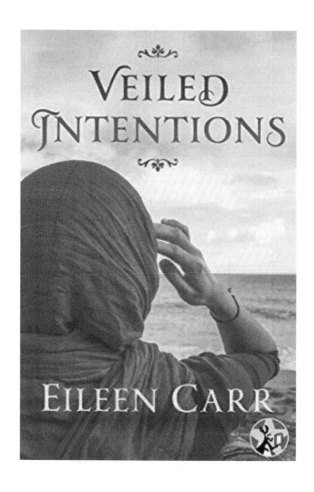

ABOUT THE BOOK

When a young Muslim high school student is accused of a crime she didn't commit, her school counselor gets involved to clear her record in this ripped-from-the-headlines romantic thriller from the author of *Vanished in the Night*.

When Lily Simon finds cops in the lobby of the high school where she's a guidance counselor, she's not surprised: cops and adolescents go together like sex, drugs, and rock 'n' roll. But when the cops take Jamila, a Muslim student, into custody for a crime she didn't commit, Lily's high school becomes a powder keg.

Police think Jamila is responsible for a hit and run, and since she's not talking, they have no choice but to keep her as the main suspect. And since the victim—a young soldier recently returned from Afghanistan—is lying unconscious in the hospital, the whole town is taking sides on whether or not Jamila's arrest is religious persecution. Determined to find the truth, Lily teams up with a reporter to uncover what really happened the night of the hit and run. But Lily didn't expect to find such a tangled web...

Each time a man stands up for an ideal, or acts to improve the lot of others, or strikes out against injustice, he sends forth a tiny ripple of hope, and crossing each other from a million different centers of energy and daring, those ripples build a current which can sweep down the mightiest walls of oppression and resistance.

—Robert F. Kennedy

CHAPTER ONE

October 11
9:15 A.M.
Yolo County Courthouse
725 Court Street
Woodland, California

LILY SIMON SHIFTED ON THE SEAT, trying to find a comfortable spot. There wasn't one. The hard chair wasn't the only thing that was going to make this a grueling day. Reliving everything would suck. Not as much as the burn treatments on her hands. Not as much as having her world turned upside down. Not as much as being more alone than she had ever felt in her life. But it would still suck. She'd been over it a million times. With the cops. With the lawyers. With the school officials. With the press. This was the last time, though. This was the time that would stick a stake in its heart and kill it dead.

At least, that's what she kept telling herself.

District Attorney Max Fitzsimmons rose to his feet. "Objection, Your Honor. Ms. Simon was a witness for the prosecution. Defense had an opportunity to cross-examine her at that time." He was a nice-looking guy. Tall and dark with a mop of blond hair that was just messy enough to be adorable.

"Your Honor." Karen Longmont, attorney for the defense broke in before Judge Kezerian had a chance to even open his mouth. "My questions exceed the issues brought up by the prosecution. It would have been inappropriate to ask them at that time."

"Inappropriate?" Fitzsimmons burst out. "This is inappropriate. It's grandstanding. Pure and simple, Your Honor."

Judge Kezerian banged his gavel and glared at both the attorneys. "I appreciate that feelings are running high regarding this case, but the two of you need to stay calm."

He let a few seconds pass while everyone simmered down, then said, "I've ruled on this. I take note of your continued objection, Mr. Fitzsimmons, but it is what it is."

Longmont turned to look at Lily. Lily took a deep breath and readied herself. She had sworn to tell the truth, the whole truth, and nothing but the truth. It had taken her a ridiculously long time to figure out what the truth was. She had no idea how she was going to explain it to the twelve people sitting in the jury box or to the child sitting at the defense table. She glanced in that direction for a moment. That's all it took to break her heart.

Longmont stood up from behind her table and walked toward Lily, on the witness stand. She looked good. A couple of the times that Lily had met with her preparing for today, she had looked tired. Not today. Today she looked cool and calm in a suit with a belted blue jacket and a black skirt that hit right at the knee. Professional, but approachable. Pretty, but not quite TV pretty. "Hello, Ms. Simon. How are you today?"

"Fine, thanks." Lily's voice cracked on "Fine," her mouth suddenly dry. It had actually been a while since she'd felt fine, but she figured that wasn't the whole truth they'd made her swear to tell. She took a sip of water, surprised that her hands weren't shaking. She felt like she was vibrating inside and that everything—her hair, her hands, her feet—should be flying in the air.

"Can you begin by telling us about the events of January twenty-seventh of this year?" Longmont asked.

Lily took a deep breath and let it out slowly, centering herself, readying herself, trying to focus. It felt like it had begun a century ago, but it was less than a year. She closed her eyes and put herself back on January 27. It was a Friday. It had been cold and foggy all week and she was looking forward to ending up on her couch with a glass of red wine by the end of the night. Then she'd walked into the school office and seen the cops.

January 27
1:45 P.M.
Darby High School
2710 11th Street
Darby, California

"Why are there cops in the office?" Lily whispered to Callie Monroe. Cops weren't unheard of in the office of Darby High School. Things happen when teenagers are around. Especially when those teenagers have access to vehicles. Hence, cops in the office on occasion, mainly to make reports so insurance claims could be filed about parking lot fender benders. Usually, however, Lily knew about it before it came to cops hanging out in the office. "Did someone not come through this morning's combat driving unscathed?"

Not sure. They want to talk to Jamila Khaury. She's in PE. I paged her." Callie's lips barely moved as she answered. She didn't pause in her typing.

"Jamila? Are you sure?"

Callie nodded.

Darby was a nice town, a family town, a university town, but that didn't mean kids didn't get into trouble. There were drugs and alcohol, like there were at any high school. There was vandalism and petty theft. There were kids whose home lives weren't perfect. There were kids who acted out for all the millions of reasons that teenagers had been acting out and rebelling possibly back to the time when they had to use stone tools to vandalize things. Lily knew most of those kids by sight and definitely knew all of them by name and reputation. It was her job.

But Jamila was not one of those kids. Lily knew her name because it showed up on the honor roll and lists of students to thank for participating in charity events.

"I have no idea." Callie looked up briefly and then went back to the papers in front of her on the desk. "They didn't offer up much information."

Lily plastered on her best pleasant professional smile and walked over to the two officers sitting in the waiting area under a bulletin board crammed with flyers about school clubs, concerts, and plays. Usually those seats held fidgety, sulky teenagers. These men didn't fidget. There wasn't a single twitch between them. "Can I help you?"

Both officers were men. Both bristled with radios and handcuffs and, of course, guns. The dark-haired cop leaned to look around Lily. "She's coming, right?" he asked Callie. "Ms. Khaury? She's on her way?"

Callie nodded without looking up. "Mmm-hmm."

The cop looked back at Lily. Great eye contact. Completely polite. Totally unhelpful. His face stayed blank and neutral. "We're fine. Thanks for asking."

"Should I call Jamila's parents?" If Jamila was really in trouble, the police would want her parents involved. She was a junior and she wasn't eighteen yet. Or at least Lily didn't think so. Jamila was still a minor, if just barely.

The two officers glanced at each other. The dark-haired one again spoke for them both. "I don't think that's necessary right now."

"What exactly does that mean? Will it be necessary soon? Is it not necessary at all?" Cryptic much? What was with the stonewalling? Lily was generally on the same side as the cops, when sides needed to be taken.

The officers exchanged a look with each other. The dark-haired one answered again. "We need to speak with Ms. Khaury."

Lily racked her brain for another way to ask what the heck was going on. Before she could figure out a way to formulate the question, Jamila came into the office.

She was slightly out of breath and her face shone with exertion. She was wearing a baggy DHS T-shirt and the regulation DHS basketball shorts and was clutching her backpack to her chest. It was not the most flattering of outfits and most girls would have looked dumpy.

Not Jamila. Jamila still looked gorgeous. Jamila was the kind of girl who made conversation stop just walking by. She was all that and a bag of chips with her mass of dark curling her hair, her café au lait skin, and her huge dark brown eyes. She didn't dress provocatively. Quite the opposite. Most of the kids were pushing the envelope, trying to figure out where the boundaries were. The culture today was all about showing more skin, looking sexy, being provocative.

But Jamila didn't push that envelope. Jamila never dressed inappropriately or was truant or failed her classes or was drunk at an assembly or gave her boyfriends blow jobs behind the oleander bushes by the back fence. At least, not as far as Lily knew.

"Someone paged me?" Jamila looked from Lily to Callie to the two police officers. She dropped her gaze to the ground, away from the cops.

Callie stood up. "I did, Jamila. These officers wanted to talk to you about something."

The two police officers stood up. Again they exchanged a glance and the dark-haired one spoke. "Ms. Khaury, were you over at the South Market Shopping Center on Ridge Line and Banks Street last night around ten P.M.?"

Jamila looked at Lily as if Lily might know the answer. Maybe Jamila had witnessed something? Seen something and not reported it? "Were you there, Jamila?"

Jamila looked at the floor a few inches away from the officers' feet and shook her head no.

The dark-haired officer's lips tightened. "Do you drive a black SUV bearing California license plate 3DHE789?"

This time, Jamila nodded, her gaze still trained on the floor.

Another glance between the two officers and then the light-haired one said, "Jamila Khaury, you are under arrest for leaving the scene of an accident."

Jamila's head shot up. She looked over at Lily, her eyes wide. "What? What are they saying?"

Lily didn't know how to answer because she was having trouble believing what she'd heard as well. Under arrest? For leaving the scene of an accident? "Are you sure you have the right person, Officers?" she asked, stepping between them and Jamila.

She got a blank, flat stare from both of them. Neither of these men was going to give anything away. "We need Ms. Khaury to come with us to the police station to answer some questions. We need her to come now."

Jamila made a little sound. Not quite a whimper and not quite a moan. Lily turned. Jamila's eyes were wide enough that Lily could see the whites all around them. Sweat had broken out on her upper lip. Lily turned back to face the officers, but didn't budge even though her heart had started to thump in her chest.

Jamila looked down at her gym clothes and then at the officers and then at Lily. "Should I change into my regular clothes?"

The lighter-haired cop spoke. "That's not necessary. It's probably best if we go now."

"Now? But the school day's not over. I have World Civ after PE." Jamila looked at Lily as if World Civ would matter to these two men.

Something was wrong, really wrong. Lily wasn't sure what it was, but she knew wrong when she smelled it. "Can't you ask your questions here? You could use my office." She gestured behind her to the door.

The dark-haired officer shook his head. "Thanks for the offer. It won't be necessary." He moved as if to go around Lily.

"It's really not a problem." Lily shifted to keep herself between the officer and Jamila.

"No, thank you, ma'am," the lighter-haired officer said. His voice had grown sharp and developed an edge. "We'd like to take Ms. Khaury down to the station. We'll straighten everything out there. Now, if you'll excuse me?" He looked at her. His gaze even and cool, but his hand went to his hip.

Was he going to Taser her in the school office? Lily doubted it, but it was also abundantly clear that this guy wasn't going to take no for an answer and she knew she couldn't really stop them. Lily stepped out of the way. She wasn't sure what else she could do. Should do.

The dark-haired officer took Jamila's arm. Jamila flinched at the contact. If that wasn't bad enough, he pulled her arm behind her and snapped a handcuff onto it and then grabbed the other. Then he led her out the door of the office toward the parking lot.

"Handcuffs? Come on, guys. That's way over the top." Even if Jamila had done something wrong, it wasn't as if they were picking up one of America's most wanted. She was a kid.

"It's standard operating procedure, ma'am. Please let us do our jobs." The lighter-haired one now stepped between Lily and Jamila.

"Callie?" Lily called. "Could you get me Jamila's parents' contact information?"

Callie walked over and put a Post-it note with three phone numbers on it in her hand. "Already on it. Something's not right here."

Damn straight.

January 27
2:15 P.M.
Darby High School
2710 11th Street
Darby, California

Lily reached Mrs. Khaury on her cell phone. Wherever she was, it was loud and Lily had to shout into the phone to be heard. After several diplomatic tries, she ended up yelling, "The police have arrested Jamila. They've taken her to the police station. I think you need to get there right away."

It wasn't the kind and gentle way she'd wanted to break the news. She hadn't, to her knowledge, ever met Mrs. Khaury. She racked her brain, but couldn't pull up a mental picture of her. It was a big school and by the time kids hit high school, there weren't any more parent-teacher conferences, just open houses with hundreds of parents milling back and forth between their children's classrooms. Generally speaking, if Lily met someone's parent, it was bad news, and until today Jamila had not been bad news. There was some kind of mistake. It would all get straightened out. Probably before Monday morning.

Her door opened and Hugh Gardella stuck his head inside. She held up a finger to hush him and gave him a scowl. He should have knocked. She might have been doing something confidential. She *was* doing something confidential. Or as confidential as it could be after the police had led Jamila out with her hands cuffed behind her back and Lily had screamed the news of Jamila's arrest over the phone to her mother.

"I don't have any details, Mrs. Khaury," she said into the phone. "The police wouldn't give me any. Jamila seemed shocked and more than a little confused. Can you get there right away? I'm sure it's some kind of mistake."

Hugh tilted his head to one side quizzically. She frowned at him again and shook her head. He rolled his eyes at her in response and mouthed, "Café Darby at six o'clock?"

She nodded her head, pointed at the phone, then made a shooing gesture while she tried to focus on what Mrs. Khaury was saying to her over the phone. Hugh ducked back out with a wave of his fingers.

What Mrs. Khaury had were even more questions than Lily had had. What was going on? Why had Jamila been arrested? What were the charges? "I'm so sorry. The police were either unwilling or unable to give me any information. All I know is that they said something about a hit-and-run accident in your SUV at the shopping center in South Darby last night."

"A hit-and-run? With our Explorer?" Mrs. Khaury asked.

"I guess so. They had a license plate number. I didn't ask what the make or model of the car was." They'd said black SUV, though. She was pretty sure of that.

"The Explorer didn't hit anything. I drove it today. It's fine. What are they talking about?" Anger tinged Mrs. Khaury's voice. Coupled with the ever so slight British accent, it made her sound arrogant and impatient.

Lily began to feel a little more impatience of her own creep up on her. She was calling as a courtesy. She hadn't had to. She could have waited and let Jamila call her parents herself from the police station. Or had Callie do it. But no, she'd tried to do the right thing and now she was getting yelled at.

Lily hated being yelled at.

"I really don't know, Mrs. Khaury. I've told you everything that I do know. I think your best course of action is to get to the police station and see what you can do for Jamila. She's all alone with the police officers right now."

"Alone with the police officers? Were they both men?" Mrs. Khaury gasped.

"Yes. Do you want their names?" Callie had probably written them down. It was the kind of detail she took care of automatically.

"Their names? I don't care about their names. I care about my daughter being alone with two men who are not related to her."

She got it now. There was some kind of religious thing where women weren't supposed to be unchaperoned with men to whom they weren't related, but that was hardly the biggest of Mrs. Khaury's worries at this point. Her daughter had been arrested. Arrested and taken away in handcuffs, no less. Lily took a deep breath, counted to ten, and said, "Again, I really think your best course of action is to go to the police station or call your lawyer or both."

"I will do that. Thank you for calling me." Mrs. Khaury suddenly went cold and formal.

Lily leaned back in her chair and let her head fall back. Great. Now she was the insensitive bad guy somehow. "You're quite welcome. I wanted to help. Jamila is a lovely girl."

"Thank you. Good-bye now." Mrs. Khaury hung up.

Lily set the phone down very very softly.

"Not so easy trying to be helpful, is it?" Callie asked from where she was leaning against the door frame, because, of course Hugh hadn't shut it after himself. "Sometimes they want to kill the messenger, don't they?"

Callie had terrified Lily when she'd first started at Darby High. The woman had a face like a tree. Weathered and lined and creased and seemingly immobile. She had a tendency to be terse and she did not suffer fools gladly. The first time Lily had gotten Callie to smile at her had been quite the accomplishment.

"Do you ever get used to it? To people yelling at you about stuff that isn't your fault?" Lily asked.

Callie waved her hand in the air. "Oh, yes. I've never gotten to the point where I actually like it, but it doesn't much bother me anymore either." She grinned. "Okay--sometimes I like it a little. It gets the blood flowing, you know what I mean?"

Lily listened to the boom boom boom of her heart and figured she knew exactly what Callie meant.

January 27
3:15 P.M.
Darby High School
2710 11th Street
Darby, California

Shelby Stedman heard the rumor that Jamila Khaury had been led out of the high school in handcuffs by two uniformed police officers right after the seventh-period bell rang. She had to hang on to her locker for a second to keep her knees from giving out beneath her. Arrested? Taken away in handcuffs? The information was not processing. That was not supposed to happen. That had not been the plan.

She leaned her head against her locker for a second, appreciating how cool the metal felt against her flushed face. A bang to her right made her jump.

"Yo, Stedman, 'sup? You already wasted? I guess it's five o'clock somewhere, right?"

Fabulous. Nick Gable. He was *so* not who she wanted to see right now. She pulled her Bio book out of her locker and crammed it into her already bulging backpack. "Go away, Gable."

"Why so hostile, Shelby?" He leaned closer. Way too close. Close enough that she could see the peach fuzz on his upper lip and a pimple starting to sprout in the corner by his nose. "You were pretty happy to see me last weekend when I had that bottle of tequila." He leered.

Shelby didn't want to think about what she'd done to have access to that bottle. It had seemed worth it at the time. Now she looked at Nick's pimply face and wondered if it had been. She wanted to forget all about it. She wanted the sick taste in the back of her throat to go away. She wanted to go home. She zipped her backpack shut.

"You got a bottle now?" She kept her voice flat, deadpan, a monotone, but she could feel the tremble in it even if no one could hear it. Would she do it again? If he had a bottle, would she go down on her knees to get it? Would she do it right now back behind the oleander bushes? Was she really capable of that? She didn't know what she was capable of anymore. She'd like to stop thinking. A bottle of tequila would go a long way toward shutting off her brain.

"Uh, no, but I could get one. I think," he said, his face flushing a mottled red.

Shelby shook her head. She didn't have to choose. The universe had done it for her. "You snooze, you lose, buddy," she said as she walked away, praying that she could stay steady and look as if she didn't care, didn't want to lie down on the sidewalk and weep, didn't wish she could disappear.

By the time Shelby got home, Kimberly Camp had posted a cell phone picture on Facebook of Jamila walking with her head down between two uniformed men. She couldn't tag Jamila. Jamila's parents wouldn't let her be on Facebook. Or Myspace. Kimberly had labeled it though. You couldn't really see the handcuffs. The photo was too blurry and the angle was all wrong. But Jamila's hands were clasped behind her. They could totally be cuffed. What must that have felt like? Did it hurt? What if you stumbled? Would the police officers help you?

Shelby looked at the refrigerator knowing that oblivion waited for her inside those pristine white doors. There was an open bottle of white wine on the top shelf and part of a six-pack of beer on the second shelf down. Her mouth got dry just thinking about them. She didn't dare, though. Her dad would definitely notice if another beer went missing. The difference between five bottles and four? That was fuzzy. Winnow that six-pack down to three? He'd totally notice. She'd learned that lesson the hard way.

The wine presented certain possibilities. She could have a glass, add some water to the bottle, and who would notice? If her mother even registered a difference in the way it tasted, she'd blame it on the bottle being open for too long and dump it. She'd done that dozens of times.

No. She didn't dare chance it. Besides, she had another option, one that had really cost her. It would be stupid to let it go to waste.

She glanced at the clock on the microwave. Her mother would be home any minute now. Maybe she should wait.

She didn't want to wait, though. She wanted that funny calming effect she got when the vodka seemed to run right through her veins and make everything a little more tolerable. She wanted that warmth flooding through her to counteract the cold pit that had formed in her chest when she'd heard about Jamila's arrest.

She wanted it now.

Shelby went to her room, pulled the basket of old stuffed animals out of her closet, and dug down under the teddy bears and bunnies and puppy dogs until she found the bottle of vodka. She ran her hand up and down the cool, clear glass already starting to feel how it would calm her, steady her, heal her.

Maybe it didn't have anything to do with her. Maybe it was all a coincidence. Maybe Miss Perfect Princess Jamila had really done something wrong and had to suffer the consequences like everyone else.

Yeah, right.

She got a juice glass from the cupboard, poured in a healthy slug of vodka and added orange juice. Then she drained the whole thing in one long gulp. She stashed the bottle of vodka, rinsed her glass and put it in the dishwasher, and started watching the episode of *Survivor* she'd DVRed. She floated on the couch, feeling warm and soft, like all the hard edges of the day had been somehow sanded off.

"Hey, sweetheart, how was school?" Her mom bustled in the front door, kicked off her shoes, and dumped her purse on the credenza by the front door.

Every day. How was school? Did you have a good day? What did you have for lunch? So many questions and none of them mattered. None of them meant anything.

"Fine." Shelby didn't look up from the TV.

"That's it? Fine?" She stood there, hands on her hips, waiting.

"Yeah, Mom. Fine. That's it." Shelby felt her heart kick up a little. It always did that when she lied. She hated it. She pulled the blanket she was under up to her chin.

Her mother came over to the couch and sat down next to her. "You feeling okay, honey?"

Thank God, she'd popped that piece of chewing gum in her mouth five minutes before. No way would her mom smell the booze on her breath over the blast of watermelon and lime. "I'm fine, Mom. Just tired."

Her mother brushed her forehead with her hand. "You look a little flushed. You sure you're okay?"

Shelby rolled her eyes. "I'm fine, Mom." If she only knew how far that was from the truth. Shelby was so far from fine, she wouldn't be able to find it with a GPS.

"Well, okay then. Your dad and I were talking about going out for sushi. Want to come with?" Her mother stood.

The thought of eating sushi made her stomach feel like a small storm was brewing in it. "Which place are you going to?" As if she didn't know.

"The boat place on Second Street." Her mother stretched her arms and rolled her neck a little. "I don't feel like cooking. It's been a long week."

Shelby wrinkled her nose. "The boat place isn't half as good as the place over in the basement on E Street."

"But it's a third of the price, so the math still works out. What do you say? Want to come? I'll split a spider roll with you." Her mother used a wheedling tone that had stopped working on Shelby when she was about three. Had her mother even noticed that? That Shelby didn't like to be wheedled? Did she see her at all? Couldn't she see how miserable she was?

Shelby burrowed down deeper into the blanket, hiding her face. "No. I'm going to go over to Lindsay's later. I'll have a sandwich here before I go."

"Suit yourself. I'm going to change." Her mother waltzed out of the room.

Shelby stared after her. Could the woman be any more blind? She tossed herself back against the cushions, wishing she could still talk to her mother like she used to. Wishing that she could dump her problems at her mother's feet and have her solve them. There had been a time when she'd told her mother everything. Everything. When exactly had that stopped? When had her mother become so freaking clueless?

What did it matter? It had stopped and Shelby's problems were big enough at the moment that she didn't think there was any way for her mother to ever fix it.

Made in the
USA
Middletown, DE